The Long
Way Home

By the same author

The Morning Promise

The Long Way Home

Margaret James

ROBERT HALE · LONDON

© Margaret James 2006
First published in Great Britain 2006

ISBN-10: 0-7090-8171-5
ISBN-13: 978-0-7090-8171-5

Robert Hale Limited
Clerkenwell House
Clerkenwell Green
London EC1R 0HT

2 4 6 8 10 9 7 5 3 1

Typeset in 11/15½pt Stempel Garamond
by Derek Doyle & Associates, Shaw Heath
Printed and bound in Great Britain
by Biddles Limited, King's Lynn

PROLOGUE

March 1925

I T wasn't so much a nightmare as a mystifying dream.
Whenever Daisy Denham had the dream, she woke up tangled
in the bedclothes and soaked with perspiration. Of course, this
wasn't unusual in India, especially when the summer was coming,
the temperature on the plains was rising, and it was time to go up
to the hills.

'What's the matter, sweetheart?' asked her mother, after Daisy
had woken up at three o'clock one morning, shouting to somebody
in her dream to wait, to *say* something! The ayah had gone running
in a panic to rouse Mrs Major Denham.

'I had that dream again.' Daisy sipped slowly from the glass of
juice that Rose had brought. 'I saw that lady, the one I always see.'

'Don't you recognize her, love?' asked Rose.

'No, I can't see her face, it's always blurred. She's young and has
black hair, like you. But she isn't you. I'm sure I've met her once in
real life. But I don't know where.'

'What does she say to you?'

'She never says anything. She just stands there, looking at me.'
Daisy clung to Rose's arm. 'Mum, she really scares me.'

'She's just a dream, my darling.' Rose stroked Daisy's golden

5

hair away from her sticky forehead. 'I dream about all sorts of things, see people I've never met, and I go to places I know I've never been.'

Rose took the empty glass from Daisy and smoothed the linen sheets. 'Try to go back to sleep, my love,' she said. 'You're going to have a busy day tomorrow.'

'Did you finish my dress?' asked Daisy.

'Yes, and it looks lovely, the style and colour are just right for you. Dad's bearer has polished up your shoes so that you can see your face in them, and I've had all your ribbons starched and ironed. You're going to be the star of Mrs Colonel Norton's little show.'

'What about my dad, do you think he'll come?'

'He says he hopes to get away. But he's got a lot to do right now, getting all the transport organized for when the mothers and children go up to the hills.'

'I wish he could come with us when *we* go.'

'So do I,' said Rose. 'But when he has some leave, I expect he'll try to join us for a week or two. Come along, my darling, settle down. Ayah, stay with missy baba until she goes to sleep.'

So Daisy's ayah sat down by the bed, patting Daisy's hair and crooning softly to her charge in soothing Hindustani. The dark lady had vanished. As her ayah sang a lullaby, Daisy felt herself falling asleep.

CHAPTER 1

March 1930

THE show had been a great success. The audience clapped and whistled and stamped their feet, and as Daisy took her final bow with all the other performers, she scanned the rows of faces. But she couldn't see the person she had hoped would come.

The clapping died away. The other singers and dancers skipped and scurried off the stage. Daisy followed them to the dressing-rooms, where the happy buzz of conversation contrived to raise her spirits – just a little.

'You were excellent, sweetheart,' said her father, when she came out of the makeshift greenroom to find Edgar Denham waiting with her hat and coat and gloves. 'Your song and dance act was the best thing in the show.'

'Do you think so, Dad?' said Daisy, looking all around for someone else.

They started to push their way through the crowded lobby of Charton village hall, where Edgar nodded to acquaintances and agreed with everyone that his daughter was a star. But Daisy still couldn't see the special person whose opinion mattered most.

'Where's my mum?' she asked.

'She couldn't make it, darling.' Edgar shrugged. 'She had one of her headaches, and she had to go and lie down. She'll be so sorry to have missed your triumph.'

Daisy's shoulders slumped. Why was her mother being like this?

When the Denham family had left India and come to live in Charton, a honey-coloured, stone-built village on the Dorset coast, Rose had made no effort to fit in. When, a few months later, Daisy had asked if she could take part in a musical evening organized by the schoolmistress, Miss Sefton, at the village hall, Rose had not forbidden it, but she hadn't shown any interest, either.

Since they'd come back to England, Rose had changed. When the Denhams lived in India, Rose had been involved in everything, and the social life of the cantonment had revolved round Mrs Major Denham. Rose had organized all kinds of shows and fêtes and parties. She'd encouraged Daisy to take part in amateur dramatics, let her perform in the variety shows in the cantonment theatre, and sent her to dancing lessons, singing lessons, made her costumes – everything.

'Where are the brats?' asked Daisy.

'In the car,' said Edgar. 'They enjoyed themselves. They were telling everybody you're their grown-up sister, and they clapped like anything. Do you want to stay for a while and chat, and have a glass of orange and a bun?'

'No, Dad, let's go home.'

So Daisy and Edgar said goodnight to a flushed and happy Miss Sefton, who had masterminded the event and looked relieved that it had gone so well. Now the local cottage hospital would be that much closer to getting its new ward.

They walked across the cinder patch where Edgar had parked the battered Riley he'd been left in Alec Denham's will. The brats were in the back, kicking and punching one other, but broke off when their father and sister got into the cab.

'Oh look, it's Greta Garbo,' sniggered Stephen.

'You were gruesome, Daze.' Robert, the bigger and stronger of Daisy's vile twin brothers, grabbed her round the neck, making her choke. 'When you croaked that song about picking lilac, I was nearly sick.'

'Yeah, and so was I,' said Stephen, Robert's faithful echo. 'Daze, when you sat on that Miss Muffet's tuffet thing, and that little kid came on, dressed up as a spider, you looked like you were going to lay an egg.'

'Your eyes were bulging, like someone on the lav. A lady said you needed Beecham's Pills.'

'Hark the herald angels sing, Beecham's Pills are just the thing,' sang Stephen, in a high falsetto.

'You danced like Mr Hobson's donkey, and—'

'Daisy, take no notice,' interrupted Edgar, glaring at the boys in the rear-view mirror. 'Belt up, you little blighters, or I'll thrash the pair of you.'

Although their father had never laid a violent hand upon them, the twins heard the authority in his voice. They belted up at once.

'We must all give it time,' said Edgar, as he drove up the rutted track that led to Melbury House. They'd come back to England the previous October, after Edgar had been injured in an anti-British riot, and forced to leave the army. 'Dorset's so very different from Delhi, after all.'

'Bloody right it is – no money, freezing cold, no servants, living in a ruin,' whispered Robert, confident he was on his father's deaf side, so Edgar wouldn't hear him, even if Daisy did.

'But we'll be fine, you'll see,' continued Edgar. 'I know this winter's been a challenge. We've all had coughs and colds, and your poor old mother hasn't been very well at all. But the spring and summer are wonderful in England. You kids can learn to swim. We'll go for picnics on the beach. I'll find some ponies for you all,

9

and then you can go riding.'

'It all sounds lovely, Dad,' said Daisy loyally, even though she didn't much like riding, and she hated England and everything about it.

The damp and dismal countryside was ugly and depressing. The glass-green sea looked freezing, and she didn't want to dip a toe in it, much less learn to swim. The beach was covered with sharp shingle or big pebbles, not with soft, white sand. The constant cold poked icy fingers through her clothes into her very bones, and she'd given up all hope of being warm again.

Every time she went into the village on an errand for her mother the locals said hello, but then they gawped and goggled so much that it was as if she had webbed fingers or three eyes. Whenever she went into the village shop, the woman behind the counter was friendly and polite, but the other customers stared and muttered, then they grinned like idiots if she turned round suddenly and caught them gawking at her, like a lot of fools.

They parked in front of Melbury House, which Edgar had inherited from his guardian, Alec Denham, along with the old Riley. In its dilapidated state, the house was probably worth about as much as the rusty motor. Or maybe even less.

'You two can go and get the coal in,' Edgar told the twins, as he parked the Riley. 'Make the fire up in your mother's bedroom, wash your hands, then go and fetch the supper trays that Mrs Hobson's left for us. Bring them to the drawing-room; there'll be a good blaze there. At the double, chaps.'

'God, we're nothing but child slaves,' groaned Stephen, but he went with his brother to the stables where the coal was kept, leaving Edgar and Daisy on the steps of the old house.

'You were very good, you know,' said Edgar.

'You're just saying that,' said Daisy, scared she was going to cry.

'I mean it, darling.' Edgar stroked a strand of her straight, blonde hair back from her forehead. 'You're very talented. Your mother and I have always thought so. Don't take any notice of the brats. They're only ten years old. They say the sort of beastly things that boys of their age do. I should know, I used to be like them, many years ago.'

'I can't believe you were as foul as those two,' muttered Daisy.

'Oh, I was *much* fouler!' Edgar grinned, then shook his head. 'I was a horror. If you don't believe me, ask your mother.'

'Why didn't she come?' asked Daisy.

'I told you, she had a headache.'

'Yes, but Dad—'

'Come on, let's go and see if she feels better.'

They found Rose lying on the sagging sofa in the twilit drawing-room. The fire had burned to ashes, and shadows danced around the walls and ceiling, so all the cracks and stains weren't quite as noticeable as in daytime. Edgar drew the rotting velvet curtains, sending them rattling along the tarnished poles.

'Edgar?' Rose opened her eyes and rubbed them. 'Daisy, love! You're back already? Well, how did it go?'

'She was wonderful. They clapped and cheered like maniacs. You'd have been so proud.' Edgar sat on the edge of the sofa, taking Rose's hands and rubbing them to get the circulation going again. 'Goodness, Rose, you're freezing! Why didn't you pull those blankets over you?'

'I fell asleep.' Rose patted the sofa, inviting Daisy to sit down. 'Now, tell me all about it, and don't miss out a thing.'

As she leaned against her mother's shoulder, inhaling her familiar scent of jasmine, Daisy began to feel a little better. She'd come home, and even if these days home was a crumbling ruin, not a British army major's splendid married quarters, she was with her parents, the people who loved her best.

Maybe her dad was right – they needed to give it time. Maybe England wouldn't be so horrible, after all.

*

Lolling against the wall of the morning-room, his hands thrust deep into his trouser pockets – a stance he knew his mother hated – Ewan Fraser scowled. 'But why do *I* have to come?' he growled, his green eyes mutinous slits, his generous mouth a stubborn line.

'I can't leave you in Scotland on your own all summer,' replied his mother tartly.

'I shan't be on my own,' retorted Ewan. 'Mr Morrison and his wife are here, and they'll look after me. They did so when you went away with Dad, when he was in hospital and you stayed in Edinburgh so you could visit him, when you had to go and see the lawyers—'

'But Sir Michael has invited you.' Agnes Fraser looked beseechingly at her tall, broad son. 'Ewan, they're your father's only relatives. They're rich, they're influential. You know that you have no one else to help you make your way.'

'I'm going to be an actor, so I don't need the help of country cousins down in Dorset,' muttered Ewan. 'Anyway, you don't like Lady Easton. You're always saying she's common. When my father was alive, you'd never have even talked to someone who had been divorced. Let alone gone to stay with her, and allowed the wretched woman to tell you what to do.'

'Well, things are different now,' said Agnes. 'Your father didn't leave us enough money, this place costs a fortune to maintain, and we have to live.'

'I still don't see why we should have to go and grovel to the likes of *them*,' objected Ewan. 'Why do you want me to go to university, anyway? Why can't I leave school and get a job?'

'A minute ago, you said that you were going to be an actor.'

'Yes, I did, and acting is a job.'

'Oh, my darling!' Agnes clasped Ewan round the waist and hugged him, laying her neat, dark head against his chest. 'My baby, you're so young and inexperienced, you don't know the world!'

Ewan knew that in a moment she would start to cry. Then he

would have no option but to agree to go to Dorset. So he might as well give in right now.

'I don't have to spend the whole time fishing, do I?' he demanded, determined to salvage something.

'I'm sure Sir Michael would be very pleased if you would go with him. When people don't have children of their own, they like to have the young around the place, and he's so fond of you.' Agnes looked up at Ewan, brown eyes bright with unshed tears. He hoped she wouldn't actually turn the taps on, because he never knew what to do. 'I knew you'd see the sense of going, my bonny boy.'

Ewan shrugged out of her embrace and slouched out of the room.

A few days later, after Agnes Fraser had agreed with Ewan's day-school that he could be absent for the summer term because of urgent family business, he and his mother left Glen Grant for the long journey south.

Agnes had arranged for the house to be let until September, bringing in some welcome cash but making Ewan feel even more gloomy. Now he'd be stuck in rural Dorset, sponging off his father's distant relatives and missing the place he loved, until the best of the year was past.

They travelled first class, which in Ewan's opinion was a total waste of the money Agnes said they didn't have. But at least they had a compartment to themselves. While his mother stared out of the window, occasionally getting out her powder compact and touching up her paintwork, Ewan lolled across three seats and read his pocket Shakespeare, a tiny copy printed on the thinnest India paper. It had been his father's, had gone with him to the trenches, and it still smelled of dirt and smoke and blood.

As Ewan read accounts of wars and tales of tortured love, he wondered if he was ever going to live up to his father, a highly-decorated hero who had died of war wounds, even though he'd taken years to do so.

It didn't look as if another war was in the offing, or at least not yet. So he wasn't going to be able to cover himself with glory on some distant battlefield. It looked as if he'd have to fall in love. . . .

'Ewan, what are you doing?' demanded Agnes, suddenly. 'You've got that strange look in your eyes again.'

'I'm just reading,' Ewan murmured, hoping she didn't want to talk to him.

'You always have your nose stuck in a book. You're always dreaming. But there's life out there, child – real life!'

Yes, hunting, shooting and fishing down in Dorset, which isn't going to compare with anything we get in Scotland, Ewan thought, but didn't say. He didn't want to provoke her into delivering yet another sermon.

Agnes rearranged her furs, peering at him over the turned-up collar of her coat like a petulant marmoset in lipstick.

'It's freezing in this carriage,' she complained. 'I wonder where the guard can be? Maybe there isn't one on this wretched train. Ewan, I don't feel well. I'm sure I'm feverish. I think I must be going to start a cold.'

Daisy had yet another cold. Since they'd come back to England, she almost always had a cold, which wasn't surprising since she was always freezing, even if she wrapped herself in layers and layers of woollens, wore itchy home-made cardigans and thick, hand-knitted socks. The spring her dad had promised them was taking its time to come.

Getting up late one morning, she found her mother in the kitchen, discussing the week's meals with Mrs Hobson, the woman from the village who did for them.

Daisy liked Mrs Hobson, an untidy, wholesome person who cooked untidy, wholesome stews with lots of carrots and potatoes, and always welcomed Daisy to the kitchen with biscuits and a glass of milk.

14

Mrs Hobson came to Melbury House each weekday morning, and she and Rose did everything between them – dusting, cleaning, scrubbing, laundry, peeling endless piles of vegetables, and laying all the fires. Daisy came home from school most days to find her mother resting with her feet up on the sofa, pale with fatigue and looking drained.

'I thought I heard some footsteps,' Mrs Hobson said, beaming as Daisy snaked a hand across the kitchen table to grab a fresh-baked scone. 'You're not at school today, then?'

'She was up coughing half the night, and so I thought I'd keep her off this morning. This old place is so damp, I'm surprised we haven't all had pneumonia this winter.' Rose brushed Daisy's fringe out of her eyes and felt her forehead. 'You're not so feverish now. If you're feeling better, you could go to school this afternoon.'

'Maybe not, it's double Latin.' Daisy grinned. 'I'll go for a walk along the beach, and blow my germs away. Unless I can do anything for you, Mum?'

'Thank you, darling, but I think we're finished,' Rose replied. But she must have known that she was never going to finish, would never have the money to run the place as it was originally intended, with a live-in staff of five or more, and extra help besides.

'Stay on the cliff path, won't you?' she reminded Daisy. 'The gated road is private. It's on someone else's land.'

'Where's my dad?' asked Daisy, changing the subject deftly.

'He and Mr Hobson are marking out the vegetable garden. Your dad has lots of plans for it this year.' Rose smiled ruefully. 'I think he intends to keep you children busy.'

'I'll go and see what they're doing.'

Daisy went to fetch her coat, but as she walked along the service passage the women's voices floated after her, and she couldn't help but hear what they were saying.

'She's grown up very pretty,' said Mrs Hobson. 'I always knew she would.'

'She's lovely,' Rose agreed. 'A regular Dorset milkmaid.' Then Daisy heard her mother sigh. 'Of course, it's rather difficult for *me*, coming back here and having to see the people I used to know. I expect there's lots of gossip in the village?'

'Well, there's still a bit,' admitted Mrs Hobson. 'But not as much as when you first came home. You and Mr Denham and the children are living here so happy and respectable that I'm sure there's nothing much to say.'

'I hope you're right,' said Rose.

'Mrs Denham – I dare say it's not my business, but does Daisy know what happened all those years ago?' asked Mrs Hobson.

'She . . . look at the time, we must get these potatoes on,' said Rose.

CHAPTER 2

DAISY and her brothers had always been taught to think of England as the mother country, and as their real home. So when they'd first been told that they were going home, they had been thrilled.

Their picture-books of England had shown them green fields, purple hills, romantic castles, black-and-white half-timbered villages, bustling cities, golden beaches, lakes and snow-capped mountains. They couldn't wait to see this paradise.

But when they had come back to England, docking in Southampton on a drizzling, dismal day in late October, everything had been a disappointment.

It was so cold and damp. They were used to cold, for when they had spent seasons in the hills, it had been sharp and chilly on frosty winter mornings. But they'd never known the dripping, miserable damp of cold, grey England.

'We're going to live in a beautiful old house,' Rose had explained, and got them all excited. 'Your father's guardian left it to him several years ago, but there's been no one living in it since. So it will be a little shabby now, but we'll soon get everything spruced up.'

Melbury House turned out to be a hideous old ruin, too far gone, thought Daisy, for any sprucing up, even if it was a fine example of a Jacobean mansion.

'Look at the period detail,' Rose said brightly, as she and their father took them round, pointing out elaborate plastered ceilings (cracked and green with mould, the plaster falling off in dirty, icing-sugar chunks), the Grinling Gibbons staircase (full of wood-worm, so there was to be no sliding down it, for fear it would disin-tegrate), and the enormous, curtained beds, made on site to fit the first floor bedrooms, swagged and draped with velvet (threadbare and full of spiders).

On their second day at home, while their parents shivered in the drawing-room, trying to keep warm beside a smoking, choking fire, and saying they must get the chimneys swept, Daisy and the twins did some exploring of their own.

Above the second storey, the main staircase had collapsed, but they went up the service stairs and up on to the roof. They found that half of it was missing, the slates blown off or broken, the wooden beams exposed.

'We can't use that part of the house,' admitted Edgar, when they'd pointed out to him that rain was getting in, and this must be the reason that everything was rotten. 'The rooms on the third floor are past redemption, and nobody's used *them* for centuries.'

'But, Dad,' said Daisy, frowning, 'why don't you get the roof fixed?'

'Money, old girl,' said Edgar, 'or rather, lack of it. Listen, you fellows, don't go on the roof. It's far too dangerous.'

By the end of their first week in Dorset, they all had streaming colds. Rose was ill all winter. She had tonsillitis, followed by bron-chitis, followed by influenza, followed by tonsillitis, round and round in circles. Edgar was still getting over wounds he had sustained the previous summer, and everyone was miserable and sluggish, unwilling to do anything but sit and dream of the beloved India they had left behind.

'But *we*'d have had to come to stinking England, anyway,' said

Robert grimly, as Daisy and the twins cleared away the breakfast things one chilly April morning.

'If Dad was in the army still, and if we had some money, *you*'d have gone to be finished off in Switzerland,' went on Stephen. 'So *you*'d have been all right. But Rob and me would be at some old boarding-school in Kent, where you have to fag for older fellows, and everyone gets flogged. So really, we're quite glad we're broke.'

'It's Rob and I,' said Daisy, absently.

She had decided she would make the best of England. It was too wet, too cold, too dull, too quiet, but once in a while a clear, bright day made everything look better. Then, the sky shone crystal-blue, the dew-sprinkled grass was the most brilliant shade of green, and in all the copses pale daffodils glowed yellow. Tiny, fragile things, these Easter lilies – as the local people called them – were nothing like the gorgeous regal lilies which had grown like weeds in India. But they were pretty, just the same.

She went to school in Dorchester, catching the early morning train from Charton. She usually walked home along a well-main-tained and gated road that went past Easton Hall, a splendid stone-built manor house. Its gleaming paintwork and new roof suggested that the people who lived there must be very rich.

But Daisy didn't know them, because they didn't mix with village people. They even had a private pew in church, with its own special entrance near the choir-stalls, which no one else could use. So, boxed into a sort of holy hen-house, they did their worshipping in secret, lurking out of everybody's sight.

Rose had told Daisy several times she mustn't go that way, because the gated road was private and she would be trespassing. But Daisy took no notice. She wasn't doing any harm, and this was the short way home.

One Friday afternoon, as she was walking back to Melbury House, she saw there was someone sitting on the gate that lay ahead. A boy of about the same age as herself – fifteen going on sixteen, she supposed – he didn't have a hat on, and his dark, reddish hair was glinting copper in the sunshine.

Probably a poacher, Daisy thought. A poacher or a vagrant. Maybe that was why her mother didn't like her coming home this way. She might meet tramps and undesirables.

'Good afternoon,' the vagrant said. Actually, decided Daisy, he looked quite respectable close up. Or at least clean and decent, anyway.

'Good afternoon,' said Daisy, carefully.

'I'm Ewan Fraser.' The boy held out his hand, but Daisy knew much better than to take it. People might look clean, but they could still have some terrible disease. This boy might be incubating cholera, perhaps, or have leprosy.

'Daisy Denham.' Daisy thought, perhaps he wasn't a vagrant after all. His clothes looked quite expensive. But he sounded Scottish, which was odd, considering this was Dorset. He must be one of the unemployed, come south to look for work.

'I live at Melbury House,' she added, pointing to the chimneys in the distance, hoping this would make him think again before he robbed her, and silently daring him to smirk, or make some smart remark about life in ruins.

'I'm staying with some relatives here,' he said.

'I haven't seen you in church.'

'Oh, I'm an atheist, so I don't go to church.' The boy looked Daisy up and down. 'Daisy Denham, Melbury House. You must be the girl my mother and Lady Easton talk about, when they think no one's listening.'

'Really?' Daisy frowned. 'What do they say?'

'Oh, how you're very talented, and such a splendid dancer, and how it's not surprising considering who your mother is – just boring women's gossip.'

'I see,' said Daisy coldly, thinking how very odd. She'd never known that Rose herself was any good at dancing. In fact, she'd never seen her mother dance. 'I need to get across this gate.'

'Where are you going now?' asked Ewan Fraser, moving to one side.

'That's no concern of yours,' said Daisy, holding down her skirt and hoping she wasn't showing too much leg.

'You're right,' said Ewan, 'but I'm bored. May I walk part of the way with you?'

'I'm sorry, I must hurry, I've lots of things to do.' Daisy climbed the gate then walked on briskly, feeling hot around the neck, and wondering if the boy was following.

But when she glanced back furtively, she saw he was still sitting on the gate and staring out across the fields.

When she got home, she found her mother in the kitchen, making one of her everlasting lists. 'Mum,' she began, 'when you were younger, did you ever—'

'You're very early, sweetheart.' Rose glanced up, and Daisy saw how tired and old she looked, how there were lines developing at the corners of her eyes. 'Good day at school?'

'Yes, it was all right. I got a merit mark in geography. Mum, when you were my age, did you like to dance?'

'Oh, goodness, yes! I loved it!' Rose smiled dreamily. 'In those days before the war, you can't imagine it now, but everything was so – well, I can't describe it. But we had such balls, such lovely parties! The men wore black or uniform, and the women, you should have seen them, lace and silk and flowers and jewellery – gorgeous.'

'You met Dad at a ball, then?'

'No, we knew each other when we were children. Edgar's guardian was my father's friend.'

'But you *did* dance with him?'

'I don't think I ever did, now that you come to mention it, but I danced with everybody else!' Rose stood up and pushed her thick, dark hair back from her brow. 'What about supper? Do you think we've had enough eggs this week? I don't want everyone to get bunged up! But it's scrambled eggs, or tinned sardines with tinned tomatoes – not very inspiring, I'm afraid.'

Daisy took the same path home on Monday afternoon. She found the boy still sitting on the gate, reading a small, brown book. 'Have you been here all weekend?' she asked.

'Most of it,' he said, and grinned, revealing perfect teeth.

'Why aren't you at work?'

'I'm on my holidays just now.'

'You mentioned Lady Easton when I saw you last, so you must be staying at Easton Hall?'

'Yes, that's correct, Miss Holmes,' he said, and slipped the little book into his pocket.

'Miss Denham.' Daisy realized that she was grinning now. She wished she wasn't blushing, too, for she was so fair-skinned, she looked like a tomato when she blushed. 'Where do you usually live?'

'In Scotland. But my mother wanted to spend the summer here in Dorset, with my father's cousins.' Ewan pulled a face. 'I'm hating every minute. All Sir Michael seems to think about are guns and fishing, he loves killing things, and Lady Easton is a bitch.'

'Yes, they don't like her in the village, they all say she's stuck up.'

'You were too busy for a walk last Friday.' Ewan looked at Daisy hopefully, and she was reminded of a friendly Labrador, who was just longing to be thrown a stick. 'Let me carry your bag a while. It looks extremely heavy.'

'Yes, actually it is,' said Daisy, handing it to him. 'So you don't like Sir Michael, then?'

'Oh, he's pleasant enough to me, but he's a crashing bore.' Ewan kicked a stone along the road. 'At this very moment, he's anxious to become a magistrate. He talks of nothing else. Apparently there's a situation vacant, and he wants it. He can't wait to hand down fines and floggings.'

'Mmm, lovely, he sounds really nice.' Daisy grinned.

'My mother reckons it's his great ambition to be Lord Lieutenant of the county,' muttered Ewan. 'But he'll need to work at it to make the people who matter forget he married a divorcee – and *she* must work hard at being a lady.'

'That's a very snobbish thing to say.'

'Och, I'm no snob,' said Ewan calmly. 'I'm a socialist. I believe in equal rights for all, and justice for the common man. Until the revolution comes, so-called ladies should at least be generous, and kindly and polite, and grateful for their undeserved good fortune. But Lady Easton's rude and selfish.'

'Oh,' said Daisy. 'I don't know much about them, actually. Do they have any children?'

'No,' said Ewan, then he grinned. 'But looking at Lady Easton, I can't say I'm surprised. She's not an appealing woman.'

'But if Sir Michael married her, surely he—'

'Oh, cousin Mike was after some heiress, but she wouldn't have him, because she was in love with someone else. Chloe was about to be divorced, and she was hanging out for a new husband. Mike was furious when the heiress went off somewhere with this other man, and he married Chloe on the rebound. Or so my mother says.'

'I'm not quite sure I follow that,' frowned Daisy.

'I'm not sure I do,' admitted Ewan. 'But it doesn't matter, it's ancient history now.'

Soon they turned off the road and took the path that led to Melbury House, skirting the cliffs and headland.

'Look, the spawn of Satan,' murmured Daisy, pointing to the twins who were skimming pebbles on the shingle beach below.

'They must be your little brothers.' Ewan Fraser grinned. 'Lady Easton mentioned them at breakfast. Apparently they've been going in the coverts, and springing traps with sticks. If Sir Michael's keeper catches them, he's going to tan their hides.'

'They don't like seeing animals get hurt. But that's the only decent thing about them.' Daisy glanced at Ewan. 'When we lived in India, they had a whole menagerie of pets. Rats and bats and mongooses, you never knew what was in their wretched pockets, waiting to leap out and bite your hand. They've probably got a new collection now. But God knows what's in it.'

'I have a pet white rat myself,' said Ewan. 'His name is Archie, and he's very clever.'

'So is he in your pocket now?' asked Daisy.

'No, don't worry,' Ewan said. 'The man who looks after our house in Scotland will be looking after Archie, too – or so I hope.'

Daisy glanced at her wristwatch. 'I have to go home now,' she said, and held her hand out for her satchel.

'I shouldn't have mentioned Archie.' Ewan sighed. 'Poor wee thing, my mother hates him, too.'

'I don't hate Archie, and I'm not afraid of rats, but Mum is going to wonder where I am.' Daisy took her bag back and slung it across her shoulder.

'See you tomorrow?' Ewan shouted, as she strode off down the path to Melbury.

'Maybe,' she called, not looking back.

As the spring warmed into summer, Ewan grew on Daisy.

It wasn't as if she was overwhelmed with friends. The girls at school were nice enough, but boring. Although she endured respectable little parties with her fellow pupils and their mothers, she didn't find a soul mate. But Ewan was good-looking, wasn't stupid, and he was an atheist, which was jolly daring. In the total absence of anyone more exciting, Ewan would have to do.

School had finished for the summer. As Ewan and Daisy lay on the headland one hot afternoon in late July, gazing towards Lyme Bay, Ewan said he was going to be actor.

'Actors are always out of work,' said Daisy.

'Thank you for your kind encouragement.' As he propped himself up on his elbows Ewan's grin was wry. 'You sound just like my mother. I thought I might expect a wee bit more enthusiasm from a seasoned trouper, who has not only trodden the boards herself, but has won great plaudits in the village.'

'I only mess about,' said Daisy, blushing. 'I'm just an amateur. A professional would laugh at me.'

'You're very good, according to Miss Sefton. She's getting up a concert party soon, and she told Lady Easton you would definitely be in it.'

'Well, she hasn't asked me,' retorted Daisy, annoyed but also flattered. 'Those village people,' she went on, 'I don't know what to make of them. They're chatting to you as nice as pie one minute, then gossiping behind your back the next. Making arrangements without even asking—'

'Well, you should be familiar with their ways. After all, you're one of them,' said Ewan.

'No, I'm not – not really.' Daisy shrugged. 'We went to India when I was a toddler. So, although I was born in England, I didn't remember anything about it. When we came home, it was like coming to a foreign country.'

'Why *did* you come home?'

'My dad was in the army. One day there was a riot, and he got shot.' Daisy shrugged again. 'Indians are always having riots. You see, they want their independence, but we won't let them have it. Anyway, my dad was badly hurt, and when he got better, he wasn't fit enough to be a soldier any more.'

'So you came back to Dorset, to the old ancestral home.'

'Well, to that dump Dad's guardian left him, not that I'd have chosen it. I don't see why we can't live in some decent modern house, with proper running water and electricity. It's money, I suppose. We haven't very much of it. Dad's only got his army pension.'

'You mother's from Dorset too, though, isn't she?'

'Yes, but I don't know exactly where, she's never said.' Daisy rolled over, lay on her back and stared up at the sky. 'Money, money, money – that's all Mum ever talks about.'

'It's all my mother talks about, as well. She's always going on about my school fees, about how much it's costing her to educate her stupid, lazy son.'

'Let's hope you're worth it, then,' grinned Daisy, turning to glance at Ewan, who wore no tie today and whose white shirt was open at the collar. She thought she saw a glint of gold beneath the thin material. 'What's that around your neck?' she asked.

Ewan fished out a chain, and showed her a ring that hung from it.

It is an honour 'longing to our house,
Bequeathed down from many ancestors;
Which were the greatest obloquy i' the world
In me to lose.

'I beg your pardon?' Daisy frowned.

'It was my dad's.' Ewan pushed the chain inside his shirt. 'He died when I was twelve; the worms have long since eaten him, but he left me his ring. Of course, we're not allowed to wear any jewellery at school, and so I got myself a chain for it, and keep it hidden.'

'What was all that stuff you said just now?'

'*All's Well That Ends Well.* But don't you know your Shakespeare?'

'Well, not as thoroughly as you do, obviously.' Daisy pursed her lips. 'I'm not an actress, I only sing and dance a bit, whatever you may have heard down in the village – and not everyone can go to Eton.'

'I don't go to Eton, my mother couldn't raise the fees for Eton!

I go to Grange Academy, one of Scotland's finest grammar schools, but I dare say you ignorant Sassenachs won't have heard of it.'

'If you want to act in Shakespeare's plays, you'll have to master English first,' retorted Daisy sharply, sticking up for the England she had hated, not so long ago.

'What's that supposed to mean?'

'Well, with your accent, the only part *you* could play would be Macbeth.' Daisy grinned at him. 'Say worms again.'

'Worms.'

'No, not wurrums, worms!' Daisy laughed. 'You'll have to go to see Miss Sefton, ask her to give you elocution lessons.'

'Away, ye saucy besom.' Ewan pushed her shoulder, and the feel of his hand through the light cotton of her dress made Daisy blush again, made her feel all hot and strange inside.

'I must go home now,' she said, and made to scramble up.

'Why, what have I said?' demanded Ewan.

'Mum has lots of things for me to do.'

'Daisy, wait a minute.' Ewan grabbed her hand and pulled her down again, so she was sitting facing him. 'All right, go home and help your mother. But I'll see you tomorrow, yes?' He leaned towards her, and she felt the butterfly touch of his mouth on hers before she had a chance to jerk away.

'Tomorrow, yes?' he said again, his green eyes meeting Daisy's blue ones.

'I must go home!' cried Daisy, leaping up and running off as if the hounds of hell were after her.

CHAPTER 3

I F only I'd had some warning, Daisy thought. Then I could have
said something smart and clever. I could have put Ewan Fraser
in his place.

Why had he kissed her, and – this was the worst part – why had
she enjoyed being kissed? That was the really awful, dreadful thing.
Why had she wanted to put her arms around his smooth, brown
neck, kiss him again, then lay her head on his broad shoulder?

What if the twins had seen them? They'd have laughed their
idiotic heads off. Then she'd have had to kill the little blighters, and
she would have ended up in prison, because she wasn't old enough
to hang.

Or she'd have had to get her lawyer to make out she was mad.
Then they'd have put her in the local bin, with lunatics who wet
themselves, who wore grey flannel uniforms and ugly, hobnail
boots. She'd watched them clumping into church, where they sat
and gibbered at the back, while their keepers shushed them.

All for a stupid kiss.

She went the long way home, taking a path that snaked through
Easton Woods, then skirting the perimeter walls which enclosed
the grounds of Charton Minster. This was some old mansion
which, the village gossips said, was a kind of prison where bad boys
were locked up, regularly birched, and fed on bread and water.

Daisy often wished the brats were locked up with them.

By the time she returned to Melbury House it was past seven o'clock. She went in round the back way, through the outbuildings, and there she found the twins.

'You've missed your supper,' Robert said.

'We ate all your scrambled eggs,' said Stephen.

'There's only sago pudding left for you.'

'It'll be cold by now.'

'Ugh, cold frog-spawn,' went on Robert, wrinkling his freckled nose. 'That's what sago's made from, cross my heart and hope to die. It will hatch inside you, and you'll sick up tadpoles all your life.'

'I wish *you* were a tadpole, then you might get eaten by a pike,' said Daisy, coldly.

The twins had commandeered the stables, and now they were mucking out a rabbit-run they'd made from bits of planking and old chicken-wire, and playing with their pets. 'What are you going to do with that lot, make them into pies?' demanded Daisy, eyeing a fat, brown doe with several kittens.

'They're pets, they're not for food!' cried Robert, scooping up a black-eared heavyweight, and rubbing his nose against its furry neck.

'We got a buck and doe down in the village. They were only sixpence each, and now we've got fifteen,' said Stephen, as he stroked a small, grey rabbit-kitten. 'We're selling some of them to boys at school for half a crown.'

'After we've checked that they've got proper hutches,' added Robert, 'and that they'd be safe from foxes, naturally.'

'Naturally,' echoed Daisy, wryly. 'Where are Mum and Dad?'

'They're in the house,' said Stephen. 'They're talking about money, and they both look pretty gloomy.'

'Now Dad's left the army and he only has his pension, we're jolly short of cash,' said Robert, putting down the rabbit. 'So, we're trying to do our bit. We told them about the rabbit farm, and how we're selling pets, and Dad said, "Well done, chaps."' '

'But when we suggested going to the village school instead of Rydale Manor, Mum got very weepy and said we ought to sell the house.'

'Then Dad said nobody would buy it.'

'Then Mum said it was hopeless and she was going to have a bath, so that's where she is now.' Stephen looked at his sister anxiously. 'Daze, we're up the creek, or that's what Dad said, anyway.'

Daisy looked back at them, seeing two black-haired, grubby kids whose anxious little faces showed how much they wished to help, but didn't know how to do it. They were just children, she reflected. They knew nothing about the world. Suddenly, she felt weary, sad – grown up.

'What's this one called?' she asked them, picking up a large, white pink-eyed rabbit.

'Freddie, he's a buck, he's very strong, he'll kick you if he can,' said Stephen, taking the squirming animal and putting it back among its many wives.

'That brown one's Emily, she's nice, she'll let you stroke her nose,' said Robert, pointing to a pretty little doe.

Daisy picked Emily up and stroked her gently, thinking hard.

'Stokeley says he saw you on the headland earlier today,' said Agnes Fraser. Ewan had been summoned to her bedroom before dinner, and now he sat watching as she rouged her face, pencilled in her eyebrows, and powdered her snub nose. 'He says you were with some girl.'

'Yes, with Daisy Denham.' Ewan didn't see what business it was of Albert Stokeley's, the Easton family bailiff who had once worked for the Denhams, but who had apparently been lured to Easton on Alec Denham's death by the promise of a better cottage and much higher pay.

'I don't think you should see her any more,' said Agnes, carefully. 'You might give certain people the wrong impression.'

'We only go for walks,' said Ewan, hoping the odious Stokeley hadn't seen them kissing. Well, hadn't seen Ewan doing the kissing, and Daisy doing the leaping up and running off, disgusted.

'Well, please don't go walking with Miss Denham from now on.' Agnes turned to face her son. 'Sir Michael is getting up a fishing-party for tomorrow, and he would like you to go along. He thinks your casting needs a lot more work.'

Ewan scowled, but then reflected that maybe he would go. It would stop his mother wittering, and Daisy had been so angry with him that he didn't think she'd want to meet him any more. 'I suppose he's right,' he muttered.

'You'll go fishing, then?'

'Yes.'

'Good, I'm glad.' Agnes came to sit beside him on the window seat. 'Chloe says Daisy Denham ... well, that girl's not quite the thing.'

'What do you mean?'

'Oh darling, I don't know, but there was some gossip in the war years. The usual business, I suppose. Maybe Mrs Denham had a baby rather soon after she married – or perhaps before.' Agnes's face was pink. 'Chloe isn't one to scandalmonger, as we know, but she wants to keep us on our guard.'

Chloe, thought Ewan, sourly. Since when had it been Chloe? Agnes Fraser hadn't had a good word to say for Chloe when she'd first married Sir Michael Easton. When Ewan's father was alive, Agnes had made remarks about divorcees and people covering up their dubious pasts, about how his father's cousin could have had just about any girl, and didn't have to stoop to marrying a common, grasping divorcee.

But it seemed that now the boot was on the other foot, that

Agnes was the pauper and Chloe the baronet's influential wife, Agnes and Chloe were the best of friends.

I could leave school, thought Daisy. I could get a job, I could learn typing, work as someone's secretary, perhaps. These days, girls are doing jobs like that. Yes, I could help them out.

She left the stables, crossed the yard and went into the house. She made her way upstairs to her parents' bedroom, where Rose would be having her bath in one of the old zinc tubs which they had to lug up to their rooms, then fill with water from the kitchen copper, jug after tedious jug.

She could hear Edgar's talking, and was about to knock on the door when something made her freeze.

'I think you're exaggerating, darling,' Edgar said.

'No, Edgar, I'm not,' retorted Rose. 'There's been so much gossip since we first came home. Someone is bound to say something soon. In fact, I'm surprised they haven't done so already. But Daisy should hear about it all from us, not someone in the village.'

'So do you think we ought to tell her now?'

'Well, not this very minute, Edgar, obviously,' said Rose. 'But soon, when the twins are out of the way, and the three of us can all sit down together quietly. Pass me that towel, darling?'

'You're sure you've got the right address?' demanded Edgar, several moments later.

'Well, I've got *an* address in Leeds,' said Rose. 'I hope it's still the right one, and I suppose they could forward something to her if I wrote. Edgar, I need another towel now, this one's very wet. I left a pile of them on the landing.'

Then, before Daisy could step back, could run away, could duck into another room, Edgar was suddenly there in front of her, a strange expression on his face which Daisy couldn't read. 'Oh, there you are, we were wondering where you'd got to,' he began, in a husky voice not like his own.

32

'You were talking about me,' Daisy said.

'You shouldn't listen at doors,' said Edgar, frowning.

'You shouldn't talk about people behind their backs. Or that's what you've always told *me*, anyway!' Daisy glared at him, her offer of going out to work and helping save the family fortunes forgotten. 'What did Mum mean, she's got an address? Who do you know in Leeds?'

'You'd better come in,' said Edgar.

Rose was sitting on the bed wrapped up in several towels, fingering out the knots in her wet hair. She took one look at Daisy's face and sighed.

'Come and sit down, sweetheart,' she began. 'We have something to tell you.'

After she'd given Daisy the bare facts, Rose kept saying over and over again, 'Daisy, it doesn't matter who your actual parents were, you're our darling daughter, and we love you.'

'But you lied to me.' Daisy looked from Rose to Edgar, willing herself to wake up from a nightmare, but aware that she was awake already. 'When I was little, and I used to have that dream, when I saw the lady with black hair, you must have known she was my mother, but you never said.'

'Daisy, you were too young to be told.'

'But now I know.' Daisy swallowed hard, as if she were trying to digest it. 'So I'm a misfit, aren't I? You're a proper family. Mummy, Daddy, your two little boys, and I'm the cuckoo in your nest.'

'Daisy, don't ever talk like that, don't ever even think it!' Edgar cried. 'We're your parents. You're our child. We'd give our lives for you.'

Rose wrapped one arm round Daisy. 'You're our lovely daughter, always have been, always will be. So don't you ever think you're not, do you hear me?'

'I suppose so.' Daisy shrugged. 'What's my mother's name?'

'It was Phoebe Gower. But now she's Phoebe Rosenheim, or she was going to be. I don't know if she married her fiancé.'

'Where does she live?'

'She came from Bethnal Green, in the East End of London, then she went to Leeds. But I don't know where she lives today.'

'Mum, don't lie to me!'

'Daisy, it's the truth, I promise you.' Rose hugged Daisy tight. 'She didn't keep in touch. When we were in India, I sent a dozen letters to that address in Leeds, I sent her photographs of you, but she didn't reply. Before we went to India, she told me she was going to America, but I don't know if she went.'

'She didn't want me, did she?'

'Darling, it was wartime, she was very young, and she didn't have a real home.'

'So she abandoned me.' Daisy was trying to digest all this, but felt that something was stuck deep in her throat, that if she breathed too deeply she would die.

'She couldn't keep you,' Rose said gently. 'So we said we'd adopt you, which we did.'

'How did you meet her, anyway?'

'She was the younger sister of a nurse I knew in France, during the war,' said Rose. 'Maria and I were working on the ambulance trains, and the Germans sometimes used to bomb them. Poor Maria was killed, but *she* would have adopted you, I'm sure.'

'Darling,' said Edgar, sitting on Daisy's other side, 'please don't think the worst of us. We did what we thought was best for everyone concerned.'

'I know you will be curious about her,' added Rose. 'Maybe you'll want to find her, get to know her, and we'll help you, if you wish.'

'Why should I want to find a woman who abandoned me?' Daisy laid her head on Edgar's shoulder. 'Dad, I hate her, I don't want you to mention her again.'

'I'm sorry we didn't tell you sooner, sweetheart,' Rose said softly.

'Oh, don't worry, Mum, I understand.' Daisy shrugged and got up from the bed. 'Get dry, you'll catch a chill.'

'Where are you going now?'

'To get some supper, if the brats have left me anything.'

'Let me put on my dressing-gown, and I'll come down and make you scrambled eggs.'

'Look, Mum, I'd like to be by myself a bit, all right?' Daisy felt she was choking. She needed to breathe some clean, fresh air. She had to leave the room.

'She didn't ask about her natural father,' whispered Rose, when they were certain Daisy was downstairs, and could hear her clattering plates and saucepans in the kitchen.

'One thing at a time,' said Edgar, and Rose could see he looked all in, grey, tired and drained.

'She's bound to want to know eventually.'

'Let's hope she doesn't ask us yet,' said Edgar. 'I don't think I could cope with it right now. Rose, come here, you're shivering. Let me dry your hair.'

Daisy spent a sleepless night, turning things over in her mind, coming to no conclusions, hating Rose and Edgar for lying or at least misleading her, loving them still for loving her so much, then hating them again.

She got up very early, had her breakfast before anyone else was up, then she left the house. She wanted to see Ewan, so she walked to the place they usually met.

She sat on a stile, waiting.

CHAPTER 4

PHOEBE Rosenheim buttoned up her dress. She met the doctor's calm, professional gaze. 'So you don't think there's any 'ope?' she muttered.

'I didn't exactly tell you that,' the doctor said, evasively.

'But I've already 'ad one baby. I didn't 'ave no bother with my labour, so why can't I have more?' demanded Phoebe. 'I'm only thirty-five, so surely I ain't past it yet?'

'My dear Mrs Rosenheim, some things aren't meant to be.' The doctor spread his clean, white hands. 'But there's nothing seriously wrong. You have a little internal scarring, so although that can make conception hard, I wouldn't say it was impossible.'

'So just keep tryin', eh?' Phoebe put on her elegant straw-hat, settled the smart, black veil over her eyes, then pulled on her new gloves. 'Nathan, he don't say nothin',' she murmured, 'an' he's very patient. But I know 'e wants kids. He's worked so hard, an' now he wants somebody to take over his business when 'e's gone.'

Phoebe's great dark eyes were full of disappointed tears. 'God knows he's done enough for me,' she cried, 'an' now I want to give *'im* somethin', too! Dr Stein, I want to make 'im happy!'

'You've had one child already,' said the doctor, as he glanced at Phoebe's notes again. 'That was back in England, was it?'

'Yeah, when I lived in London,' Phoebe nodded. 'It was born in Bethnal Green, poor little bleeder, just like me.'

'So don't give up all hope.' Then the doctor coughed, clearing his throat. 'I'm sorry, Mrs Rosenheim, but did your baby die?'

'No, it was fine,' said Phoebe. 'But I wasn't married then, an' so it was adopted.'

'Do you know by whom?'

'Oh, yeah, the bloke was in the army. The woman 'ad been a nurse with our Maria – that's my sister, but she's dead – durin' the war.' Phoebe shrugged, as if to suggest all this was ancient history. 'They was good, kind people, so I didn't mind leavin' it with them. Then I married Nathan an' we came to the States, but I couldn't 'ave brought the kid along. It wouldn't have been fair to Nathe, not after all he'd done.'

'The child was not your husband's, then?'

'Oh, no, she was some soldier's.' Phoebe shrugged again. 'You wouldn't think it now, seein' me dressed up so nice, an' all respectable, but I used to go with soldiers then. It was that or starve, durin' the war. Anyway, the people who 'ad the kid wrote to me when I was livin' in Leeds – that's back in England. But I didn't keep the letters, didn't want to know.'

'Where are these people now?'

'God alone knows, Dr Stein.'

'You surely have their names?'

'Of course I have their names, but – doctor, I want *Nathan's* baby, not some other bloke's! I want to be a proper family!'

'Just give it time.' The doctor stood up then, led Phoebe from his office and asked the receptionist to call a cab.

Soon she was in a taxi, all her senses stimulated by the noise and bustle of New York City.

But Phoebe's heart was back in Bethnal Green.

Daisy had waited most of the morning before she realized Ewan wasn't coming. She wondered how he knew. But then she told herself, oh, don't be so ridiculous, of course he doesn't know!

But then she remembered what he'd said the first time they had met, about how his mother and Lady Easton talked about her, how they knew her name and where she lived. They probably knew everything else, as well.

The week went on, the glorious Dorset summer of blue and gold contrasting cruelly with the bitter winter that had frozen Daisy's heart. She must have looked so miserable, she realized, that even the brats were pleasant, and this was restful but alarming. Rose insisted that the twins knew nothing, but the boys were acting as if somebody had died, and Daisy was in mourning.

Mealtimes were impossible. She was given the best of everything, but didn't feel like eating. 'Why don't you have another pilchard, Daze?' asked Robert, one bleak supper-time, on the third or fourth day after Rose's revelations. He didn't wait for Daisy to reply, but slid one off his toast, then plonked the blank-eyed corpse on Daisy's plate.

'You can have one of mine, as well.' Stephen wobbled a fish across the table on his fork.

But Daisy couldn't have eaten the wretched pilchards if she'd tried. Their blind, dead eyes seemed to stare up at her reproachfully. The tomato sauce looked just like blood. Gagging, she got up and left the table.

She knew she had to pull herself together. She was Rose's and Edgar's daughter still. They'd said so, and she knew they really meant it, that they loved her dearly and would always be her mum and dad, no matter who her natural parents were.

But she was in such a muddle.

Superficially, everything in Charton was the same. The people in the village were as pleasant as they'd ever been. But now all their enquiries about her parents and her brothers seemed sarcastic, not polite.

Now, she could imagine all the whispering and gossiping there had been when the Denhams first came home again. She wondered just how much these strangers knew, when she'd known nothing.

Even kindly Mrs Hobson had become an enemy – one of them – and Daisy had stopped going to the kitchen when she was there. Sometimes, Daisy even hated Rose.

She thought, I need to get away from Charton.

But where could I go?

One hot morning, she was making for the headland, meaning to sit on the cliffs and think the whole thing through again, when she saw Ewan coming down the path that led from Easton Hall.

She turned back, walking quickly, hoping that he hadn't seen her yet. But he ran after her and caught her, falling into step beside her, hands thrust in his trouser-pockets, staring straight ahead.

They walked in silence for a hundred yards. But this silence gradually became so heavy and oppressive that Daisy couldn't bear it any more. 'You never came to meet me!' she began. 'I waited hours that morning!' But then she was furious with herself for letting him know how much he had upset her.

'I thought you were so angry with me that you wouldn't come,' he muttered, scowling at the path.

'Why should I be angry?'

'I – well, because I kissed you.'

'Oh, *that*,' said Daisy, somehow knowing that if she dismissed it out of hand, this would hurt him more than getting angry. Glancing at him, she saw his ears and the back of his neck were red. 'I was just startled. You bashed my nose, as well,' she added, pushing the blade in deeper. 'You made me start to sneeze.'

'Sorry,' muttered Ewan, growing even redder.

'I should think so, too.'

39

'Look, can we forget about it?'

'I suppose so,' Daisy murmured, wishing now she hadn't said all that, for there had been no need to be unkind.

Ewan stopped walking. 'Come and sit on the beach a while,' he said, and looked into her eyes, his own beseeching.

'I've things to do at home,' she muttered, feeling her colour rise.

'Just for half an hour?' Ewan reached out and touched her arm as if he would detain her, fingers lying lightly on her flesh. Then he smiled, but nervously, as if afraid she'd bite him.

'Oh – very well.' Daisy became aware that she was actually smiling back, that she was feeling happy for the first time in days. 'Just for half an hour, mind, and then I must go home.'

'I'm really sorry I didn't come that morning,' Ewan murmured as they scrambled down the cliff path, all the tension magically gone. 'But I thought I had annoyed you, and that you'd never speak to me again. Then Sir Michael asked me to go fishing.'

'Well, that must have been a lot more fun than kissing me.'

'God, no, it was deadly. Casting lines, then sitting there for hours. Sticking hooks through worms—'

'Och, those poor wurrums,' teased Daisy.

'Aye, the puir wee beasties.' Ewan grinned. 'Come on, then, sit down. I promise I won't lunge at you again.'

'On your honour?'

'On my father's grave.'

'So what have you been doing?' Daisy asked him. 'Apart from sticking hooks through helpless worms?'

'Nothing,' Ewan said. 'Absolutely bloody, boring nothing. It's good to see *you*, Daisy. But honestly, I've had enough of Dorset, and my mother's driving me insane.'

'Why, what is she doing?'

'Oh, it's all Sir Michael this, and Lady Easton that, and let Sir Michael show you how to shoot and how to fish. Let him get to know you, worm your way into his heart, then he might leave you all his money. Aye, I know, fat chance – he has a dozen brothers and sisters, nephews and nieces, cousins by the score. I don't want his rotten, stinking money, anyway.'

Ewan turned to Daisy. 'I know fine how to shoot and how to fish. But I do both for food, not entertainment. I don't sit on a bank for hours and days, throwing out lines and torturing blind maggots. God, I'm sick of bloody Easton Hall. I miss the Highlands, Daisy, and I miss my home.'

'So do I,' said Daisy. She suddenly remembered India, where there had been certainty, where she'd never doubted that Rose and Edgar were her parents, where they'd had enough to live on, had a host of servants, didn't scratch and forage like wild animals for their food. 'I miss India every day.'

'What do you miss the most?' asked Ewan.

'I – I miss the snow,' she told him, choosing something neutral and impersonal, something safe.

But actually, she realized, this was true. She *did* miss the clean, sharp air and distant snowy peaks of the great Himalayas, which had been clearly visible from the summer residences where she and her mother and the twins had spent the worst of the hot weather, leaving Edgar toiling on the plains.

'Every March,' she told him, 'we left Delhi, and went up to the stations in the hills. Some years, we stayed for months and months, till it got cold and snowed. Then we'd go tobogganing. I don't suppose there's ever any decent snow in Dorset. Last winter, there was some in January, but it soon melted. It turned to slush and mud.'

'I know what you mean about the snow,' said Ewan, nodding. 'A field of clean, white snow, it lifts your spirits. It makes you feel alive. I wish I could see some now. If I were at home, of course, I could.'

'But surely there won't be any snow in August, even up in Scotland?'

'Oh, there'll be a little still on the highest peaks, and in the northern corries.' Ewan caught Daisy's hands and held them, looking earnestly into her eyes. 'Daisy, I've got a plan. Why don't we go and see the snow?'

CHAPTER 5

'WE can't just disappear,' objected Daisy.
'I don't see why not,' retorted Ewan.
'Oh, don't be so stupid! Your mother will wonder where you are, my parents' – yes, they *are* my parents, Daisy insisted to herself – 'will be really worried if I don't come home for lunch.'

'Well, if you ask permission to go on a jaunt to Scotland, do you think you'll get it?' countered Ewan. 'They'll say, "Where are you going, and who's this Ewan person? We don't know his family, so no of course you can't go off with him." Listen, Daisy, you could leave a note.'

'Mm. I suppose I could,' said Daisy, wondering what she'd write. But, since Rose's revelations, she'd been dying to get out of Charton, and suddenly she couldn't wait to leave. 'But what will we do for money?' she asked. 'I have about twelve shillings, I think, and that won't get us far.'

'I have enough to get us to Pitlochry, if we go third class, and after that we'll walk, or find a wagon going up the glen.'

'What about your mother?'

'What *about* my mother?' Ewan grimaced sourly. 'She's so busy sucking up to bloody Lady Easton that she'll never miss me. But don't worry about my mother, I'll be leaving her a note.'

'All right, we'll do it.' Now, for the first time in days, Daisy felt excited, and glad to be alive. 'I'll meet you at Charton station in an hour. We'll tell them in the ticket office that we're only going to Dorchester—'

'Why should we do that?'

'So they don't get suspicious and telephone our parents. Then, when we get to Dorchester, we can buy tickets there for the express.'

'My, what a canny plotter!' Ewan grinned. 'I only suggested this five minutes since, and we're away already!'

'You weren't joking, were you?' Daisy asked him, suddenly anxious.

'No,' he said, and pulled her to her feet. 'Let's go and see the snow. Away and pack your bag now, and don't let anybody see you leave.'

Daisy ran home to Melbury House, grabbed an old oilskin shopping-bag from a hook behind the kitchen door, then quickly ran upstairs, hoping she wouldn't bump straight into Rose.

What should she take to Scotland? She'd never packed for herself before and didn't know how to do it. In India, her ayah had always looked after her clothes, and since they'd lived in Dorset, she hadn't been away.

'A change of things,' she muttered, shoving a clean cardigan, dress and various bits of underwear into her oilskin bag. 'Soap and a flannel, toothbrush, money. . . .'

She scribbled a hasty note to say that she was going to Ewan's house in Scotland for a week or so. But Rose and Edgar shouldn't worry, because she'd soon be home again. Then she sneaked down the service stairs which no one ever used because they were unsafe, went out the back way past the stables, and she was on her way.

They caught the local train from Charton, changed at Dorchester, and two hours later they were on a fast express to Glasgow.

In all her haste to get away, Daisy hadn't had time to think or worry. But, as they sat back in a third-class carriage and watched the West Country scenery speeding by, she suddenly felt sick. Did her note explain things properly, would her parents worry, and would they be furious when she got home?

'A penny for them?' Ewan grinned.

'I was just looking at the cows.' Daisy smiled back wanly. 'Dad's getting into dairy farming soon, or so he says. He wants to buy a herd of Jerseys. Mum is going to manage it, and sell the cream and butter. She's also going to get some laying hens and sell the eggs. How long is it going to take to get to Scotland?'

'Oh, hours and hours yet.' Ewan's eyes were bright and almost seemed to give off sparks. 'Well, I'm getting hungry. Let's go and have some lunch.'

But Daisy's stomach was in knots, and she found she couldn't force down a thing. So Ewan ate her ham and eggs and polished off her pudding.

The journey seemed to go on and on for ever, with everlasting changes after Glasgow as they zigzagged up into the Highlands, with Ewan getting more excited as they went further north.

When they reached the halt that served Glen Grant, it was pitch-dark and raining hard, so it was just as well that Ewan had thought to bring a torch. 'Here, have my jacket,' he began. He took it off, draped it round Daisy's shaking shoulders, and turned up the collar against the downpour.

'But you'll get soaked,' objected Daisy.

'Oh, it's just a shower, and anyway, we Scots are no' afraid of a wee drop of rain.' Soon, Ewan's shirt was sodden, but he didn't seem to mind. In fact, he was grinning broadly. 'Come along, step smartly, and we'll soon be warm and dry.'

Daisy could see that Ewan was delighted to be home. As they squelched along the gravel road that led to where he lived, he hummed and whistled, shaking his wet hair out of his eyes and darting sudden glances all around, chatting about what they would do tomorrow, and wondering aloud if Archie would be pleased to see him. Did Daisy think she might be able to love a wee white rat?

Daisy was more interested in keeping her feet out of the deeper puddles, and wishing she had the excellent night vision that Ewan evidently possessed.

Mr and Mrs Morrison didn't seem to mind being woken in the small hours of a filthy night. They didn't seem especially surprised to see either Ewan or his friend, making Daisy wonder if he had a habit of wandering where he pleased, and bringing people home.

Mrs Morrison made up beds for them in their own cottage, since the big house was let. She made them drinks and sandwiches, then suggested they should go to bed.

'You must telephone your parents in the morning,' she told Daisy, as she lit a candle to light her up the stairs. 'Mrs Gordon at the post office will let you use her phone. She'll put the cost on Mrs Fraser's bill, I have no doubt.'

Daisy went up to bed, where she slept much better than she would have dared to hope, waking to the smell of frying bacon, and to see sunshine streaming into her attic room.

'It's a lovely day,' said Mrs Morrison, as she filled their breakfast plates with bacon, eggs and dubious-looking sausage, which Daisy later learned was properly called pudding, in the perverse way of Scots.

'You say you're going up Ben Grimond, Ewan?' Mr Morrison asked. 'The wireless says we'll have more rain a wee while later on today, so we must find your friend some proper clothes. There'll be a mackintosh in the gun-room, and some boots to fit, I'm sure.'

'But don't forget to go and phone your people,' Mrs Morrison reminded Daisy.

Daisy had expected a little ticking-off. But when she eventually managed to put a call through to her parents, she had to hold the phone a foot away while Edgar told her what a thoughtless, selfish beast she was, how her mother had been beside herself, and how she was to come home straight away.

'Ouch,' she said, as Ewan took the mouthpiece from her trembling hand and hung it up again. 'I forgot my dad was in the army.'

'Lady Easton says he's very aggressive,' murmured Ewan.

'I wasn't aware she knew him.' Daisy had forgotten about the snow. Now she was desperate to go home, see Rose, give her a hug, and say that she was sorry. 'Dad's not at all aggressive, in fact he's very kind. But he's never yelled at me before.'

'I tell you what we'll do,' said Ewan. 'Today, we'll climb Ben Grimond, see the snow, then we'll go back to Dorset.'

'You don't have to come,' said Daisy.

'Yes, I do,' grinned Ewan. 'I need to see your father, let him take a swing at me.'

'*Blow winds*,' cried Ewan, as they climbed the mountain. '*You cataracts and hurricanoes, spout!*'

'*Till you have drench'd our steeples, drown'd the cocks!*' gasped Daisy, feeling the first fat drops of rain come down, and glad of the protection of the bulky and unflattering mackintosh.

'*And thou all-shaking thunder, strike flat the thick rotundity of the world!*' continued Ewan, grabbing Daisy's hand to haul her up a bank of scree.

'*Crack nature's moulds, all germens spill at once, that make ingrateful man!*' wheezed Daisy, watching with awe as lightning forked on a bare ridge a mile or two away.

'I see your education hasn't been totally neglected.' Ewan dragged her panting up the path. 'But God, you are unfit!'

'You don't believe in God,' puffed Daisy, 'and so you shouldn't take his name in vain.'

'I most sincerely beg your pardon,' murmured Ewan, looking anything but sorry.

Daisy's hand was warm in his, and she felt cherished, treasured

– which was quite ridiculous, she decided, considering she was halfway up a mountain with a boy she'd known five minutes, hardly able to get her breath and scared the storm would hit them, then blow them of off the crag.

'It's all right, it's going the other way,' said Ewan, smiling like a guardian angel, and suddenly looking so strong, so brave, so handsome that Daisy felt a stupid urge to fall at his feet and worship.

'I don't much like lightning,' she confessed.

'You mustn't worry, I'll protect you,' Ewan said, his smile as radiant as the sun.

'You'd better, you brought me up here. I thought we were going to look for snow?'

But even though they reached the top of the mountain, they didn't find much snow – only a little tucked deep in a corrie, left there by the blizzards that had scoured and carved the landscape.

Ewan scooped up a crystal handful, and offered it to Daisy.

'It smells of the North Pole,' she said, and licked it, feeling it dissolve upon her tongue. 'It tastes of winter.'

'You're so lovely, Daisy.' Ewan was looking at her so intently that his eyes glowed like green fire. 'So pretty, so bewitching. *Chaste as the icicle that's curdied by the frost from purest snow, and hangs on Dian's temple.*'

Daisy blushed. 'More Shakespeare?' she said lightly, wishing and yet not wishing to defuse the electricity that she could feel flickering between them.

'*Coriolanus.*' Ewan took Daisy in his arms. 'I mean to play him one day,' he said softly, as he held her tight.

'Then I'm sure you will.'

'What about you?' asked Ewan, tipping up her chin and making her look up at him. 'You could be my Juliet, my Rosalind, my Beatrice.'

'I – *'tis an honour that I dream not of—*' said Daisy, laughing.

'You'll be my Juliet,' repeated Ewan. Then he kissed her with such fervour that it didn't matter when their noses bumped, and she could do nothing but kiss him back with clumsy but rising passion, as the stinging rain came down.

'We should go home,' he said, five minutes – or it could have been five hours – later. 'Daisy, take my hand.'

They got down from the top of the mountain somehow, holding each other tightly, terrified but exhilarated by the worsening storm.

'Just as well you never wanted to be a meteorologist,' gasped Daisy, as they forded torrents and slid down gullies, grazing their bare hands.

'I – come here, hold on to me down this bit,' Ewan said, as Daisy slid and scrabbled down the rocky apology for a path.

'Do you know where we are, then?'

'Somewhere on Ben Grimond,' Ewan replied, and grabbed at Daisy's hand just as she began to slide towards a sheer drop and certain death.

To Daisy's huge relief, Mr Morrison came to look for them, then led them home.

'You need your heads examined,' Mrs Morrison clucked, as she dried Daisy's hair. 'How far did you go?'

'To the top, of course,' said Ewan, grinning.

'You'll be the death of Mrs Fraser, and of this young lady's mother,' Mrs Morrison scolded. 'Well, you'll be doing jigsaws and playing cribbage for the next few days. The weather's turned. A bit of the railway line's been washed away. I don't know when you're expected back in Dorset, but you've no chance of getting away this week.'

They had to go for walks. There was no other way that they could be alone, and kiss, and talk, and kiss again. In wellington boots and hats and mackintoshes, they went for rainy hikes all round Glen Grant. Mrs Morrison gave them severe, old-fashioned looks, but didn't say anything.

Daisy was in love, she decided, for there could be no other explanation for the delicious warmth that made her glow, for the silly smile she couldn't keep from curling around her mouth, for the need to be close to Ewan, even if that meant being close to Ewan's Archie, too. She found she was prepared to find the rat's pink eyes, white whiskers and long, scaly tail enchanting – just for Ewan's sake.

They waited for the storm to die away, and then went back to Dorset. The journey took for ever, but although Daisy actually wished that it would never end, of course it did.

The train pulled into Charton, and to Daisy's horror she saw Edgar waiting for them on the station platform, looking grim.

'I'm for it now,' she said.

'Listen, he can't kill you,' murmured Ewan. 'It's against the law.'

'I somehow doubt if that would bother him,' said Daisy, who felt sick.

'Good luck, then,' said Ewan.

Daisy stepped down from the train.

'Dad, I'm really sorry,' she began.

'Where is this boy?' demanded Edgar.

'This is Ewan.' Daisy felt as if she were throwing Ewan to a lion, a very angry, fierce lion who hadn't eaten anything for weeks, and had a taste for human flesh.

'Good afternoon, sir.' Ewan held out his hand.

'Ewan Fraser, is it?' Edgar ignored the proffered hand. 'I suppose you realize Mrs Denham and your mother have been frantic?'

Every word was like a blow, and Daisy expected to see Ewan flinch, but he held his ground and didn't drop his gaze.

'I'm sorry to hear it, sir.' Ewan's face was red, but he stood straight and tall and didn't try to bluff his way out of the situation. 'Mrs Denham will be happy to have Daisy home.'

'Yes, I'm sure she will.' Edgar turned and walked towards the car, and Daisy scuttled after him, much to the interest of the ticket man who didn't dare ask Daisy for her ticket, and she didn't blame him.

Edgar didn't say a word as he drove back to Melbury House. But the very moment Daisy got out of the car, the twins came hurtling out of the front door, and launched themselves at her like small torpedoes.

'Daze, you've been so *wicked*!' Stephen cried. 'The old man's been so *angry*! We haven't dared to cheek him for a *week*! God, it's been *agony*!'

'A boy in the village said you were a hoyden,' Robert added, grinning. 'We had to look it up, it means a rude and ill-bred girl, and so we thumped him. He's got two black eyes.'

'Daze, we've got some cows!' Stephen started pulling her towards the cowshed. 'Come and see them, they're—'

'Daisy, go and see your mother,' Edgar snapped, and Daisy followed him into the house. 'She's waiting for you in the drawing-room.'

Daisy was expecting tears, reproaches and some kind of punishment, but Rose looked calm and placid. 'Come and sit down,' she said, patting the place next to her on the ancient, sagging sofa.

'Mum, I'm sorry,' Daisy said, and meant it.

'At least you left a note, and rang us up to tell us where you'd gone.' Rose took Daisy's hand. 'Er – Daisy, love, the boy you went with, he and you—'

'Oh, don't worry, Mum, Ewan and I are just good friends,' said Daisy, reddening.

'So, sweetheart, what's the matter, are you very unhappy here in Dorset?'

'No,' said Daisy. 'Well, actually, I was upset. When you told me about what happened, I thought everyone in Charton must be looking at me, and laughing at me behind my back. I wanted to get away.'

51

'Yes, I can see why.' Rose stroked Daisy's fingers. 'But darling, please don't run away again. Your father and I were so upset and worried. When we realized you'd gone with the boy from Easton, Edgar had to go and see Sir Michael and his wife. I believe it was an awkward meeting. He's never liked the people at Easton Hall.'

'Ewan says Lady Easton is a bitch,' said Daisy. 'As for Sir Michael, he—'

'I think we should draw a line under all this,' Rose interrupted. 'Darling, promise me something – don't upset your father again, and don't hurt him like you've done this summer. Remember that he loves you.'

'I'll remember,' Daisy promised, getting up.

It wasn't until she was in the peace and solitude of her bedroom that Daisy realized Rose herself hadn't mentioned loving Daisy, had not asked Daisy not to hurt her mother.

So didn't Rose think of herself as Daisy's mother, after all?

So didn't Rose really care?

After Edgar had dropped Daisy off, he went to Easton Hall again, and came home looking blacker than the last time.

'What exactly did you say to Michael?' Rose asked him gently, when she was sure all three of the children were in bed, the doors were shut and nobody could hear them.

'I told him to see his bloody cousin doesn't come near our daughter,' Edgar replied, raking his fingers through his greying hair. 'Chloe then reminded me that Daisy's not our daughter.'

'I hope you didn't rise to that?'

'Rose, it's fine for you to sit here being calm and reasonable! It was different for me to have to walk into their den, to see them sitting there so rich and smug.'

'Darling, I made my choice,' said Rose. 'I've never regretted anything, you know that.'

'Then you're a saint. Or mad – one or the other.' Edgar shook his head and looked away. 'Easton said he'd heard we'd bought some cattle, and that dairy farming was a waste of effort on land like ours.'

'But you didn't comment?'

'I didn't give him the satisfaction of seeing I was riled, or that I thought he might be right.'

'What about the Fraser boy, did Michael say he'd speak to him?'

'He said that Ewan, or whatever he's called, is seventeen, that he's not a child, that he has no authority over him. The mother just sat there snivelling and dabbing at her eyes. I didn't see the boy. I suppose he was avoiding me. So I imagine we must appeal to Daisy's common sense. If she has any common sense.'

'Edgar, we need to tell her the whole story.'

'Open a can of worms that would stink out Dorset?' Edgar turned to look at Rose. 'We don't know if Phoebe told the truth, and we could never prove it if she did. So why spoil everything for Daisy, and maybe even lose her?'

'It wouldn't come to that, she knows she's ours.'

'You're forgetting she ran away.' Edgar shrugged, then grimaced. 'Easton said his keeper's seen the twins going in the coverts. He suspects they're springing traps. So he's told Stokeley he may thrash them, if the keeper catches them.'

'What did you say to that?'

'I told Easton that if any of his servants touch my children, I will have the bloody servants up before the bench, and I will personally thrash *him*.' Edgar's grin was humourless. 'You should have seen his face – and Chloe's.'

'Edgar, it wasn't wise to make such threats.'

'Well, that's too bad, I've made them now.'

'Do you think we ought to tell the children about you and Chloe? Or at least tell Daisy?'

'Why?' asked Edgar. 'It's water under the bridge now, isn't it?'

'Well, I suppose so.'

'You just suppose so? Rose, didn't we both make choices, and haven't we both paid for what we did?'

'Yes, you're right, it's water under the bridge,' said Rose.

Edgar got up and stretched. 'Mr Hobson said he'd get the cows into the shippen, so they'll be ready for the vet when he comes first thing tomorrow morning. I'm just going to check he's shut them in. We don't want them wandering round the yard.'

Edgar left, but ten minutes later he was running back in again, followed by the scent of smoke sharpening the summer night. 'Ring the fire brigade!' he cried, as he burst into the drawing-room, his clothes begrimed with smoke. 'The shippen is on fire!'

Rose was on her feet at once. 'What about the Jerseys,' she began, pulling on her shoes.

'I've let the cows out, they're running round the paddock, I just hope the gate's shut and they don't get on the road. Rose, forget the cows. Go and wake the children. The wind is blowing the fire towards the house!'

CHAPTER 6

ALTHOUGH they threw buckets of water at the blaze, although they dragged out bales of smouldering straw and tried to contain the fire inside the shippen, the wind was blowing off the sea that night, and drove the smoke and flames towards the house.

The sparks from burning timbers danced and flew like wicked fairies. Some beams in the roof of Melbury House, exposed to all the elements, and tinder-dry from three or four weeks of glorious summer sunshine, soon caught fire.

'Me and Rob'll go up on to the roof, Dad,' offered Stephen.

'You'll do no such thing!' cried Rose, grabbing each twin to stop them running into the blazing house. 'Oh, Edgar, where's the wretched fire brigade?'

'They're on their way,' said Daisy. 'I can hear the bells. They must be coming down the road from Dorchester.'

'But that's the long way round,' cried Rose. 'Why aren't they coming down the gated road?'

'It would take too long, getting out and opening all those gates. Come on, you chaps,' said Edgar, wiping his arm across his soot-streaked brow. 'A few more bucketsful should get the fire in the shippen out.'

But although the shippen was gradually damped down until it became a steaming, blackened ruin, the Denhams could do nothing to stop the house from burning down. Daisy, Robert and Stephen, still in their bedraggled pyjamas, stood with their parents as the firemen – who had at last arrived, but admitted they were far too late – failed to do anything but contain the blaze, and stop it spreading to the stables, too.

Mr and Mrs Hobson and other people from the village had smelled smoke, had seen the flames, and they came running across the fields to help put out the fire. But although they made up bucket chains, the old house burned like matchwood, defying any attempts to stop it turning into its own funeral pyre. By the morning, Melbury House and most of the range of outbuildings behind it were reduced to one great, smoking ruin.

'Just as well we have the Stokeleys' cottage,' Rose observed, as Edgar stared shell-shocked at the soot-stained walls and charred oak timbers of his childhood home. 'We can move in there for the time being.'

'We've still got the cows, Dad,' added Robert.

'The rabbits are all right as well,' said Stephen, who had been to check.

'It's just a house,' said Daisy.

'Yes, it's just a house, but it was mine.' Edgar turned to Rose. 'This is down to Easton,' he growled, through gritted teeth. 'He'll never let me forget I took you from him. Although he got his filthy hands on everything that's yours, he still can't allow us to be happy.'

'Dad, what do you mean?' asked Daisy. 'Did Sir Michael want to marry Mum?'

Edgar put his arm round Daisy. 'Yes, he did,' he muttered. 'A long time ago.'

'A *very* long time ago, love,' Rose said quickly. '*I* never wanted to marry anyone but your father, and Mike Easton doesn't like being thwarted. But Edgar, I can't imagine he'd do anything like this.'

'Oh, Mrs Denham!' Mrs Hobson loomed out of the early morning mist. 'What will you do now?'

'We'll manage, Mrs Hobson.' Rose's tired, pale face looked bleached and ghostlike in the misty morning light. 'We'll move into the bailiff's cottage.'

'But Mrs Denham, dear, you can't live there! It's just a hut!'

'Well, it will have to do.' Rose smiled wearily at the other villagers clustered round. 'Thank you, everyone, for all your help.'

'We'll find you sheets and blankets,' promised Mrs Hobson. 'Me and Mrs Dale, we'll get our brooms and soap and buckets. We'll sort the cottage out.'

'We'll get you food, bring up some bread and milk,' announced Miss Sefton.

'There's tins of cream distemper in the village hall,' went on the parish clerk. 'I'll go up and fetch 'em.'

'You'll need some firewood,' said the postman.

'I don't think so, Mr Tranter,' Rose said wryly. She turned to look at Melbury House, at the fallen timbers that were smoking in the dawn. 'We already have enough of that.'

'I'll kill him,' muttered Edgar, who was still standing with his arm round Daisy, and staring into space. 'I'll finish him. I'll deal with Chloe, too.'

'*What* did Mr Denham say?' Mrs Hobson asked, peering at Rose.

'Oh, nothing important – he's upset.' Rose put her arm round Edgar's waist. 'Come along, my love, there's work to do.' Rose led him away, leaving Daisy standing there alone.

'It must've been a cigarette,' said Robert, as he and his brother came out of the ruined shippen, carrying various trophies like blackened, twisted nails, and bits of charcoaled wood.

'Yeah, probably,' nodded Stephen. 'It was one of Dad's butt-ends, I reckon. He chucks them everywhere. Or it was Mr Hobson's stinking pipe.'

'Listen, brats, don't share your thoughts with Dad,' said Daisy, rounding her little brothers up like sheep, then shepherding them towards their parents. 'He won't want to hear them.'

'But why didn't I know?' demanded Ewan, when he heard what had happened and came rushing over to see what he could do to help.

'The wind was coming off the sea, blowing the smoke away from Easton Hall.' Daisy was unpacking groceries in the cottage kitchen. 'There's a hill between us, so you wouldn't have seen the flames.'

'But – oh, Daisy, you could have been killed!' Ewan raked his hands through his red hair, shuddering as if he had a fever. He said he'd come to help and comfort Daisy, but she soon found that she was comforting *him*.

Rose and Edgar were very cool with Ewan. Edgar said he didn't need Ewan to help him with the cows, that they were traumatized enough already, and anyway if he needed anybody's help, he had the twins. Rose had a dozen village women sorting out the cottage, scrubbing floors, and clucking like so many broody hens.

'Daisy, if you want to be useful, go and sort through the stuff the firemen managed to pull out,' said Rose, ignoring Ewan completely. 'It's piled up on tarpaulins in the stable yard. See if you can find us any clothes.'

'I'll come and help you, Daisy,' said Ewan, eagerly.

'Be careful, Daisy, and don't go in the house,' continued Rose, as if he hadn't spoken. But then she turned to Ewan, her grey eyes cold. 'Mr Fraser, I'm sure your mother must be wondering what's become of you. I don't imagine she'd be pleased to know you're here.'

'I'm being sent home,' said Ewan, three days later.

'Well, that was what you wanted, wasn't it?' countered Daisy, as they walked or rather as they skulked along the shingle beach, keeping close to the overhanging cliffs, unwilling to attract the attention of the odious Stokeley or of anyone else from Easton Hall.

'I want to be with you.' Ewan took Daisy's hand. 'When we got back from Scotland, I told my mother I was going to marry you.'

'I'll bet that went down well!' said Daisy. 'What did she say?'

'She laughed.'

'Oh, Ewan!' Daisy stroked away his frown, then kissed him on the cheek. 'We can't get married. I'm not old enough. I'm still at school.'

'You'll soon be sixteen.'

'Nobody gets married at sixteen!' Daisy knew instinctively she mustn't laugh as well. But honestly, she thought, this is insane. 'Anyway, you're going to Oxford, aren't you?'

'I'm not going to Oxford. I'm going to be an actor. I've written to dozens of companies this week. I've made a list of the theatres in the district, and I'm going to see their managers. I'm sure I'll find a rep to take me.'

'Ewan, don't be silly, I'm sure you can't just walk into a theatre and say you're going to act.'

'No, so I'll be an ASM, paint scenery – do whatever it takes to get me started.' Ewan turned to her, his green eyes bright. 'Daisy, you don't *have* to go to school. In fact, your parents need your help. You ought to get a job, in Dorchester or Weymouth. Why don't you—'

'Run away again? My Dad would kill me.'

'Daisy, don't be like this!'

'Like what?'

'So cold, so calculating!' Ewan grasped her hand so tight it hurt. 'You don't have any notion of what I feel for you. Or if you do, you think it's funny.'

'Ewan, that's not fair! You know I'm very fond of you!'

'You're *fond*. Oh, that's fantastic.' Ewan turned on her, his green eyes blazing. 'I *love* you, Daisy – don't you understand?'

'I love you, too.' But right now, Daisy felt she couldn't deal with being in love, as well as with the fire, as well as with her father's misery, as well as with her mother's obvious worry about how they'd all survive.

'I can't think of anything but you!' continued Ewan.

Oh, *and* of being an actor, Daisy thought, but didn't say out loud.

'I'm going to be a star, you'll see,' said Ewan, as if he'd read her mind. 'I'm going to be Hamlet, Romeo, Antony – I'm going to do them all. I want you to come with me. I want you to be my leading lady. I want you to be my Juliet.'

Daisy could see he meant it, and suddenly felt a great surge of affection for him, wanted most of all to be with him. Yes, she was in love. In spite of life being such a mess, in spite of having lost her home and almost everything she owned, being with Ewan made her feel alive, feel she could do anything, feel happy.

'Ewan, don't look so gloomy. I'd love to be your Juliet,' she said. 'I'll talk to Mum and Dad tonight.'

She found her parents sitting in the kitchen of what had been the bailiff's cottage, poring over catalogues of farm machinery. 'So if I leave school, and earn some money, that will help,' she said, looking from her mother to her father, hoping they would see the sense of it.

'But what about School Certificate?' asked Rose. 'Sweetheart, you don't need to find a job. We'll get the insurance money soon, then we'll be on our feet again, you'll see.'

'You'll need that money for rebuilding Melbury House.' Daisy looked at Rose, her blue eyes bright. 'Mum, Dad, I don't need to pass exams, not for the kind of work I want to do.'

'What *do* you want to do?' asked Edgar, looking up from photographs of tractors.

'Well, I was wondering if I could join a rep?'

'You mean you want to be an actress?' Rose's look of horror was almost funny. 'No, I'm sorry, Daisy – that won't do at all.'

'I don't understand.' Daisy frowned at Rose. 'When we were in India, I was always in productions. You encouraged me to sing and dance. You even sent me to have drama lessons with Mrs Abercrombie.'

'Yes, I know, but that was amateur stuff,' said Rose, and looked down at the table. 'You were just performing for our friends. You didn't do it for anyone who had a spare half-crown.'

'So if I do it for nothing, it's all right, but if people pay me, it's not on? Mum, you're just a snob.' Daisy looked at Edgar. 'Dad, do you agree with Mum?'

'Well, if you're serious, maybe you could go to drama school,' said Edgar, carefully, but he was obviously hedging.

'You don't have any money for drama school!' Daisy glared at him. 'Listen, I want to help! I want to work!'

'You'd meet some very strange people in the theatre,' said Rose.

'You mean they would be common.' Daisy scowled. It's like I said, Mum – you're a snob.'

'Let's think about it, shall we?' Edgar glanced at Rose. 'Your mother's right, you know. You'd meet all kinds of people in the theatre, not all of them agreeable.'

'By the way, I'm not happy about you seeing so much of that Fraser boy,' said Rose.

'You don't need to worry about Ewan,' muttered Daisy. 'He's going home next week.'

'I'm going to see a chap in Weymouth,' Ewan said the following day. 'I wrote to the man who runs the company in rep there for the summer season, and he said he'd talk to me.'

'That's great,' said Daisy, beaming, delighted to see Ewan so happy. 'What did your mother say?'

'Oh God,' sighed Ewan. 'She and the gruesome twosome, they got the heavy guns out, didn't they? "If you don't go to Oxford, I'll disinherit you," my mother told me, weeping into her wee lace handkerchief. Honestly, Daisy, Mum missed her vocation. She should be on the stage herself.

'Sir Michael and his ghastly other half stood up for Mum, of course. Lady Easton told me that if I went to see this chap in Weymouth, I wouldn't be welcome at the Hall.'

'What did you say?'

'I told the bitch I had enough money to pay for digs in Weymouth for a month, and that if I didn't get into a rep, I'd find myself a job.' Ewan grimaced wryly. 'Then Sir Michael said that maybe I wasn't aware there were about three million unemployed. At this, my mother started *howling*. I was most impressed.'

'So what will you do now?'

'I'm still going to see this chap on Wednesday. Come with me?'

'Yes, of course I will.'

'I want to do the balcony scene for him,' continued Ewan. 'So you'll have to be my Juliet.'

'Fine by me,' said Daisy. 'I can feed your lines to you.'

But Ewan didn't just want feeding. He wanted feeling and commitment, too. He found a copy of the play in the library at Easton Hall and set about directing Daisy, making her say the lines again and again until she spoke them naturally, breaking her of the histrionic delivery that Mrs Abercrombie had fostered in her pupils, and making Daisy feel that she *was* Juliet.

They spent the rest of the week on a deserted little beach that holidaymakers never used because it was miles from any road and totally submerged when the tide came in. An overhanging rock made a convenient balcony for Juliet. They played to an audience of seals and gulls.

At last Ewan was satisfied with Daisy. But she could see that *he* was born to be an actor, that he came alive when he was Romeo.

'*At what o'clock tomorrow shall I send to thee?*' asked Daisy, as they reached the stile where they parted every evening.

'*At the hour of nine,*' said Ewan, kissing her goodnight.

'*I will not fail,*' said Daisy.

'See,' said Ewan, 'you can do it now, you speak the verse as naturally as breathing. But maybe we'd better make it eight o'clock, at Charton station. I don't want to keep this fellow waiting.'

Wednesday dawned cold and dull, with a sea mist hanging over everything. After a lovely summer, autumn was on its way.

'You're up bright and early. Where are you going?' asked Rose.

'To Weymouth,' Daisy said. 'I need to buy some things for school. A new geometry set, some pencils, stuff like that.'

'You could get those in Dorchester,' said Rose. 'Your father's going to Dorchester this morning, he could give you a lift.'

'I know, Mum, but I fancy going to Weymouth. I've saved my pocket-money, so I've got the fare.' Daisy pulled on her jacket. 'I should be back by lunchtime.'

'I'll need you to help me turn out the bedrooms later, don't forget!' called Rose, as Daisy left the house.

She and Ewan caught the train to Weymouth. 'My mother isn't speaking to me now,' said Ewan, as they settled down in a compartment. 'She's been having breakfast in her room for the past week, and she has the vapours every evening. She says she can't believe how I've turned out, and that my father must be turning in his grave.'

'Mine knows I'm up to something,' Daisy said.

The theatre was in a sidestreet near the sea-front, and proved to be a tiny little playhouse whose faded plush, unpolished brass and threadbare, dirty carpets had all seen better days. It wore an end-of-season, tawdry air, its posters faded, and its handbills in their holders yellowing and curling in the dusty foyer.

Ewan walked in boldly, with Daisy close behind him, breathing in the familiar scents of dust and sweat and greasepaint that she remembered from the garrison theatres back in India, where she had played fairies, elves and maidens. 'Ewan, are you nervous?' she whispered.

'Terrified,' he replied, but she could see his eyes were bright.

'Ah, you must be Mr Fraser,' boomed a middle-aged man with mutton-chop whiskers, a huge belly and tiny feet in spats, who suddenly materialized out of nowhere, like a ghost. 'I'm Alfred Curtis, pleased to meet you. Your letter was most timely. One of my juveniles has just walked out on me, his understudy broke his arm last week, so we've been doubling up the parts. But that's not very satisfactory.'

He hadn't seemed to notice Daisy, but she followed as he led Ewan into the darkened, silent theatre. 'Hang on a minute,' he said, 'let's get some lights on. Tom!' he shouted to some invisible being. 'Let's have a spot or two down here! There, that's much better. Now, what have you prepared?'

'A scene from *Romeo and Juliet* – I hope that's all right?' Ewan turned to Daisy. This is Miss Denham, she'll be Juliet.'

'We could have got a lady from the company to be your Juliet,' said Mr Curtis, plumping himself down like a cigar-scented, hound's-tooth-suited walrus in the front row of the stalls. 'But since your friend is here – very well then, off you go.'

Ewan helped Daisy climb on to the stage.

Daisy's first few lines came creaking out, and sounded false and artificial. But Ewan spoke so naturally, so earnestly, that soon she started to relax and speak only to him.

She forgot about fat Mr Curtis, forgot she was in a musty English theatre on a damp September morning, balanced on some rickety wooden steps which did duty as a balcony. Instead, she was in Verona, on a warm, velvet night, and she'd just fallen desperately in love. . . .

'Mr Curtis?' Ewan snapped out of being Romeo and walked downstage.

'Yes, Mr Fraser, that was very good.' Mr Curtis grinned. 'I have a bit of trouble seeing Romeo as a Scot, but – yes, you're hired, my boy.' He rubbed his several chins and looked at Ewan sideways, as if measuring him. 'Actually, we're not going to be doing any Shakespeare,' he continued. 'It would be wasted on the Midlands, which is where we'll be this winter.

'But you'll be fine for general modern drama, I can tell. You've got that look about you. Do you have a suit of evening dress, some casual flannels, shirts and things?'

'Yes – er – I can find them.'

'You'll need to supply your make-up. You must work on your accents, too.' Mr Curtis grinned again. 'On the English stage, you see, you ought to sound as if you come from Surrey – not from Aberdeen.'

'I can do English accents,' Ewan said, and rattled off some lines which Daisy didn't recognize, but which he later told her were from one of Mr Noel Coward's plays. 'Mr Curtis – er – what could you pay me?'

'Three pounds a week until next March, and then we'll see.' Mr Curtis glanced at Daisy. 'What about your lady friend? Where is she working now?'

'I'm not working,' Daisy told him, curtly. 'I still go to school.'

'Two pounds ten a week?' suggested Mr Curtis, doing his measuring-up look once again.

'Doing what?' asked Daisy.

'Mostly walking on. Maids and cooks and nurses or whatever, but a bit of understudying, too.'

'I'm not sure if my mother—'

'Mrs Curtis chaperons the ladies, so you can tell your mother she doesn't need to worry about you getting into trouble. All our digs are proper boarding-houses, they only take theatricals. I'm happy to meet your mother, if you wish.'

Ewan took Daisy's hand and squeezed it.

'Thank you, Mr Curtis.' Daisy met the manager's gaze. 'I accept your offer.'

Daisy walked into the bailiff's cottage feeling very nervous – far more nervous than when she'd been on stage, which in a curious way had felt like home.

'You can't,' said Rose, at once. 'You're far too young.'

'Rose, let's talk about it.' Edgar looked at his wife and smiled. 'You weren't much older than Daisy when you went to nurse in France.'

'There was a war on, Edgar – I was needed!'

'Where are these people based?' asked Edgar.

'They travel around the country. They've been in Weymouth for the summer, but they'll be in the Midlands all this winter.'

'Birmingham, Wolverhampton.' Rose shuddered.

'Dad?' said Daisy, looking at Edgar.

'Maybe we should go and meet these people,' Edgar said, looking at Rose.

'Mum, I'll be with lots of other people,' continued Daisy. 'Mr Curtis says he'd like to meet you, then he can tell you what goes on. You can meet Mrs Curtis, too. Listen, Mum,' said Daisy, desperately. 'It's what I really want to do.'

'This is all ridiculous,' said Rose. 'I'm going to bed.'

Daisy met Ewan on the shingle beach the following day. 'What did your parents say?' he asked.

'Mum is dead against it. She's being really horrible. She doesn't want me to have any fun.' Daisy glanced up at Ewan. 'She thinks I should do my School Certificate, then be a clerk – or something.

But Dad might be persuaded.'

'Shall I have a word with him?'

'Yes, if you want him to put his foot down, and forbid it after all.' Daisy's grin was wry. 'You might not have noticed, but you're not very popular with Dad. What about your mother, what did she have to say?'

'Oh, nothing much, but she'd be spitting pins and throwing carving knives, if she had any handy.' Ewan grinned. 'I'm leaving Easton Hall tomorrow morning.'

'Where will you go – to Weymouth?'

'Yes, I'll find some digs.'

'Ewan, will you do something for me?' Daisy looked into his eyes. 'I'm not sure I should ask you this. . . .'

'What do you mean? Daisy, I'd do anything for you.'

'Even help me find my real mother?'

CHAPTER 7

'WHAT do you mean?' asked Ewan.
'Obvious, isn't it?' Daisy looked down at her hands and wished she didn't bite her fingernails. It didn't look very grown-up, and she must stop.

'Well, it's not obvious to me.'

'I was adopted when I was a baby. My mother came from the East End of London. She wasn't married. I only found out a couple of weeks ago.' Daisy looked up at Ewan, challenging him. 'I dare say you're disgusted.'

'Oh, Daisy, don't be silly. Of course I'm not disgusted. But I wish you'd told me.'

'It's not the kind of thing one brags about,' said Daisy, half-wishing she *hadn't* told him now, afraid that she might cry.

'My poor wee girl, come here.' Ewan put his arm round Daisy's shoulders. 'I'll help you find your mother, of course I will.'

'I don't have much to go on,' murmured Daisy, snuggling up against the Harris tweed of Ewan's jacket. 'Just that her name was Phoebe Gower, and now she might be Mrs Rosenheim. She could still be in Britain, or she might be in the USA.'

'Well, that's just two countries out of dozens, she's not called Anne Smith or Mary Brown, so don't worry, we'll soon find your mother,' said Ewan, cheerfully. 'Now, about the other matter – do you think your father is going to be persuaded? Or shall you have to run away again?'

'I can usually get my way with Dad. It sometimes takes a while, but if I keep on at him, he generally gives in. But Mum's determined to spoil everything.'

'Let me come and talk to her, maybe?'

'Oh, Ewan! She'd throw you out, and then she'd lock me up for ever.'

Daisy gradually wore Edgar down.

While he was always strict with the two boys, he was lenience itself with Daisy. Or he had been up to the time he'd yelled at her and ordered her to come back home to Dorset.

But he'd calmed down now. While Rose was still adamant that the whole scheme was ridiculous, and wouldn't talk about it, Edgar went with Daisy into Weymouth to meet Mr and Mrs Curtis.

Looking at the manager and his wife through Edgar's eyes, Daisy suddenly saw a pair of strangely dressed, Micawberish small-time actors. Mr Curtis's white spats looked stupid, his loud check suit was grubby, and he had a silly little monocle hanging round his neck.

Mrs Curtis wore a calf-length dress of faded purple velvet with some oddly puckered segments in the skirt, which made Daisy wonder if it had once been a curtain. She also wore a horrid orange wig, a huge amount of rouge, and lots of rings with diamonds which were obviously fake. She had the stubble of a grey moustache.

They were both well into middle age. Their dreams of thespian glory must have faded long ago. Now they eked out an existence in the sticks, putting on shows for easy-to-please provincials, and hoping to save enough for their retirement.

She shook her head, and looked at them again, saw two people who'd help her start to realize a dream – or Ewan's dream, at least, and Daisy knew how much it meant to him.

Yes, said Mrs Curtis, she would see Miss Denham wrote to her parents once a week at least. She would make sure Miss Denham had good lodgings, ladies only. She and Mr Curtis had a daughter of their own. Mr and Mrs Denham needn't worry about a thing.

Please, Dad, don't say anything, thought Daisy, as Mrs Curtis gushed on like a geyser, now and then reaching out to pat his hand, which made him flinch.

'Thank you, Mrs Curtis,' Edgar said politely, as she finished her monologue and stuck a hairpin back into her wig.

'So we'll look forward to Miss Denham joining us,' said Mr Curtis, baring yellow dentures that would have looked more natural inside a tiger's mouth.

'Well, Dad?' Daisy asked him anxiously, as they walked along the street towards the railway station.

'Well, Daisy – is it what you really want?' asked Edgar.

'I'd like to try it, Dad.'

'If it doesn't work out, if you get stuck, if you're in any kind of trouble, you tell me right away.' Edgar stopped and looked at Daisy. 'I'll come and fetch you. Wherever you are, whatever you've done, it makes no difference, I'll be there. So promise me you'll phone, and you may go.'

'I promise, Dad,' said Daisy.

'I didn't know Mum knew words like that,' said Robert, as Daisy, Stephen and he sat on the staircase that same evening, as their parents argued in the kitchen. 'Daze, do you think Dad will be all right?'

'He was in the army, he killed a thousand Germans, of course he'll be all right.' Daisy scowled at him. 'Shut up, I want to listen to what they're saying.'

'Look out, here they come!' hissed Stephen.

The three of them ducked back as Edgar walked out of the

kitchen and left the house, slamming the front door behind him.

'What are you children doing, lurking there?' Rose had followed Edgar, and now she glared upstairs, hands on her hips, her dark hair a wild halo, her grey eyes flashing fire. 'I dare say you were listening?'

'You were shouting at Dad so loud we couldn't help but hear!' cried Daisy, determined to stand her ground. 'Mum, I know it wasn't like this in your day. I know girls stayed at home and did embroidery, then married some boring man and had a dozen ghastly babies—'

'Don't you talk to me like that, my girl!' retorted Rose. 'You're still a child, you know!'

'For God's sake, Mum, you can't afford to keep me!' Daisy shouted. 'Since we came back from India, we've been paupers. We're camping in a hut, we never have new clothes, we live on turnips. So let me help, why don't you?'

'I can't think what's come over you,' said Rose. 'You used to be so sweet. You were a charming little girl.'

'Maybe I've grown up. Mum, I want to start to live my life, do what I want, and you should just accept it.'

'Daisy, don't you spout that modern-woman stuff at me!'

Robert and Stephen knew when it was wise to keep their counsel. They melted into the shadows and went to bed.

'So may I go, or not?' Daisy asked Rose at breakfast the next morning.

'If I say no, you'll only run away, or do something else ridiculous.' Rose wouldn't look at Daisy. 'Apparently, your father says you may. So I've been overruled in any case.'

'Mum, I'm sixteen later on this month. I'm not a baby. Most girls in England start going out to work when they're fourteen. I know actors are often out of work, but so are lots of other people these days. I want to make a career on the stage.' Daisy looked at Edgar.

'Dad, say something, please!'

'You'd better go and pack your things,' said Edgar. 'I'll run you into Weymouth. Does that Fraser fellow want a lift?'

'Ladies and gentlemen, may I present Miss Denham and Mr Fraser!' Alfred Curtis had the whole company up on stage to meet the new arrivals. 'Mr Fraser's kindly taken over Mr Atterbury's roles, and he'll be understudying Mr Morgan, Mr Reed and Mr Kenton. Miss Denham's going to take some smaller parts and female walk-ons. She'll also understudy Miss Hart and Mrs Nightingale.'

Mr Curtis pointed to a pile of scripts lying on the piano in the wings. 'The new stuff came this morning, so we'll have a read-through in ten minutes.'

Daisy looked nervously at Miss Hart and Mrs Nightingale, who lounged against the flats. Two divinely dressed and made-up creatures in their twenties, their scarlet lips were curved in – what? Amusement, welcome, scorn?

Ewan looked all right, she thought, he'd fitted in at once. One of the older actors was grinning at him matily, while another was offering him a light.

Daisy felt a pang of loneliness, a sudden wish to be in the kitchen of the bailiff's cottage, shoving books into her satchel, getting ready to go off to school.

In spite of what Mrs Curtis had told Edgar, her digs in Weymouth weren't exactly homely. The whole house smelled of mice and onions. The mattress on her bed was stuffed with straw, and it was freezing in her attic, but the attic was all she could afford.

'Miss Denham?' Alfred Curtis tossed a script her way. 'Do wake up, my darling. You're the office girl, and later you'll be the woman at the bus-stop. So, my loves – Act One, Scene One!'

*

'You look like you've lost a hundred quid and found a sixpence.' Miss Hart caught Daisy as she left the stage. 'Hey, don't look so worried, I won't bite.'

'I'm not worried,' Daisy lied.

'You are, but you were doing fine.' Miss Hart lit up a Craven A then offered the pack of cigarettes to Daisy, who declined. 'I'm Julia, and Lady Muck is Amy Nightingale. She has the room right under yours, so don't you go thinking it's *me* who snores all night! We're going to the pub, d'you want to come?'

'I can't, I'm under age.' Daisy was now convinced of the stupidity of this. Rose was right, she was a child, she ought to be at school.

'We'll sneak you in,' grinned Julia Hart. 'Stand tall, girl, stick your chest out, put on a bit of lipstick and you'll pass. I'll buy you a lemonade.'

'I – er – I've left my make-up at my digs,' said Daisy, feeling really stupid, young and small.

'Jesus and Mary, child – here, borrow mine.'

Ewan came up then and put his arm round Daisy's shoulders. 'What would your mother say?' he whispered, as she put on lipstick, frowning at herself in Julia's powder-compact mirror.

'She'd say I told you so,' said Daisy, snuggling up against him, enjoying the familiar feel of him and breathing in his special scent. 'She'd say I was well on the way to being a fallen woman.'

'There's no chance of that with me around,' said Ewan, suddenly serious. 'I'll look after you.'

'Come on, you two, before they close,' said Julia Hart. 'We're wasting precious drinking-time.'

The men were nice, thought Daisy. George Reed and Francis Kenton, middle-aged inseparable friends who always shared a double at their digs, so Ewan said, treated her like a child, but not in a nasty, patronizing way. 'If you need advice or anything, you just come see your Uncle George,' said Mr Reed.

'Or your Auntie Frank,' said Mr Kenton, grinning. 'We'll see you right. Go on,' he added, holding out a bag, 'have a liquorice allsort, take a few.'

Mr Morgan was a little younger, rather flashier in looks and manner, and Daisy wouldn't have trusted him with sixpence. But with his pencil-thin moustache, his snap-brim trilbies and his two-tone shoes, he was a comically obvious seducer, an end-of-the-pier romancer. The kind of man who'd always be a rather pathetic joke, even though he thought he was a charmer and was always touching her, patting her bottom, stroking her shoulder, coming up behind her and playing with her hair.

Ewan said that one day very soon, he was going to beat Bryn Morgan up.

'Oh, he doesn't mean any harm,' said Daisy.

'You're a flirt,' said Ewan. 'You like it when men look at you and want you.'

'Well, I'm supposed to be an actress, so men are supposed to look at me – and women, too.'

'You know what I mean,' said Ewan, scowling. 'You just remember, you're *my* girl.'

The women weren't as easy to work out. Julia Hart was usually friendly, but she often drank too much, and then she could be waspish. Amy Nightingale was rather frosty, curling her lip disdainfully if Daisy fluffed her lines, and making loud remarks about certain people who should still be in the kindergarten.

'She's jealous of you, that's all. She thinks you want her parts,' said Julia, who told Daisy she'd been born in Liverpool, and was the eldest in a Catholic family of nineteen. 'So they don't miss *me*,' she said, and grinned – but then looked tragic, and added that she missed *them*. 'I never had a mother,' she said, sadly. 'Well, I did, but she was always pregnant, and she never had any time for me.'

Edgar brought the brats to see the last of the shows in

Weymouth. Much to Daisy's great surprise, the twins were well-behaved, and didn't make any remarks about the smallness of her parts.

'Mum sends you her love,' said Robert, colouring as he always did when he was telling fibs.

'Mind you write, Daze,' Stephen said. 'Our form's task this term's collecting picture-postcards of the British Isles. So send us some, then we'll get loads of house-points and we'll win the cup.'

'I'll send you lots,' said Daisy.

'Look after yourself, old girl,' said Edgar, kissing her on the cheek, and making her want to go back home, to tell Rose she was sorry, that she'd made a big mistake.

'I'll look after Daisy, Mr Denham.' Ewan came up and put his arm round Daisy, and she saw Edgar wince. But he seemed to hear her silent pleading, and was polite to Ewan, shook his hand and wished him well.

The following day the company packed up, got out, and caught the train to Walsall. 'You'll be playing the daughter of the vicar in the next one we do,' said Julia, lighting up although it was No Smoking. She had told the others this compartment was Girls Only, and made the middle-aged couple who were already sitting in it glare. 'I heard old Alfred telling Mrs C last night.'

'But don't go getting a swollen head,' said Amy Nightingale, who'd set out all the equipment for an in-depth manicure, and now began to file her long, sharp nails. 'God, it's really stuffy in here. There's a bit of a pong as well, like last night's fish and chips. Mind if I open a window, anyone?'

The middle-aged couple got up and left the compartment, huffing crossly.

'Good riddance to them,' grinned Julia, putting her feet up on the opposite seat. She opened her case and took out several greasy paper bags. 'Here, Daisy, have a cheese-and-pickle sandwich. Now I'm going to tell you all my secrets.'

Eating in public, putting one's feet on railway carriage seats, smoking, wearing make-up in the daytime – Daisy was glad Rose wasn't there to see.

As soon as they arrived in a new place, Ewan and Daisy got hold of the telephone directory and town gazette and looked up all the Gowers and Rosenheims. They checked electoral registers, and even knocked on doors, alarming several innocent Gowers and Rosenheims, who were usually very nice about it, but who couldn't help.

They never found a Phoebe Gower or Rosenheim, not even in Leeds, where Rose said Phoebe lived, or had lived – once upon a time. 'She must have gone off to America,' said Daisy.

'Then we'll go there, too,' said Ewan. 'One day.'

'We'll never find her in America!'

'We might, you never know.' Ewan smiled encouragingly. 'Chin up, my brave wee girl. Look on the bright side, eh? We none of us know what the future holds, or what might happen.'

'Nathan, I don't think it's going to happen.'

Phoebe was sitting at the breakfast table in the newly fitted out apartment in Lower East Side, drinking cup after cup of fragrant coffee, and smoking endless Lucky Strikes. 'I'm bein' punished for givin' Daisy up. God don't want me to have no more children.'

'Phoebe, darling, it's nothing to do with God.' Nathan took her hand in his, and gave her his usual reassuring smile. 'You're still young. There's plenty of time to have another child. Do you remember Sarah, Harry Goldman's wife? She was nearly forty when she had her twins.'

'I'd better go to work.' Phoebe stood up and smoothed her smart, black dress. 'We're gettin' a delivery this morning.'

'Your hat shop's doing very well,' said Nathan, happy to change the subject. 'I was looking at the books last night. You're going to make a handsome profit this year.'

'That's something, I suppose.' Phoebe sighed. 'If I'm not goin' to be a mother, I need something else to do.'

'Phoebe, listen to me.' Nathan pulled her down on to his lap. 'I'm not saying I don't want children. Of course I do, it would be wonderful. But if it never happens, we mustn't let it blight our lives.'

'You're far too good for me, you know that?' Phoebe kissed his cheek and forced a smile. 'Tell you what we'll do. We'll give it another couple of months, all right?'

'Then what?'

'Then if nothin' happens, I'm goin' back to England. I'm gonna find my daughter.'

'Do you want me to come with you?'

'No, I know you 'ate the place, an' I can't say I blame you. England ain't done much for you, or me. But – I gotta go.' Phoebe looked anxiously at Nathan. 'Look, I promise I'll come back. So don't you go divorcin' me?'

'I won't divorce you,' Nathan promised. 'You're my life.'

'So when I got divorced, my parents said they didn't want anything more to do with me. It was just as well I could earn my living on the stage,' said Amy Nightingale, in a cut-glass accent which Daisy recognized as genuine. They were having an after-theatre drink back at their digs, Amy and Julia drinking gin, and Daisy lemonade.

'Come down in the world a bit now, ain't you, Lady Muck?' asked Julia, filling Amy's glass and her own again. 'Daisy, you wouldn't know it, but our Amy used to be a nob, an' married to an honourable, no less.'

'Who beat me up and had a string of mistresses, so I had an affair, to pay him back.'

'So then he threw her out and got his lawyers on the case, an' soon old Amy was beggin' in the streets.'

'The woman always loses everything.' Amy stared into her glass of gin. 'Daisy, darling, we're going to need another bottle soon. Nip round to the offie, there's a love.'

Daisy did as she was told.

Amy and Julia let Daisy off for being younger, prettier and slimmer. After all, Daisy was a dope who couldn't do her make-up properly, and blushed when people swore. Daisy knew when she was being patronized, but also knew she had a lot to learn. So she was grateful when Julia or Amy heard her lines, told her company secrets, and – most important – explained where babies came from, and how she should conduct herself if she didn't wish to make additions to the population.

They also advised her not to get too serious with Ewan, a boy who thought too much of himself, they said. They'd met his kind before, and Mummy's boys like him were always trouble, used to getting their own way in everything, which was bad news for girls. They lent her clothes, which Ewan didn't usually like, saying she looked too flashy.

'He means you'll start attracting other men,' said Julia, grinning as she buttoned Daisy into a very flattering black jacket with a smart fur collar that set off her blonde hair. 'You ought to get a permanent wave, you know – that would make you look much more grown-up. You need to get your ears pierced, too. We'll do it with a needle and a cork. Then you can wear my rhinestone earrings.'

Daisy shut her ears to Rose's voice inside her head saying that rhinestone earrings would look vulgar, that permanent waves were common, and that using corks and needles would lead to septicaemia and make her ears drop off.

Ewan kept his promise to Edgar, looking after Daisy, seeing she wasn't out alone at night, and letting everyone know she was his girl. Daisy found this gratifying, but irksome. She still loved him, but. . . .

'We don't *always* have to go around together,' she told him. These days, she was feeling very much more secure, and Ewan was managing at last to speak as if he came from Surrey.

'But I like to be with you,' he said. 'No matinée today – what shall we do?'

'I'm going to the talkies with Julia and Amy.'

'Oh.' Ewan shrugged, but then braced up. 'Well, that's all right. I know you ladies like to have an all-girls outing, every now and then.' Daisy suddenly thought, he sounds as if he's fifty, not eighteen. 'I'll go and play a bit of hockey with the chaps.'

'Ewan, just a minute. I need to tell you something, so you don't find out from someone else.'

'What's that, then?' Ewan took out the nasty, smelly pipe he'd recently started smoking, knocked it against his heel and smiled indulgently at Daisy.

'You know we're starting reading for that new play next month? Mr Curtis says I'm going to play the *ingénue*. So I'll be kissing Mr Morgan.'

'On the mouth?'

'Yes, so Julia says.'

'I see.' Ewan stuck his pipe between his teeth, doing a very creditable impression of a heavy father being asked if his daughter could stay out till eight o'clock at night. 'Well, I suppose it can't be helped. As long as you don't mean it, eh?'

'I certainly won't mean it!' Daisy shuddered. Bryn Morgan always stank of whisky and Capstan Extra Strength.

'That's all right, then.' Ewan grinned. 'Anyway, I know something, too. Bryn Morgan's leaving us quite soon. He's going to do some concert parties, then he's got himself a summer season in Torquay.'

'You ready, Daisy?' Amy and Julia came bustling up, dressed to the nines, enveloped in clouds of scent, their hair spun satin and their faces gorgeously made up.

'Oh, Daisy May,' sighed Julia. 'Why aren't you wearing that green coat I gave you? This old red jacket makes you look thirteen.'

'Hello, Mr Wolf,' said Amy, smirking at Ewan foxily. 'We're taking Miss Red Riding Hood away.'

'We're going to corrupt her innocence.'

'We're off to see a talkie Snow White here shouldn't see till she's eighteen.'

'Then we're going to take her to the pub and get her plastered,' went on Julia, lighting up.

'Just kidding, Aberdeen Angus, no need to look so worried!' said Amy, pinching Ewan's cheek. 'You shouldn't smoke that thing, it makes you cough, an' it'll rot your teeth. You could get a dummy if you want something to suck.'

CHAPTER 8

DAISY had noticed Julia wasn't well, but Amy told her not to worry. Julia was a moody cow who had her ups and downs.

But there were downs and there was hitting rock-bottom, Daisy thought, and all that week Julia had been missing cues, getting on stage with seconds to spare or even seconds late, and making Alfred Curtis tear his hair – or what remained of it. She was drinking gin from thermos flasks and smoking like a pot bank.

Then, one Sunday morning, Daisy caught her coming out of the bathroom at their digs, as green as Banquo's ghost, and carrying a mysterious parcel wrapped in pages from the *Daily Sketch*.

'Goodness, what's the matter?' she demanded. 'Julia, you look awful! Why don't you go back to bed? I'll go and get you some tea and toast.'

'I couldn't eat any toast, and for God's sake keep your bloody voice down, Fairy Fay. I don't want that old bag who owns the place up here.' Julia glanced over the banisters to see if anybody was lurking in the hall. 'D'you know if she's gone to church? Or to her coven, with the other witches?'

'She's gone to morning service, and she won't be back for ages. Julia, do you need—'

'I need a fag,' said Julia. She thrust the parcel into Daisy's hands. 'Do me a favour, love? Go and shove that in the dustbin, eh? Make sure you push it right down to the bottom, so the cat can't get it.'

'Yes, of course, but what—'

'You know that chap I picked up in the pub in Wolverhampton, a couple of months ago? The one with the cheeky grin and Oxford bags and Brylcreemed hair?' Julia scrabbled in the pocket of her dressing-gown, found her cigarettes and lit one, drawing greedily. 'Well, the bugger got me up the duff.'

She tottered into her bedroom, then sank down on her bed. 'But now I've dealt with it, so everything's tickety-boo again, all right? Be a little angel and don't say anything to Lady Muck, or any of the others? I don't think I could stand a bloody chorus of I-told-you-so.'

'I won't say anything.' Daisy could almost feel the parcel writhing in her hands, and although she knew she must be just imagining movement, it was certainly still warm.

She shuddered as she realized *she* could have been a parcel, if her natural mother hadn't been too – what? Too ignorant, too religious? She hurried off down the stairs and did what Julia had asked her, shuddering still. She slammed the lid back on the bin.

'What's up with Fanny Anne this morning?' When Daisy went back into the house, she found Amy at the breakfast table, smoking and eating kippers and feeding titbits to the cat.

'She – she's not feeling very well. She's going to stay in bed a bit.'

'I saw you sneaking something to the bin.' Amy leaned back and blew a perfect smoke-ring. 'She wants to watch it. Takes too many chances, does our Fanny Anne. If I've told her once, I've told her half a million times, she wants to make the buggers use a thing. But her religion says you can't, or something daft like that.

'You watch it, too, young Daisy May,' continued Amy. 'I've seen the way your Ewan looks at you, eyes undressing you, tongue hanging out. He'd have you in the pudding-club as quick as bloody winking, then blame *you*.'

Amy watched as Daisy put the kettle on. 'I'll have another cup,' she said, 'and if you're going back upstairs, make sure that trollop hasn't left the evidence in the bathroom.'

'Evidence?' said Daisy.

'Yeah, like knitting needles, messy towels. We don't want the landlady to find them, the old bag would throw us out, and anyway, I want to have a bath.'

Bryn Morgan's concert party offer was too good to refuse. He needed to leave the company even earlier than expected, making Alfred Curtis curse and say he'd never again employ a Welshman – and there'd be penalty clauses in all contracts from now on.

'Alfred's been on the telephone all week,' said Amy, as the ladies got made up and ready for a matinée in Stoke. 'He can't find anyone at all, so Mrs C was telling me. Of course, there are all the usual drunks and layabouts, people with one leg or half a brain that no one wants to work with, but everyone who's any good appears to have a job.'

'I reckon he's going to have to promote your boyfriend,' Julia told Daisy. 'So you two will be kissing in the spotlight after all.'

'Sweet,' said Amy, grinning at Daisy's blush.

'Alfred's got someone coming here tomorrow,' added Julia. 'I heard him telling Mrs C, name's Jessie something.'

'Why do we need another girl?' Amy rolled on her stockings. 'What's the old bugger got up his sleeve now, eh?'

'A play with decent parts for women?' Julia slicked on lipstick. 'Now, girls, that *would* make a flippin' change.'

'God, more rehearsals. Daisy, love – lend me your number five.'

*

Daisy was tired after two performances, a matinée and an evening played in a half-empty theatre which left all the cast feeling low and unappreciated.

'Nobody's got any money in the Potteries, they're all on the dole,' said Julia, creaming off her eye-paint. 'I dunno why Alfred took these lousy bookings.'

'The premises are all cheap,' said Amy, scowling round the dressing-room in which the paint was flaking, and which smelled of ancient sweat and tomcats. 'Come on, girls, let's go and have a drink or several, drown our bloody sorrows.'

'See what we can find,' said Julia, winking.

'Oh God, Miss Holy Innocent, don't look at us like that,' said Amy, catching Daisy's eye. 'We can't keep ourselves in gin and knickers on what that old skinflint pays us, and a girl needs company now and then, in any case.'

'That bloke I was chatting to in the Lamb last night, he was a proper gent,' said Julia, smugly. 'A travelling salesman, so he said and it might be true, he had a case of samples.'

'Yeah, married, though,' said Amy. 'I can always tell.'

'So much the better,' Julia grinned. 'Well, if he's in the bar, I'm getting off with him tonight. He should be worth a couple of gins, and a bit more beside. If he's a *very* naughty boy, I could always threaten to tell his wife.'

'I think I'll go home,' said Daisy, yawning. 'I need to write to Mum and Dad before I go to bed.'

'Oh, don't be such a little Goody Two Shoes.' Julia had redone her make-up, and now she checked her lipstick one last time. 'Come and have a bloody gin. It's time you learned to drink.'

Daisy had a dandelion and burdock, which tasted very nasty and medicinal, then told Amy she was going back to their digs. Amy was only half-inebriated, so she wouldn't be going home just yet, Julia was wrapped around her salesman, and Ewan was rather obviously reluctant to tear himself away from hearty masculine company, beer and darts. But he said Daisy couldn't go home alone.

'I'll be all right,' she told him.

'No, I promised Mr Denham.' Ewan told the others he'd be back, and they waved Daisy and Ewan off with several crude remarks.

They got the bus back to the boarding-house where Daisy meant to make herself some cocoa, eat whatever sandwiches the landlady had left out for them, then have an early night.

'No, don't come in, I'm tired,' she said, after Ewan had given her a not very passionate kiss goodnight. 'You go back to the pub.'

'You're sure?'

'I'm sure,' said Daisy, yawning.

'See you tomorrow, then.'

Daisy put her key in the lock, opened the door and walked into a scene.

'I don't care what the manager told you, I'm not going anywhere else this evening,' said the owner of a broad, strong back and a head of coal-black hair. 'We'll sort it out tomorrow morning. I'm sleeping in your sitting-room tonight.'

'This house is ladies only,' said the landlady. 'I never have any men.'

'My dear Mrs Fisher, what do you think I'm going to do?' the owner of the coal-black hair demanded. 'Roast your canary, rape the parlourmaid?'

'Good evening to you, Miss Denham,' said Mrs Fisher, who looked flushed and cross. 'Your Mr Curtis made a big mistake, he called round to ask me if I could put up a Jessie Trent, and here's this man, instead.'

The man turned round and stared at Daisy. 'It's J-e-s-s-e Trent,' he sighed. 'Jesse, as in the outlaw Jesse James, and father of King David.'

85

Daisy stared back into a pair of piercing, dark-brown eyes. 'Er – Mrs Fisher,' she began, aware she sounded strange, but totally unable to do anything about it, 'surely you don't mind if Mr James here – I mean Mr Trent – sleeps on your sofa, just tonight?'

'Well, I *do* mind, as it happens.' Mrs Fisher grimaced. 'I never have men here, never,' she continued, testily. 'I don't like men, I never have, they leave the bathrooms in a shocking state, bits of whisker stuck all round the basin, and they never lift the seat. But if you and the other ladies don't object, and I suppose it's late. . . .'

'It looks like rain, as well,' said Daisy.

'I'll fetch you a couple of blankets,' Mrs Fisher muttered. 'But tomorrow, Mr Trent. . . .'

'I'll leave at crack of dawn.' Jesse Trent smiled gratefully at Daisy. 'Thank you for speaking up for me, Miss Denham. Mrs Fisher, I promise on my honour that I'll behave myself.'

'You'd better,' said Mrs Fisher. 'Miss Denham, what's the matter, have you got something in your eye?'

'No, Mrs Fisher, I'm just tired.'

Whoever loved, thought Daisy, as she rubbed the eye which Cupid's dart had pierced so suddenly and unexpectedly, *who loved not at first sight?*

She didn't sleep that night, and when she got up next morning she felt feverish, almost queasy, but excited. She stayed in bed until she heard the front door slam, until she hoped the newcomer had gone.

'He was here when I arrived, talk about an early bird, and he sounds as if he comes from Yorkshire,' Amy told the rest of the cast assembled in the rehearsal room above a dirty spit-and-sawdust pub. Jesse Trent was now closeted downstairs with Mr Curtis, sorting out his contract and the other paperwork.

'Anyway,' continued Amy, 'he told me that he was with a company which got flooded out, and so they've all dispersed. He only found out about us because that miser Curtis was desperate enough to put a small ad in *The Stage*.'

'Well, I'm very glad he did.' Julia put on yet more lipstick, even though it was only a read-through and the cast all wore old slacks, old jumpers, and most looked very morning after a heavy night before.

'All right, people, settle down.' Alfred Curtis came in with the newcomer. 'This is Mr Trent. He's kindly agreed to join us at short notice. He'll be replacing Mr Morgan, who has got himself a *far* superior engagement.'

Jesse Trent smiled genially all round, and Daisy's heart did back-flips.

'So Mr Trent will be playing Piers Montgomery in our drama *Blighted Blossoms*,' continued Mr Curtis, 'and David Hammond in our brand new comedy *Down the Drain*. All got your scripts?'

So they began the read-through of *Blighted Blossoms*, in which Daisy played the innocent girl corrupted by her brother's evil friend.

'How old, do you think?' hissed Amy, as Jesse and Ewan read a scene together.

'Oh, twenty-eight, perhaps, or maybe thirty.' Julia stubbed out a cigarette. 'Older than you and me, my love, but none the worse for it. Dangerous, don't you think? A charmer, but a bastard, too. Me, I always like that well-worn look. . . .'

'Miss Hart, if you don't mind!' Mr Curtis glared at Julia. 'Miss Denham, lost your place?'

'No – I -er. . . .'

'Act Two, Scene Four, wake up, please!'

Daisy found it hard to concentrate on anything but Jesse Trent's dark eyes. Julia was right, he looked well-worn, but he was also very attractive. He wasn't very tall, but he was broad and didn't carry any fat, and he moved like a dancer, light upon his feet.

He smoked, of course, and so he smelled of cigarettes. But since he smoked Black Russians, the scent was quite a novelty and Daisy found it appealing – not disgusting, like Ewan's horrid pipe, which smelled of dog-mess and old hay.

'Ready, Miss Denham?' Jesse's voice was low, husky without being harsh or rough, warm without being slimy or suggestive. When they reached the kissing scene, she was aware of Ewan's gaze upon her, proprietorial, jealous. 'Relax,' said Jesse, as he held her in his arms and tipped her back a little, but not enough to make her feel off balance, as Ewan often did.

But Mr Curtis didn't like the way that Daisy moved, said he wanted her to be more flirtatious. But then he told her not to look so arch, she wasn't in a blasted pantomime. She ended up kissing Jesse Trent a dozen times or more, and every time she could feel Ewan's glare, burning through her cardigan, scorching her back.

'You mustn't worry, you're doing fine,' Jesse said much later, as they were all packing up to leave. 'But maybe you haven't actually done this kind of thing before? Stage kisses can be tricky, I admit. Especially when you don't know the kisser very well.'

Jesse's dark eyes sparkled, Daisy noticed, and his smile was warm, appealing, comforting, sincere. As Julia and Amy had agreed, he was a very dangerous man.

'I – er – I haven't kissed anyone on stage before.' Daisy felt the blush creep up her neck, and hated herself for being so gauche and young. 'But I dare say I'll get used to it.'

'I'm sure you will.'

'I hope you've got your digs fixed for tonight?'

'Yes, thank you – I'll be with the other boys.' Jesse's smile was gently mocking, wry and confidential. 'So you ladies will be safe.'

'Coming for a snifter, Daisy?' Ewan came up and put his arm around her shoulders, kissed her on the cheek in a way that wasn't remotely stagey. 'Mr Trent, do you fancy a beer or two?'

'Yes, Frank and George just asked me, thank you.' Jesse smiled again, and Daisy's heart did somersaults. 'The Hope and Anchor, isn't it? I need to talk to Alfred for a moment, then I'll join you. See you, Daisy.'

'Look at those shoulders,' Amy said to no one in particular.

'Alfred, do you have a second?' Jesse strolled back across the room to talk to Mr Curtis, and Daisy thought, look at him move, I'd love to see him dance. Or dance with him, a little voice inside her head went on, disloyally.

'Who does he think he is?' huffed Ewan, as he and Daisy crossed the road. 'Frank and George and Alfred! The fellow's only been here twenty minutes, and he's behaving as if he runs the company. We'll have to take him down a peg or two.' Ewan fished in his pocket, took out his stinking pipe and jammed it in his mouth.

'Letter from Daisy, Rose!' Coming in from the cowshed, which had cost a fortune to rebuild to modern standards, and had swallowed up a lot of the insurance money, Edgar had met the postman at the gate. Now he put the post on the kitchen table, poured himself a cup of strong, black tea, and then picked up the *Farming Times*, from which he was trying to learn to be a farmer. Whatever Rose said, he knew she liked to be the first to read her daughter's letters.

She wrote at length to Daisy – not reproachfully, Edgar hoped, but didn't like to say. His own letters were factual accounts of what was happening in Charton, and much shorter.

'Goodness, what a pile,' said Rose, as she lugged a basket full of washing over to the copper. 'I hope it's not *all* bills. I always seem to be paying bills. Cattle-feed, and visits from the vet, and school fees for the boys – God, it's never ending.'

She turned to shout upstairs. 'Stephen and Rob, get *up*!' she called. 'I shan't tell you again!'

'You also have a letter from America,' said Edgar. 'Who do you know there?'

'I don't think I know anyone.' Frowning, Rose picked up the thin, blue, foreign-looking envelope. She slit it open, scanned the letter quickly, then sat down, looking winded. 'Edgar,' she whispered, fearfully, 'I never thought we'd hear from her again. She – she wants Daisy back.'

CHAPTER 9

THE company moved on each week, playing to half-empty theatres all around the Midlands. When they arrived in each new place, Julia and Amy got painted up and went round all the shops to hand out playbills, dragging Daisy along with them and hissing at her to stick her flippin' chest out, to stop looking thirteen. The men were sent out after dark to stick up bills on lampposts and on hoardings.

They'd got the new plays sorted out, and now it was the morning of the dress-rehearsal for *Blighted Blossoms*. The *only* rehearsal on a stage, in fact, so everyone knew they'd have to get their moves right, cues right, props assembled, entrances and exits understood, while Tom, the general factotum, had to sort out all the scenery and lighting, in just a few short hours before they opened for the paying public, that same Monday night.

Daisy had meant to get in bright and early, to see how big the stage was, or how small, to see what kind of dressing-room she'd have – the usual sort of horror, or something even worse, knee-deep in pigeon droppings, with no running water and no electricity, up four steep flights of stairs.

But she found Jesse there already, sitting on the edge of the stage, swinging his legs and looking as if he'd grown there.

'Good morning,' she began, aware that she was blushing scarlet.

'Hello, Daisy.' Jesse smiled, and his smile lifted Daisy's heart. 'Where's everybody else?'

'I don't know.' Daisy shrugged. 'Well, Amy and Julia must be on their way, but they had to get some cigarettes. What about the other boys?'

'George and Frank were still locked in the bathroom when I left.'

'What about Ewan?'

'*He* said he was going for a run.' Now, Jesse shuddered. 'Got up at crack of dawn, he did, put on his old school plimsolls, off he went. Maybe he's having so much fun he's lost all track of time.'

Jesse grinned and lit a cigarette, then blew a stream of fragrant Russian smoke across the stage. 'When I look at Ewan,' he drawled, 'I can't help remembering how wonderful it felt to be so young. So full of energy. I'm such a slug myself. Any outdoor exercise has no appeal for me. Although I like to dance, of course.'

Daisy glanced at him, at his narrow waist, broad chest and well-developed shoulders, and thought that if a body like that had come naturally to Jesse, then he was very lucky.

'You can't be very old,' she said.

'Alas, I won't see twenty-five again.' Jesse stood up and stretched, and then began to pace around the dimly lit, dusty stage. Daisy was reminded of a panther she had seen in India, a dark and dangerous thing. She stared in fascination, then realized that he had noticed she was staring, and that his eyes were bright.

Julia and Amy came bustling in, lighting up and giggling. 'Ooh, are we interrupting something?' sniggered Amy, grinning.

'No, why?' said Jesse, turning to her to smile his lazy smile.

'My mistake, I'm sure,' said Amy, giving him a wink.

'You want to watch that fellow, sweetheart,' murmured Julia, as she brushed past Daisy. 'Stick with the baby boyfriend, that's my advice to you – don't go for someone right out of your league.'

*

'But how did Phoebe find us, after all this time?' demanded Rose.

'She must have kept a note of this address,' said Edgar, shrugging. 'She stayed here once, when Alec was alive, don't you remember? It must have been in 1919. Or in 1920. It was during that hot summer, anyway. Daisy was two or three.'

'Yes, of course, you're right.' Rose nodded. 'It was just before we went to India. Phoebe said she couldn't take Daisy to the USA, and you suggested we adopt her.'

'May I see?' asked Edgar.

'Yes, of course.' Rose handed him the letter, watched him read.

My dear Rose, wrote Phoebe, *I'm sorry it's taken me so long to write to you again. I'm not too smart at putting things in writing, like you know. So please forgive mistakes, and also sorry for the blots. My pen don't work too good.*

I thought you'd like to know that me and Nathan have settled down very well in New York City. He's got some cousins here, and when we come they made us very welcome straight away.

Now we got a swell (that's an American word, it means it's good) apartment, it's got a bathroom and a sitting-room and a lovely kitchen with hot water and a little balcony. We got spare bedrooms, too. We're in Lower East Side, where all the garment factories are, and Nathan's cousin took him into wholesale, and now he's gotten his own business.

Me, I got a hat shop, and it's doing fine.

But we don't got any kids. Nathan and me's been trying for years, and nothing's ever happened. So, Rose, I need to see my little girl. You been her mother, and I'm sure you been a good one, but I want to see her, get to know her, and surely that's not much to ask?

I'll wait for you to answer this before I book my ticket on Cunard.

I hope this finds you, Rose, and finds you well. I hope whoever is living in your house (if it's not you) will send my letter on.

Rose, I haven't forgot about all what you did when I had Daisy. You was a friend in need.

Give my best to Edgar, and hope to hear from you.

Yours very truly

Phoebe (Rosenheim)

'What shall we do?' asked Rose.

'You must write back inviting her to visit us, of course,' said Edgar, calmly. 'Daisy is Phoebe's daughter, and Phoebe has a right to know what's happened since she saw Daisy last.'

'Edgar, Phoebe *left* her daughter! If it hadn't been for us, Daisy would have ended up in some vile orphanage. What earthly right has Phoebe—'

'She is Daisy's mother.' Edgar put down the *Farming Times* and poured his white-faced wife a cup of tea, then spooned in two sugars. 'Rose, we have to welcome Phoebe. What else can we do?'

Daisy was getting better and better – everybody said so. She was getting flattering notices in all the local papers, and even the most curmudgeonly of the provincial critics – a bunch of ignorant old drunks who couldn't find the way to their own arseholes, as Mr Curtis eloquently put it when they trashed a show – were kind to Daisy.

Although the play itself was somewhat plodding, and the end predictable, the entire production was enlivened by the presence of a charming juvenile, announced the *Stafford Echo.*

The casting of the beautiful Miss Denham in a tiny part gave life and spirit to a tired evening, said the *Hanley Chronicle.*

'They mean they liked your legs,' said Amy sourly, one afternoon before a matinée that looked like playing to an almost empty house. 'So don't get too big-headed and think you're going to be a star.'

'Oh, give the kid a break, she's doing fine,' said Jesse Trent, and Ewan scowled at him.

'Daisy, darling, over here a minute.' Julia motioned Daisy to the wings, then handed her a package nicely wrapped in clean brown paper. 'I got you this. It's a little thank-you for helping out that time, know what I mean?'

'What is it?' Daisy asked, remembering the last time that Julia had given her a parcel, and not especially keen to open this one.

'It's for your notices. You're the only one who's getting any, after all. Go on, you goony-looking ha'porth – open it.'

So Daisy did, and she was pleasantly surprised.

'It's lovely, Julia – thank you!' she exclaimed, leafing through the leather-covered album, its pastel-coloured pages and pockets tied with ribbon, all waiting to record her life. 'I'll paste the first ones in tonight.'

'Come along, Miss Twinkletoes, you're on,' hissed Amy Nightingale. She yanked the album out of Daisy's hands, plonked it among the props, then almost dragged her on. 'You mustn't disappoint your fans,' she added, acknowledging the applause that greeted Daisy through clenched and gritted teeth.

Ewan *wasn't* doing very well – his heart was just not in it, and it showed. He wanted to play Romeo, Mercutio, Benedick, not a succession of idle bounders, tennis-playing chumps, and hero's friends or brothers.

'I'd like you two to stay behind for a moment, dearest boys,' Mr Curtis said to George and Ewan, after a bad rehearsal for the comedy *Down the Drain*. 'Mr Fraser, you've got the voice at last, the gods of drama all be praised. But this is supposed to be a farce, and quite frankly *you're* not going to get a single laugh.

'You must work on your moves, as well. You clump around the

stage like the milkman's horse, getting in everybody's way. You masked poor Mr Reed through one whole scene. Darlings, we can't afford a bad review. We're going to have our work cut out making *any* money in this god-forsaken town. So let's run through Act Two, Scene Three once more.'

Ewan was obviously annoyed, but Mr Curtis jammed his monocle in his eye and fixed him beadily. 'Daisy, if you could wait ten minutes,' Ewan began, as the rest of the company disappeared, like genies going back into their bottles.

'It's all right, I'll walk Daisy to the pub,' said Jesse, getting Daisy's coat.

'Or we could wait for Ewan,' said Daisy, longing to be alone with Jesse Trent, yet also anxious to avoid it.

'I don't want Mr Fraser being distracted by Miss Denham, he needs to get this right.' Mr Curtis waved them off. 'He'll see you later, girls and boys.'

Daisy and Jesse walked out of the rehearsal room, down the stairs and into the dusty street. Jesse had a new trilby, Daisy noticed, with a very up-to-date soft brim, which shaded half his handsome face and made him look impossibly romantic.

'It seems strange to come out of rehearsals when it's light,' she murmured, glancing up at him. 'Somehow, I always think it will be dark.'

'Yes, daylight's too much like real life, with all its boredom, pain and irritation,' he agreed. 'We actors are creatures of a brighter, more exciting world. We only come alive when we're on stage, in the glare of artificial light.'

'Yes, that's right, we do.'

'Let's go through this little park, and get a bit of air.' Jesse took Daisy's hand and held it as they crossed the road, but then he forgot to let it go again. She didn't like to pull away. 'How long have you been with Mr Curtis?' he enquired.

'I joined the company last September.' Daisy blushed and stared down at the gravel path, aware of Jesse's fingers stroking hers, his pressure on her hand. 'This is my first professional engagement.'

'I never would have guessed.' Jesse laughed, but warmly, not unkindly. 'I'm sorry, I didn't mean to laugh,' he added. 'You do very well indeed, Miss Denham.'

'Thank you, Mr Trent,' said Daisy, primly.

'Jesse, please.' Jesse sat down on a bench, and since his hand still held hers prisoner, Daisy had no option but to sit down too.

'Where do you come from?' Daisy asked him, staring straight ahead. 'I mean, where were you born?'

'In Yorkshire.' Jesse stroked her fingers gently, slowly, thoughtfully. 'My father is a preacher, so you could say that acting's in my blood.'

'You're a son of the vicarage, then?' asked Daisy.

'Good heavens, no!' cried Jesse. 'Nothing as respectable as that! My people are members of a strict and frankly weird nonconformist sect. They disowned me when I started acting in return for money.'

Daisy warmed to Jesse as a kindred spirit. 'My mother isn't a member of a sect,' she told him, confidentially. 'But *she* feels acting and getting paid for it is vulgar, too.'

'You didn't have a happy childhood, then?'

'I had a lovely childhood, but—'

'Mine was truly awful.' Jesse sighed. 'I've had the devil beaten out of me so many times that – well, see for yourself.' Jesse turned back a cuff to show a pattern of angry welts encircling his wrist. 'My father used to tie me up and thrash me.'

'Oh, that's terrible!' Daisy had never been so much as slapped, and suddenly her heart contracted as she imagined Jesse as a frightened, lonely child, loomed over by a monster of a father. 'I'm so sorry.'

'Oh, don't be sorry, at least I got away.' Jesse pushed his cuff back down, stood up. 'Let's get going, shall we? The others will be wondering where we've got to.'

'Daisy, wait for me!' Running footsteps pounded on the path, and Ewan came panting up. Grabbing Daisy's arm, and almost overbalancing her, he made her stumble. 'Where are we going, to the Crown?'

CHAPTER 10

ROSE wrote back to Phoebe, inviting her to visit them in Charton, and Phoebe sent a wire to say that she was on her way.

After Rose had panicked quietly for a day or two, she went to see Mrs Hobson in the village, and told her what had happened. Mrs Hobson said, while she wasn't bothered about that Mrs Rosenheim, they couldn't let young Daisy down. Well, could they, Mrs Denham?

So, for the next week, the two of them worked night and day to make the bailiff's cottage look like a real home, not like a temporary gypsy camp. They cleared out all the rubbish, putting stuff which they'd salvaged from the house, but which there'd been no time to sort out, wash or mend, in one of old stables.

They polished and they painted. They spruced up bits of bedroom furniture they'd taken from the ruins of the house. They starched and ironed the curtains, they found some decent bedclothes and a pretty eiderdown, and at last they managed to make the house presentable. They even managed to make the visitor's bedroom look quite pretty.

Or so Rose had hoped.

But then the guest arrived, and she was totally appalled. 'Oh, Rose, whatever 'appened?' Phoebe stared round the kitchen as if she couldn't believe her eyes. 'This place is a slum! You look like some old cleanin' woman in that nasty jersey two-piece! It's all saggin' round yer arse! Rose, what are you *doin'*, dressed up like a char, an' livin' in a bloody *slum?*'

'There was a fire at Alec's house, and we lost almost all our things.' Rose had been brought up to be a lady, and now she did her best to smile politely as her visitor ranted on.

But having Phoebe standing there and wailing about charladies and slums, when enormous efforts had been made to make the cottage bright and welcoming – well, comparatively – was mortifying.

'There was some insurance money, of course, but we're ploughing that into the farm,' Rose went on, gamely. 'If the farm does well, we'll think about rebuilding Melbury House.' She glanced down at her cheap, brown knitted skirt, 'and buying some new clothes.'

'But you was so rich, Rose!' Phoebe cried, distraught, 'an' you 'ad all them lovely things! All them silk dresses, all that jewellery, all them furs!'

'But then she married me.' They hadn't heard Edgar come into the kitchen. But as they turned, he smiled in welcome, bent to kiss Phoebe on the cheek, and then stood back to take in all her splendour.

'You're looking very well,' he said. 'That's a most extraordinary hat! You're quite a bobby-dazzler these days – wouldn't you say so, Rose?'

' 'Ello, Edgar, love. It's good to see you.' Phoebe preened and smirked, smoothing the expensive, soft material of her smart, black coat. 'I – listen, you wasn't meant to 'ear me goin' on an' on. I don't mean no offence.'

'I know you don't.' Edgar sat down and rubbed his tired eyes. 'Rose, what about some tea – or coffee, as I dare say Phoebe must drink nowadays?'

'A cuppa would be wonderful.' Phoebe sat down too, and started to unskewer all her hatpins. 'Strong an' black, two sugars. They don't know 'ow to make a decent cuppa in the States. They just pours warm water over tea-leaves. God, I ask you!'

Rose moved Phoebe's feather-and-net creation to a safe place high up on the dresser, then put the kettle on. 'Where did you get your gorgeous hat?' she asked. 'One of those expensive New York stores?'

'No, I got a hat shop of me own – didn't I say?'

'Oh, yes – you did,' said Rose, remembering. 'I hope it's doing well?'

'Not 'alf it's doin' well!' Phoebe grinned delightedly. 'Listen, I got four girls in the workroom, an' a lady in the shop itself. She speaks so nice, she does the business with the toffs like I could never do.'

'I was just thinking, you haven't lost your accent,' Rose continued, smiling in spite of herself at Phoebe's blatant showing off.

'Well, Rose, love, you know what they say. You can take the girl out of the East End, but you'll never take the East End out of the girl! But I was tellin' you about my shop. I'm the brains. I does all the designs, I makes the models. Yeah, I done all right – I'm really in the money these days.'

Phoebe looked round the kitchen again, and frowned. 'So where's my Daisy, Rose? One of your letters said she was goin' to dancin' classes, didn't it? Must 'ave been a while back now? I'd love to see her dance.'

'I'd love to see you dance.' Jesse moved Daisy's lemonade to make room for his pint of bitter, then sat down on the wooden bench, making Ewan Fraser glare at him. 'You have the perfect body for a dancer. You're not too tall, but you've got nice, long legs.'

'I do like to dance,' admitted Daisy, going red as Jesse used words like *legs* and *body*, which seemed a bit too intimate for general conversation.

'Ballroom, ballet, tap?' asked Jesse.

'Anything and everything,' smiled Daisy.

'We'll go dancing, then,' said Jesse. 'On the next rest day, we'll try out the local palais, shall we? Give the regulars some entertainment? Show them how to do it.' Jesse looked round the table. 'All of us,' he added, hastily, as the others stared at him and Ewan looked apoplectic.

'Oh, I thought you and Daisy May were fixing up a private date,' said Amy, caustically.

'Good of you to let us tag along,' said Julia, taking out her compact, then starting on her mouth.

Ewan didn't say anything, but Daisy felt his arm slide round her shoulders, then pull her close to him. She didn't know if this was comforting or annoying. Where Ewan was concerned, she was confused. She couldn't wait to dance with Jesse Trent. She knew it would be wonderful. . . .

Back home at her digs, Daisy looked at herself in the cloudy, spotted wardrobe mirror. She thought that yes, she *did* have nice long legs. Yes, her still rather childish figure actually *was* perfect for a dancer. She'd been inclined to envy Julia's and Amy's generous curves. But now she thought, who needs to have a bosom like a bolster, anyway?

Jesse made her feel attractive – even beautiful. When he smiled, she felt so warmed, so bathed in radiance, that it was as if the sun shone brightly, even on the dullest, rainiest day.

But, she loved Ewan Fraser – didn't she?

'She's not here at the moment,' Rose told Phoebe, as she poured tea and offered the visitor Mrs Hobson's rather solid seed-cake, which Phoebe took one look at and declined. 'She's followed in your footsteps, actually.'

'She – Rose, you don't mean to say she's 'ad a kid?' demanded

THE LONG WAY HOME

Phoebe, looking shocked and horrified.

'No, she's on the stage,' said Rose. 'Just like you were, Phoebe, all those years ago. She's very talented. She can act and sing *and* dance – do everything, in fact. She's had some lovely notices. I'll go upstairs and get them.'

'Later, Rose,' said Phoebe. 'She don't take after me,' she added, in a smaller voice. 'Yeah, I wanted all the glamour, people lookin' at me and clappin', but I didn't 'ave no talent, not a stick of it. Took me years to admit it to meself.'

'Oh, Phoebe, you enjoyed it, you were probably very good.'

'You never saw me, Rose.' Phoebe shook her elegantly coiffed head. 'All I did was stand there, twitch me arse and show me drawers, get those poor buggers up on stage to take the bloody shillin'.'

'But you've done well in business.'

'Yeah, with my Nathan's 'elp, I 'ave.' Phoebe shrugged, and looked down at her painted fingernails. 'Rose, us talkin' about Daisy – well, I'm feelin' all of a shiver now. I could use another cup of tea – or a drop of brandy, if you got it.'

'You and Mr Smartarse, you should be in revue, that Mr C.B. Cochran fellow doesn't know what he's missing,' Amy said sarcastically to Daisy, as the company straggled back to the bus stop, hoping they hadn't missed the last buses going past their digs.

As they had arranged, on their next rest day everyone went dancing. Ewan couldn't dance, and as he stumbled round the floor, treading on Daisy's toes and pushing her into other dancers, she began to wish she'd never agreed to this daft outing.

But eventually Jesse couldn't stand to watch them any more. Gently disentangling her from Ewan, he took Daisy in his arms. Then they showed the whole hall how to do it.

'Where did *you* learn to foxtrot like a pro?' demanded Jesse grinning, when at last they took a break and went up to the bar to get a drink.

'In India,' said Daisy, aware that she was glowing and feeling gloriously alive, all lit up with the happy satisfaction of doing something that she did so well. 'My dad was in the army there, and Mum sent me to dancing lessons. Singing lessons, too.'

'Give us a tune, then?' Jesse whispered, slipping his arm round Daisy's waist and pulling her close to him again.

Daisy was aware of Ewan watching, of Amy screwing up her face and scowling, but she was enjoying herself so much she didn't care. As the band struck up again, she sang for Jesse Trent, keeping perfect time with the middle-aged, over-made-up dance-hall vocalist, her pure soprano ringing true and clear.

'You're very good, you know.' Jesse pulled back a little, his gaze met Daisy's own, and when he smiled her heart turned joyous cartwheels. 'You need more lessons to teach you how to move and breathe, of course. You're not too well co-ordinated yet, and you tend to take the initiative when the man should lead. But your voice is lovely, and you dance like thistledown. Adele and Fred Astaire had better watch it when we two get to London!'

'We're going to London, are we?' Daisy breathed. 'I mean, just you and me?'

'Daisy, love, you bet we are,' said Jesse.

'When?'

'Let's finish this tour, shall we?' Jesse whispered, winking as if she were a fellow-plotter. 'You try to save a bit of money, Daisy. Then we'll see.'

Ewan's face was thunderous, but Daisy was in heaven.

'Do you see much of *'im*?' asked Phoebe, as she sat and smoked and drank her tea, fiddling with her rings and teaspoon. Edgar had gone off to get the cows in, the twins weren't back from school yet, so the women were alone. 'I mean, I thought you said 'e lived round 'ere? Or 'e used to?'

'Oh, he's still in Charton.' Rose took one of Phoebe's cigarettes.

She lit it and inhaled, coughing because she wasn't used to it, but then inhaling yet again, needing the nicotine. 'His father died a couple of years ago, so he's Sir Michael now. He lives about three miles away from here, at Easton Hall.'

'What about that big posh 'ouse of yours?' demanded Phoebe, sticking the knife in deeper and deeper, twisting it round and round inside the wound. 'You know – that castle sort of place you showed me when I come down 'ere to visit you, just after the war? Charton Minster, ain't it?'

'My father wanted me to marry Mike. I married Edgar, so Daddy left the Minster and the whole estate to Michael.' Rose looked down at the floorboards of the cottage kitchen. 'Mike didn't want to live in it, of course, so now the Minster is a school for wayward children.'

'Your father never left you without *nothin'*?' Phoebe looked aghast. 'Rose, for God's sake, how could he?'

'It was his house and his estate.' Rose shrugged.

'Oh, Rose!' wailed Phoebe. 'All this stuff that's 'appened to you, it's all because of me!'

'It's nothing to do with you.' Rose stood up, stubbed out her cigarette. 'I need to get the supper on. The twins will be home in about five minutes, and they're always starving. I have to see to the hens, as well.'

'I'll 'elp you – if you'll let me?' Phoebe shrugged off her coat. 'I could feed the 'ens, or peel the spuds.'

'You'll stay with us?' Rose looked round her kitchen, taking in its shabby furniture and bulging, damp-streaked walls that not even coats of paint could hide. 'It's not at all luxurious, I'm afraid.'

'Oh, I been in worse,' said Phoebe, rolling up her sleeves. 'Yeah, I'll muck in, and I can—'

'Mum?' Robert came bursting into the kitchen like a small tornado, closely followed by Stephen in a flurry of boots and bags and coats.

They were stricken speechless, something Rose had never thought to see, and for twenty seconds they simply goggled at the scented, gorgeous vision that was Phoebe Rosenheim.

'Er – hello,' said Robert, who recovered first.

'Good afternoon,' said Stephen, slightly breathlessly but more politely.

'Blimey, you never said you 'ad two *boys*, Rose!' Phoebe beamed at Rose's muddy, tousled, scruffy sons. 'What *'andsome* boys, as well! A regular pair of lookers! They'll break all the ladies' 'earts!' She turned to Rose. 'Takes after Edgar, don't they?'

'Who's this lady, Mum?' asked Stephen, frowning.

'This is Mrs Rosenheim.' Put on the spot, Rose couldn't think of anything to say, and so she told the truth. 'She's Daisy's mother.'

Daisy couldn't be bothered with Ewan's sulking. She didn't *belong* to him. She wasn't doing anything wrong. So why was he so tetchy and disgruntled all the time?

She couldn't wait to be on stage each night. When Jesse kissed her, she could feel he meant it, and for a few short, precious moments she could forget the audience noisily sucking boiled sweets, or rustling their boxes of cheap chocolates half-filled with shavings, bran or crinkly paper, forget old ladies coughing, fidgeting and whispering to their next-door neighbours.

For every night, she fell in love.

CHAPTER 11

Aᴴᴛᴇʀ they had wowed the Potteries, as Jesse put it, the company would be going north to Yorkshire.

'You're going home,' smiled Daisy, as they all piled on the Sunday train to Doncaster.

'What do you mean?' frowned Jesse.

'You're going to Yorkshire – where you come from, don't you?'

'Oh – yes, of course.' Jesse grimaced sourly. 'But I'm from Wakefield. Miles from all the places where we'll be going.' He lit a cigarette and slumped down in his seat. He stared out of the window, making it clear he wasn't in the mood for conversation.

Daisy realized she'd been tactless. Of course he wouldn't be happy to be going back to Yorkshire, the scene of all his childhood misery.

Monday morning saw the company members trooping from their various squalid digs to a shabby theatre in a rough part of the town, where they would spend the next two weeks giving twelve evenings and four matinées to a hopefully receptive audience of shop assistants, mill-hands, clerks and general tradesmen and their wives.

'All right, girls and boys, less gossiping!' Alfred Curtis strode on to the stage, his monocle in place and white spats gleaming.

'We've three hours to get everything set up. The property- and costume-skips will still be at the station. So if Mr Trent and Mr Reed could go and fetch them? You may take a taxi, gentlemen. If you can find one in this god-forsaken town.'

Then Mrs Curtis, clad as usual in regal purple, and wearing an amazing hat that looked as if she had the entire chicken nesting in her wig, came up to join her husband.

'Ladies, your dressing-room leaves quite a lot to be desired,' she told them, all her chins a-wobble with disapproval. 'There's no basin, the wretched roof is leaking, and there's an inch of water on the floor. I've asked the management to find duckboards, but God knows if they will. You've got facilities down the passage.

'Gents, you've got a khazi in the yard, and it looks disgusting. But there are chamber-pots in all the cupboards, so use them, not the basins. . . .'

When they scanned the local papers after their first night, Daisy found she'd got some decent notices again. She cut them out to stick them in her album, which she meant to send to Rose.

Then, to her surprise, she got a pay-rise, to a magnificent four pounds ten a week. 'It's your legs, my love,' Julia Hart said with a grin as they stood waiting in the wings that evening. 'Alfred can't resist a pair of pins, and yours are up there with the best. If I had legs like yours, I'd walk round in me knickers all the time, so everyone could see.'

'He's still exploiting you, like he exploits the rest of us,' said Amy. She shot a poisonous glance at Alfred Curtis, who was standing on the opposite side and arguing with a lighting-man who seemed both daft *and* drunk.

'Leave the kid alone,' said Julia, elbowing Amy sharply in the side. Then she lowered her voice. 'Daisy, darlin', I don't like to ask, and you'll get every penny back, I swear – but lend me a quid till Friday?'

'I wouldn't if I were you,' warned Amy.

'Who asked your opinion, dough-face?' Julia looked beseech-ingly at Daisy. 'Sweetheart, fifteen bob?'

'Yes, of course,' said Daisy. 'Just remind me after we come off.'

'God, Miss Goody Two Shoes, you're greener than a bowl of garden peas,' sneered Amy Nightingale, hitching up her stockings and smoothing out the wrinkles at her knees. 'That leech will bleed you dry. Come on, love, we're on.'

'Who's your letter from?' demanded Ewan, as Daisy sat on the edge of the stage the following afternoon, costumed and made up for the matinée, swinging her legs and reading, and laughing now and then.

'My mother,' Daisy told him, not bothering to look up.

'Oh, which one?' asked Ewan.

'I beg your pardon?'

'As I remember, you have two.'

'Ewan, don't be silly.' Daisy stuffed the letter up her sleeve. 'It's from Dorset. Mum sent it to the last address but one, so it's been following me around, and it's all old news now. But it's so nice to hear from them. I miss them, actually.'

'It wasn't so very long ago that we were searching every tele-phone-book and street-directory in England for Gowers and Rosenheims,' Ewan reminded Daisy. 'You seem to have forgotten about all that.'

'I've sort of come to accept I'm never going to find her, I suppose.' The sounds of other people gathering, and the auditor-ium doors being opened, now had Daisy scrambling to her feet to duck behind the curtain. What's the matter with *you* these days?' she asked, as Ewan followed her on to the silent stage.

'You know very well,' said Ewan.

'No, I don't,' said Daisy. 'All *I* know is you're miserable and grumpy, that you snap at everybody and forget your lines.'

'That's right, rub my nose in it, point out I'm a rotten actor, too.'

Ewan grabbed Daisy by the shoulders, spun her round and made her look at him. 'Why do you spend all your time with bloody Jesse Trent?'

'I don't spend *all* my time with him,' said Daisy. 'But, if I did, why shouldn't I?'

'You're supposed to be *my* girl, that's why!'

'So that means I can't have a conversation with another man?' Daisy wriggled free. 'I spend time with George and Frank, as well. You don't mind that.'

'George and Frank are – well, they're not interested in girls,' said Ewan, curtly.

He scowled at Jesse, who'd just walked on to the stage with George and started to do stretches, while George checked that all the chairs and other things they needed were where they ought to be. 'George is not like *him*.'

'What's that supposed to mean?'

'Oh, don't be so ridiculous!' cried Ewan. 'You know very well!'

'Ewan, hadn't you better make sure you know where all your stuff is?' Daisy asked him, coldly. 'You couldn't find your boots last week, and don't forget you're going to need the violin today. You can't really do Scene Three without it.'

'Less chattering, now,' hissed Mrs Curtis, bustling up behind them. She took them by the shoulders and marched them off the stage. 'Darlings, if could you possibly save your lovers' tiff till later, I'd be very grateful. The audience is coming in, and they've paid their money to see the play, not to hear Mr Fraser carrying on.'

Ewan glared at the manager's wife, then stomped off to find his violin.

'There's not a bad old crowd out there today,' said Julia, as the beginners for *Blighted Blossoms* huddled in the wings.

'Jolly good,' grinned George, patting first his padding and then his crepe moustache.

'Daisy, I must have a word.' Jesse Trent took Daisy's arm and pulled her to one side, turning his back on George and Julia. 'It's no good,' he whispered. 'You must know how I feel about you. What are we going to do?'

'Well, we can't do anything right now, we're on in about two minutes.' Gratified, embarrassed, confused, delighted – Daisy didn't know what else to say.

'Oh, Daisy, don't be such a flirt!' cried Jesse, making Julia stare at him, and glaring at her until she eventually shrugged and looked away. 'You and I, we're not meant for this dull provincial stuff!'

'One minute, boy and girls,' called Mrs Curtis, who was stage-manager that afternoon. 'Miss Denham, you look flustered, are you well?'

'Yes, Mrs Curtis, I'm all right.'

All the time they were in Doncaster, Jesse stuck to Daisy like a debt-collector's runner, appearing out of nowhere when Ewan was rehearsing, squashing himself down next to her when Ewan went to the bar, and even making use of those spare minutes when Ewan was in the gents to talk to her, or smile a confiding, secret sort of smile.

One evening in the pub, Daisy happened to remark to no one in particular that she had ambitions to play Juliet one day.

'You can't be a tragedienne with a name like Daisy Denham,' Jesse told her, laughing.

'So, I could change it, couldn't I?' Daisy retorted, crossly.

'No, my love, don't change your name, or anything about you.' Jesse's hand caressed her neck, stroking away an errant strand of hair. 'You could be wonderful in a musical comedy, you know. Or I can see you in revue. Ginger Rogers, Gertrude Lawrence, Daisy Denham in *Good Evening, London.*'

'Or *Hi There, New York*,' said Daisy, drily.

'Yes, that's it!' cried Jesse, as Ewan came back carrying some drinks, and glowering to see Jesse sitting in his place. 'They'd love you in New York.'

'How do *you* know?' Julia asked him, pursing scarlet lips. 'You been there, have you?'

'No, but – well, I'll certainly go there one day.' Jesse got up, and Ewan sat down next to Daisy, scowling furiously. 'Daisy, you and me, on Broadway, eh?'

'It's a date.' Daisy smiled.

'But meanwhile, the Majestic, Doncaster.' Amy picked up her drink. 'Thank you, Ewan, darling. You might not be a star like Mr Trent here, but at least you stand your round and pay your way.'

A few days later, Jesse was watching Ewan from the wings. 'Fraser's yelling at them again,' he said, as his right hand lay on Daisy's shoulder, idly massaging her collar-bone. 'Listen to him, you'd think this bloody audience was deaf as well as daft. Well, actually, they might be – all mill-hands have cloth ears, it stands to reason. But Fraser should be playing in a field, not on a stage.'

'Don't you be so rude, he's very good!' retorted Daisy.

'He *could* be good, admittedly.' Jesse shrugged and turned to smile at Daisy. 'But our Mr Fraser has no humility. He doesn't watch, he doesn't learn. He thinks that since he was the star of all his school productions, he knows it all already. I was like him, once.'

'I suppose you think *I'm* young and stupid, too?'

'Young, yes,' Jesse smiled, 'but stupid – no.' He leaned towards her, looking deep into her eyes. 'You're a natural. Even that old idiot Curtis says so. Daisy, darling, watching you lifts everybody's heart.'

'Oh – thank you.' Daisy looked away, blushing red beneath her number five.

'But you're not a Juliet or Cordelia,' said Jesse. 'You're too light for tragedy and all that heavy stuff. You're made for fun. When this season's over and I've got a bit of cash saved up, I'm going to go to London, try to get into revue. If you have any sense, you'll come along.'

'You're going to do a song and dance act?' Daisy stared at him. 'I didn't even know that you could sing.'

'Oh, I can sing all right – better than Fred Astaire, at any rate.' Jesse shook his head. 'This country's in recession. Millions are out of work or on short time, everyone's fed up, so when they go out they want to have a bit of fun – not sit in the darkness, listening to a load of silly rubbish like *Blighted Blossoms*. I doubt if many of them want Shakespeare, either. Daisy, people like you and me can make their hearts grow lighter. Right now, musical comedy's the thing. So are you up for it?'

'I'm on,' said Daisy, straightening her skirt before she walked on to the stage.

'Break a leg.' Jesse smiled, patting her on the bottom as she went. 'Take it fast tonight, then we can all go down the pub.'

The next engagement was a week in Birmingham, but after that the company would be breaking up – George was off to Skegness for a concert party season, Mr and Mrs Curtis would be taking the summer off, Julia and Amy would be unemployed, and Jesse was wearing Daisy down about trying her luck in London.

Eventually, he talked her round.

'You're going to London?' Ewan stared at Daisy. 'You mean, you're going with *him*?'

'I'm going with Jesse, certainly,' said Daisy. 'But it's not like that.'

Daisy and Ewan had gone shopping for a few bits and pieces, and were on their own for once, because everyone else had other business. Jesse had gone off somewhere for the morning, muttering something about seeing an old friend. Now Ewan and Daisy were in a coffee-shop, eating toasted teacakes as the rain poured down on Doncaster, making it look even more depressed.

Daisy snuggled up to Ewan, took his hand and held it. 'Don't worry, I'll still see you,' she promised. 'I'll still be your girl. I know

113

– why don't *you* come to London, too?'

'I can't,' said Ewan, pulling his hand away.

'Why, what will you be doing?'

'I'm going back to Scotland. I'm going to join a company in Glasgow. It's at the Comrades Theatre, and it does experimental drama.'

'You never said!' cried Daisy.

'You never asked,' said Ewan. 'You've been so busy canoodling with Mr Jesse Trent that you've not had time to speak to anybody else.'

'So there'll be five hundred miles between us.'

'Yes, looks like it,' said Ewan. 'What do your parents say about this London scheme?'

'I – well, I haven't told them yet.'

'I'm not surprised. I don't suppose they'd be delighted to hear you're going to London with that man.'

'I wish *you'd* come to London.' Suddenly Daisy felt alone, and scared of the unknown. 'Ewan, you'll write to me?'

'If that's what you want.' Ewan stood up, brushing the crumbs off his lap. 'If you want to know about what's happening to me.'

'I'm still not sure a letter will be enough,' said Rose, as she and Phoebe talked about how Phoebe should get in touch with Daisy, for the hundredth time.

'But I'm scared,' said Phoebe. What if she don't want to know me, eh? What if I goes up to 'er, if I says, " 'ello, darlin', I'm your mum", an' then she gives me one across the chops?'

'She won't do that,' said Rose.

'Give me another day or two, an' I'll make me mind up, yeah?' said Phoebe.

'No hurry,' Rose replied.

'You 'aven't told her that I'm 'ere, then?'

'No.' Rose shrugged. 'I wondered whether you might not come

to England, after all. Or, if you did, you might decide you didn't want to meet her. I didn't want to raise her hopes, then have her disappointed.'

'Yeah, I suppose I ain't very reliable – or not where she's concerned, at any rate.' Phoebe looked ashamed. 'You often go an' see 'er, do you, Rose?'

'I haven't seen her since she went away. But I write once a week, and Daisy writes back when she can, and so we manage to keep in touch. I hope she'll get some time off when this tour is over, and she'll come and visit us.' Rose picked up a basket. 'Let's go and see how many eggs there are today.'

Rose liked having Phoebe staying in Charton. She hadn't realized quite how lonely she'd become, how much she missed her friends. Now she was back in Dorset, she'd lost touch with the other army wives, for she hadn't the time to write the long and newsy letters they demanded, and she didn't have much to say to them, in any case. She didn't know about the latest fashions, who was seeing the Prince of Wales, whether diamond clips were in.

The women of Rose's age who lived in Charton remembered her when she had been Miss Courtenay, the spoiled and cosseted daughter of the squire, whose parents had never let her mix with any local children. So although the women were polite, there was too much history dividing them and Rose, and they could never be her friends.

She didn't wish she'd never set eyes on Edgar Denham, and she loved her boys. But she knew she must keep busy, must not think too much. Or the black dog of melancholy would catch her, drag her down.

'I could get used to livin' in the country,' Phoebe said, as they stood together at the kitchen table one sunny April morning, mixing up a mash for Rose's hens.

'What shall we tell Daisy?' Rose asked, for the thousandth time.

'Nothin', Rose – not yet.' Phoebe poured the mash into the bucket. 'Come on, we've lots to do.'

Phoebe stayed for a further week, mucking in and feeding hens and even helping get the cows in, smacking them smartly on their backsides like a country milkmaid born and bred.

The twins thought she was wonderful. She was from America, she knew the latest songs, and sang them like a proper entertainer, doing all the actions. When Rose explained that she was Daisy's mother, but had been too young to care for her, the boys accepted everything and didn't seem to think the worse of Phoebe.

'Well, Mum – Daze is very blonde, but you and Dad are dark,' said Robert, sagely. 'So Daisy's actual father must have been fair-haired.'

'Or ginger,' added Stephen.

'It's sort of obvious that you and Dad—'

'Well, if you mate a dark one with another dark one—'

'If you take a white one and a black one – I'm talking about rabbits, Mum, don't look at me like that – you don't get many white ones in the litter,' went on Robert.

'Most of them are black or grey. It's like Rob and me, we're dark, so obviously we're yours. But it would be very strange if you and Dad had bred a Daisy.'

'Oh, I see,' said Rose, who'd never thought the rabbit farm could be so educational.

'They're lovely boys,' said Phoebe, as she watched the twins set off for school one sunny morning, running across the field like two young animals, darting here and there, pushing each other, trading punches, laughing, skipping, gambolling like lambs. 'You an' Edgar must be proud of them.'

'We are,' said Rose, and she thought, yes, I'm really very lucky.

'I never 'ad another kid.' Now Phoebe looked despondent, and there was tragedy in her brown eyes. 'The quack says give it time, but I don't think it's goin' to 'appen.'

'It might,' said Rose, and felt how rich she was, in spite of living in a hovel and dressing like a cleaning-lady.

'Do *you* think I ought to go an' see 'er?' Phoebe asked.

'It's a decision you must make.' Rose picked up a bag of kitchen scraps to add then to the chicken-bin. Nothing was wasted in that house, and when she thought about her privileged childhood at the Minster, she was appalled by how much waste there'd been. 'I'm sure she'd like to know you. She's in Birmingham this month, I think. I've got the tour dates somewhere, so I'll go and look them up. Phoebe, why don't you go and see her there?'

'Well, maybe.' Phoebe looked uncertain. 'You'll come with me, Rose?'

'I can't, I've far too much to do here on the farm. Anyway, you should see her by yourself.'

'I'll sleep on it,' said Phoebe, chewing at her lower lip. 'Then I'll let you know.'

CHAPTER 12

THE tour wound up with a half-capacity house in one of Birmingham's seediest, dirtiest theatres. But Mr and Mrs Curtis didn't complain about the miserable takings. In fact, they seemed quite pleased with the way that everything had gone, and after the show they told the company they'd see them in the pub, where it would be drinks all round, all night.

'We're going to take a break,' said Mr Curtis, leaning on the beer-swilled counter, creaking his spats and giving the waiter three more one-pound notes to put behind the bar. 'We want to visit our daughter down in Reading. Maudie's not been well just recently. We won't be putting together another tour until the autumn.'

'If at all,' said Mrs Curtis. 'It's getting hard on the old bones.' She squashed the bones and all the rest of her velvet bulk into a seat by Daisy. 'We might even retire. Alfred and I have saved a little bit. I tell you, Daisy love, the thought of a cottage on the Berkshire Downs is quite appealing.'

'Drink up, boys and girls,' said Mr Curtis, jamming in his monocle and catching the barman's eye.

'Come round and get your money first thing tomorrow morning,' Mrs Curtis told them, as they all said affectionate goodnights. 'Alfred will have sorted things out with the theatre management by then, and I'll have done my sums.'

'*For they are jolly good fellows*,' prompted Frank and George, the rest of the cast joined in, and Mr and Mrs Curtis blushed and grinned.

'Pay-day, girls and boys,' said Frank, when they all met at the bus stop the next morning to get the bus to the posher end of town where Mr and Mrs Curtis had their digs. 'I reckon Alfred sounded as if we'd done all right.'

'So there should be bonuses all round,' said George, rubbing his small, plump hands. 'Julia, where's Amy?'

'Just popped up the road to get her cleaning, she'll be here in a minute,' Julia replied. 'Look, she's coming now. I need to get my roots retouched,' she added. 'So that's what I'll do this afternoon. I think I'll have a manicure, as well. Then I'll go to Rackham's and try on all the latest frocks. Georgie, love, don't look at me like that. I won't pinch anything! I might even *buy* a dress or two. If they're going cheap.'

'Remember you haven't got a job, my dear, so don't go raving mad.' Amy dumped her parcel of cleaning on the dirty pavement, and lit a cigarette.

'Yeah, but I'll be making an investment,' Julia retorted, getting out her compact and touching up her mouth. 'If I get all dolled up to the nines, then go and sit in a cocktail bar and flash me pins about, I'll soon find a gentleman, and he'll see me right. Well, maybe for a week or two.'

When the bus came, Jesse took Daisy's hand in his and pulled her up the stairs. Sitting down beside her, he stretched his arm across the seat and idly stroked her shoulder, playing with her hair.

'What are those marks around your wrist?' asked Julia, who'd sat down behind them.

'His father used to tie him up and beat him,' Daisy said, looking at Jesse sympathetically.

'He must have been some bastard of a father – they look more like S and M to me,' said Amy, grinning. 'Well, Jesse Trent? Did you really have a frightful childhood? Or are you a pervert?'

'Shut up, Amy,' muttered Jesse, as he fumbled for a cigarette.

'Yes, Amy, don't be so unkind,' said Daisy, thinking she must ask Jesse later, what was S and M?

'Well, children, this must be the place.' Amy led them up the neat and tidy garden-path, then rang the bell.

'Come on,' Julia murmured. 'I'm not standing here all day, looking at the bloody scenery. I've got to find myself a job. Mr Curtis, if you please,' she said, when the door was opened.

'He's gone, love,' said the woman in a grubby floral apron, folding her arms beneath her generous bosom and scowling at them all.

'We'll see Mrs Curtis, then,' said Amy, stubbing out her cigarette and dropping the butt end on the clean-swept path.

'They've *both* buggered off!' The woman glared at Amy. 'You can pick that fag-end up as well, you mucky trollop. I don't keep a doss-house.'

'But how will we get our money?' demanded Frank.

'How will I get *mine?*' The landlady began to close the door. 'Theatricals,' she growled. 'Bloody 'ad enough of 'em, I 'ave. Professional gentlemen – that's all I'm takin' now. They smuggle floozies to their rooms, they leave the toilets looking quite disgustin', they drop their fag-ash everywhere, *but they pay their way!*'

The door slammed shut.

'The thieving, rotten bastard,' Julia muttered, as they all stood shocked and disbelieving and staring at each other on the steps, aware of the woman twitching her net curtains, glaring at them and willing them away. 'He's been planning this for months, I betcha.'

'Where exactly does this daughter live?' demanded George. 'Does anybody know her married name?'

'Oh, for God's sake, idiot, they ain't flamin' got no bloody daughter.' Julia was groping for her compact and her lipstick. 'They wasn't even married. Dolly Curtis is a bloke, as you'd all have realized if you'd ever listened to her language. Ladies don't say *khazi*, they say *bog*.'

'What?' Ewan stared in puzzled disbelief. 'But Mrs Curtis, she can't be a man. She had—'

'Enormous saggin' whatsitsnames? Oh, grow up, sonny boy.' Julia looked at Ewan with patronizing scorn. 'I seen her in the buff once, an' a horrid sight it was, the flab all hanging everywhere, but she 'ad a little pecker, too. You got the money for your fare to Glasgow?'

'I – no, I don't think so,' Ewan said. 'What shall I do now?'

'Lurk in the bogs pretending to be ill,' said Amy briskly, slapping him on the shoulder and grinning in derision at his worried frown. 'If you see a guard, just say you've got diphtheria. That'll make the bugger keep his distance. When are they expecting you in Scotland?'

'Oh – er – early evening.'

'Better get your skates on then, my darling. Got your case?' Julia led the company down the path. 'Come on, girls and boys. Let's go and see this highland laddie off to bonny Scotland.'

'Ewan,' said Daisy softly, so that no one else could hear, 'I can lend you the money for your fare. You don't have to pay me back until—'

'Keep your lousy money,' interrupted Ewan harshly. 'You'll need it if you're going to London with that bugger Trent. I'll bet he has expensive habits. *I* don't want your charity.'

'Oh, Ewan, please don't be like this!' cried Daisy. 'The Comrades Theatre, isn't it? I'll write to you next week.'

'Please yourself,' said Ewan, striding off.

'Come on, love,' said George, as Daisy's eyes filled up and overflowed. 'Young Fraser's just upset.'

'Yeah, aren't we all,' said Jesse, hugging Daisy round the neck.

'You watch your step, my girl,' said Amy, sternly. After seeing Ewan off, Frank and George had gone back to their digs to pack their things. Julia went off to hang around in one of the big hotels, hoping to find a salesman who would buy her a few drinks. But Amy had stayed with Daisy and Jesse on the station platform, waiting for the train to Euston.

'What's that supposed to mean?' asked Jesse, slapping at his pockets. 'Damn, I'm out of fags. Amy, I don't suppose you could—'

'You'd better go and buy yourself some,' Amy told him, tartly. 'Well, go on, then! Shoo! You've only got five minutes.'

As Jesse went hurrying off to find a kiosk, Amy looked hard at Daisy. 'Well?' she said.

'Well what?' countered Daisy.

'Julia and I are going to find some summer-season work,' said Amy, urgently. 'There's always something going. End-of-the-pier shows if we're really desperate. Pierrettes and blackface sort of thing. Girls are always pulling out because they're getting married or up the duff or something, so we'll soon get sorted out. Come with us, why don't you? We could do a sister act. They always come in threes.'

'I want to go to London,' Daisy said.

'You're besotted, aren't you?' Amy made Daisy meet her gaze. 'Well, if you change your mind, you can write to me care of my mum. The old bitch doesn't speak to me, but I expect she'll send a letter on.' Amy stuffed a piece of paper into Daisy's hand. 'Just don't believe a word he says, OK? I've met his sort before, all mouth and Brylcreem, hard-luck stories. All that stuff about his father bashing him is rot, believe you me.'

'Amy, he has the marks!' cried Daisy. 'Poor Jesse, he's told me all about it, have some sympathy—'

'God, you're as green as lettuce.'

'Lettuce?' demanded Jesse, coming up behind them and laying his hand on Daisy's shoulder. 'Lettuce what?'

'Oh, lettuce pray, what else?' Amy scowled at Jesse. 'Listen, Mr Smartarse, look after this little girl, all right? I've got a couple of brothers – you know what I'm saying?'

'I wouldn't hurt a hair of Daisy's head.' Jesse looked at Daisy tenderly, and she felt a flood of warmth wash over her, she felt so cherished. 'I'd defend her with my life.'

'Yeah, well – I hope for Daisy's sake it never comes to that, because I'd put my money on you scarpering, not staying around to fight.' Amy put down her parcel of cleaning which she'd lugged round Birmingham all morning, then she rapidly untied the string. 'Here, Daisy, love,' she said.

'What's that?' asked Daisy.

'My best suit.' Amy shoved the bundle of tweed at Daisy. 'Go on, take it! You haven't got any grown-up clothes. You look about eleven in that coat. If a copper notices you getting on the London train together, Mr Smartarse here will be had up for kidnapping a child.'

'But Amy, I can't take this!' cried Daisy.

'Yes, you can,' said Amy. 'It doesn't fit me any more. I'm getting fat. I can't do up the buttons on the skirt.'

The train came roaring in, belching clouds of smoke and steam. Amy darted forward, kissed Daisy on the cheek, and glared at Jesse. 'Look after Daisy, Mr Smartarse Pervert,' she said, thickly. 'You never know who might be watching you.'

Ewan got off the train at Glasgow Central, feeling more desolate than he ever had in all his life. He wondered where he ought to go – straight to the theatre, to try to see the manager and ask for an advance? That would make him popular, he reflected miserably. Get the whole engagement off to a cracking start.

But what else could he do? He had five shillings, one tarnished threepenny bit, and sevenpence in coppers, which wouldn't get him far. He should have taken Daisy's money – could have saved it, for as luck had had it, there hadn't been a single ticket inspection on the train.

He wasn't going to ring his mother, have her say she'd told him so – he would sooner die. But if he didn't have anything to eat within an hour or two, he was afraid he might.

'Hello, there,' said a small, dark girl in a long, unflattering over-coat and dark-blue tam o'shanter that looked like her school beret. 'I've come to meet a Mr Ewan Fraser off the London train. You wouldn't happen to be him, would you, now?'

Ewan glanced down and saw a cheeky-looking imp of a woman smiling merrily up at him. 'Yes, I'm Ewan Fraser,' he replied.

'I'm Sadie Lawrence,' said the imp. 'So how are you, and did you have a pleasant journey here?'

Ewan swallowed hard, and then burst into tears.

CHAPTER 13

P HOEBE stood in front of the theatre, trying to screw her failing courage to the sticking-point.

She looked the building up and down. God, it was a horrible, tawdry place, far worse than the Haggerston Palace music-hall in the East End of London, where she'd been in variety, and which she'd always thought must be the dump to end all dumps. She'd never have thought a kid of hers would sink as low as this.

It was a drizzly Monday afternoon, the sort of day that never got really light, and there was nobody about. But Mondays were always dead, she remembered, even in the war years when people were desperate for entertainment, when they didn't begrudge a bob or two to take their minds off all the awful things that were going on.

There wouldn't be a matinée on a Monday. But there must be somebody about, she thought, painting scenery, checking the lights, or something.

She tried the double doors and found them locked. She went round to the side and picked her way along a dirty alley strewn with litter. She found the stage-door, which was also locked, but there she found a little ginger ferret of a man, snoozing at the window next to it.

'I can't do nothin' for you, ma'am,' he said, when she eventually roused him. 'They done their last show 'ere on Friday, an' that was the end of their engagement 'ere in Brum. I dunno where they've gone. But I tell you now, you ain't missed much.'

'You must know where they stayed? They'll 'ave given their landladies their forwardin' addresses, for their post an' stuff.' Phoebe hadn't come so far and taken so much trouble to give up now. 'Where are the theatrical digs round 'ere? You got a list?'

The doorman scratched his head, uncertain what to do. The only folks who asked him for that sort of list were debt-collectors, chasing actors who had run up bills, then done a bunk. But this pretty woman in her expensive coat, and what he would have sworn were real silk stockings, couldn't be a debt-collector's runner. She wore a proper whizz-bang of a hat, all feathers, lace and velvet, the sort of hat you never saw in Brum.

Now she was rummaging in her crocodile-skin handbag and getting out her purse, and in her purse he could see rolls of banknotes. 'I think we got a list somewhere,' he said.

'Well then, my good man, I'd be very obliged if I could see it,' Phoebe told him, smiling. She offered him a couple of crackling, green pound-notes.

Euston was dark and gloomy, suiting Daisy's gloomy mood. On the train, Jesse had talked her into a splitting headache, regaling her with all his past successes, and bragging about the star he meant to be, either on the stage or in the talkies. Yes, he reckoned, the talkies were definitely the coming thing. He would be in the talkies. He'd have such good parts. . . .

He didn't have any money, though. He'd spent his last two shillings in the buffet car, on beer. Daisy had three pounds, nine shillings and eleven pence, and that wouldn't get them very far. It was just as well that Ewan had refused her cash.

They got off the train. 'But how could they bring themselves to do it?' she demanded crossly, as they made their way across the concourse. 'I thought we were a company. We had contracts. We'd worked so hard for them—'

'Oh, touring managers, they're all the bloody same,' said Jesse, shrugging. 'The Curtises won't be the first or last to run off with the takings.'

'You mean it happens often?'

'Yes, of course, and in these dismal days it's going to happen more and more.' Jesse put his arm round Daisy's shoulders. 'Come on, blossom, let's look on the bright side. You're in the capital of the British Empire with a handsome man.'

'I have no job, I can't afford to pay for a week's lodgings—'

' We'll sort something out, my dove, don't worry.' Jesse grinned. 'Let's go and treat ourselves to pie and chips, and then we'll find a mission.'

'A mission?' Daisy frowned. 'We had those in India. They were where beggars went to get deloused, to beg some rice or dump their grannies.'

'Well, we're almost beggars – actors are traditionally rogues and vagabonds.' Jesse picked up their cases. 'There's a place in Edgware Road that's run by Church of England nuns. It's just for women, so it shouldn't be too squalid.

'Daisy, don't tell anyone you're an actress,' added Jesse, as they walked out of the station. 'Or they'll think you mean you're on the game, and throw you out. You need to say you've just come up from Dorset, that you're looking for domestic work, that you don't have anywhere to stay, and a kind policeman told you to try the mission.'

'But what will you do?' Daisy asked him.

'Oh, don't you worry about me!' Jesse grinned and winked. 'I'll find a corner somewhere. Listen, they'll chuck you out at eight o'clock tomorrow morning, tell you to go off and look for work, even though it's Sunday. Whatever you do, don't let them keep your luggage, even if they offer. You'll never get it back.

'I'll meet you at a Lyon's Corner House, there's one near Trafalgar Square, at nine or half past nine. Daisy, I don't like to ask, but could you let me have a bob or two?'

'Yes, of course,' said Daisy. 'But hadn't I better keep some change? Why don't you take a pound?'

'Oh – well, OK.' Jesse took the note and stuffed it in his trouser pocket. 'I'll pay you back, I promise.'

'That's all right,' said Daisy, glad he seemed to know his way about, since she was lost. 'Let's go and have a meal now. I'm starving.'

They found a dingy café near the station, shared a meal of gristle-pie and chips, then went to find the mission. Turning left down Baker Street, and then right into George Street, Jesse eventually brought them out on to the Edgware Road.

'This is it,' he said, stopping beside a tall, gaunt, soot-stained building. 'Go on, ring the bell. I'll see you in the morning.'

Jesse kissed Daisy briefly on the cheek, then strode off down the road. After staring at his back for twenty or thirty seconds, in two minds about running after him, she rang the mission bell.

Eventually, a black-robed, stern-faced nun came to the door. Daisy told her story in her best Dorset accent, and was finally admitted.

'You're in luck,' the nun said briskly, as she led Daisy up some bare, stone stairs, her robes swishing behind her on the treads. 'The casual ward has just the one bed left. Otherwise, we'd have had to turn you away. Or send you to the Salvation Army hostel in the Marylebone Road, and a little country girl like you would have found the hostel very rough.

'This is where you leave your case,' she added, pointing to an empty, padlocked cage. 'I'll just get you a ticket.'

'But Oi'll need moi case,' objected Daisy, clutching it.

'Quite, so you can have it back tomorrow.' The nun looked

Daisy up and down. 'You're not in Dorset any more, my dear. This is the big, bad city, and it's full of wicked people who would cut your throat for half a crown. If you take your case up to the ward, it will be empty in the morning. Just take out your washing things tonight.'

Daisy did as she was told, sneaking out her purse as well and slipping it in her pocket, and wondering how much rougher it could get.

She'd thought she was used to slums and ruins, but this was something else. The mission was a musty, fusty building that had water running down its pea-green painted walls, that smelled of dirty laundry, and was lit by gas that stank. She thought she could hear reedy, plaintive crying. Or perhaps it was a cat?

'Be very quiet now,' said the nun, as they climbed and climbed, passing grim stone landings which led to double doors. 'Try not to let your heels click on the stairs, or else you'll wake the babies.'

'Babies?' Daisy frowned.

'The babies and their mothers, poor foolish girls who let men take advantage,' said the nun, severely.

The ward to which the nun took Daisy was high up in the roof. It was unfurnished except for rows and rows of iron beds, on which a strange assortment of women, girls and hunched-up bundles snored or lay like corpses.

Daisy used the horrid, dirty washroom, then lay down fully clothed upon the bed, which smelled of something nasty. She pulled a hairy blanket over her, trying not to notice that it stank.

But although she didn't think she'd sleep, she closed her eyes. When she opened them again, the morning light was streaming through the windows, brightly illuminating all the squalor. She could hear London pigeons courting, chattering and squabbling on the roof.

'Get up,' said a dark-haired, dough-faced girl, who was sitting down on the next bed, and pinning up her hair. 'You'll miss your breakfast, else.'

'They give us breakfast?'

'Yeah, of course they do, if you tells 'em you ain't got no money.' The girl grinned slyly. 'Sister Mary Agnes always noses through the stuff they got locked in the cage. So I 'ope you 'ad the sense to stick yer lolly down yer drawers?'

Breakfast turned out to be a bowl of lukewarm, stiff, grey porridge, full of hairy lumps and gluey globules. 'That's the snot the nuns put into it, to mortify our flesh,' observed the dough-faced girl.

But Daisy was very hungry, so she choked the porridge down.

'Good luck, my child,' said the middle-aged sister who'd reunited Daisy with her case, and who made Daisy think of Mrs Hobson back in Dorset. 'Tell me, my dear, why did you come to London?'

'To look for live-in work,' Daisy replied.

'But if you don't find any, what will you do then?'

'Oi've got the addresses of all the domestic agencies, an' so Oi 'ope Oi will,' said Daisy, edging towards the stairs.

'Then you'll need some bus fares,' said the nun. 'Do you have any money?'

'Oi got a little, thankee, Sister.' Daisy thought, I won't accept more charity, even if it's offered. I feel enough of a fraud already.

'Then please leave your offering in the box,' the nun said, nodding towards a crucifix on the wall which Daisy hadn't previously noticed. On a shelf beneath the crucifix was a wooden box with a small slit in it.

'Yes, of course. Oi'm sorry.' Daisy found her purse, then in her confusion she slipped in half a crown, which was far too much.

'It's usual to kneel and say a prayer,' went on the nun, pointing towards a greasy velvet cushion on the floor. 'Even if you're a Methodist or Presbyterian, you should know to bow and cross yourself before Our Lord.'

*

'You survived, then,' Jesse said, and grinned.

'Yes, just about.' Daisy thought the smell of coffee was the scent of heaven after the various stinks she'd had to deal with at the mission, which had been worse than anything in any provincial theatre. 'What about you, where did you spend the night?'

'Oh, I found a bar, got into conversation with a bloke, and he bought me some drinks. Then, after chucking-out time, I walked the streets until the cafés opened in the early hours.' Jesse yawned. 'If I have another cup of coffee, I'll be all right.'

'Thanks for looking after me,' said Daisy.

'My pleasure.' Jesse smiled. 'That place, was it OK?'

'Well, it was a roof over my head,' said Daisy, wrinkling her nose.

'Yes, I've heard it's grim. I'm sorry it couldn't be the Ritz.' Jesse took the previous evening's paper from his pocket. 'I forgot to say – I hope you didn't tell them you had money? They'd have tried to get you to make a contribution to their funds. So now, we have to find a room to let.'

'Two rooms, actually.'

'I was afraid you might say that.' Jesse's grin was wry. 'A common lodging-house, I think. Somewhere south of the river will be cheaper.'

'What about theatrical digs?' asked Daisy.

'In London?' Jesse laughed. 'You're obviously joking. We can't afford theatrical digs in London.'

They walked all day, looking at dingy lodging houses, dirty tenements and filthy basements. At last they found a place in Clapham, two so-called furnished attic rooms in a crumbling fire-trap that smelled of cats and sewage, for which they had to pay two pounds up front to a woman living in the basement.

'So now we're on our uppers,' said Jesse, cheerfully.

131

'What shall we do now?'

'Go and have some supper – there's an eel-and-pie shop on the corner.'

They fed their faces, and as they walked home again, Jesse's arm round Daisy's shoulders as he hummed some catchy little tunes she didn't recognize, she felt how lovely it would be to snuggle up to him tonight, to cuddle up together, and. . . .

But that was just it. That was how so many girls got caught, and she didn't want to end up like her missing mother, pregnant at sixteen, having her baby in some place for girls who had no sense and let men take advantage, and having to hand her child over to a married stranger. Or, which was even worse, having to hurt herself with knitting-needles, then dispose of blood-soaked parcels. . . .

They let themselves into the smelly, gloomy hallway. 'Goodnight,' she said to Jesse, as they reached their attic rooms. 'You must be really tired.'

'Actually, I'm exhausted.' Jesse bent to kiss her on the forehead. 'Go on, Daisy, get your beauty sleep. You're going to need it, and I sure as hell need mine.'

But Daisy couldn't go to sleep, not yet. She was too wound-up, too high, too low and too confused to sleep.

She found some paper in her case and wrote to Ewan. As she wrote, she felt how much she missed him, missed knowing he was there, always looking out for her and always on her side.

At first, she wrote a lot of nonsense, about how she and Jesse had found somewhere nice to live, and how they were going to see some agents, how they were sure they'd get themselves fixed up with something soon.

But then, as tears blurred her vision, and the asthmatic clicking of the meter warned her that the gas would soon run out, and she knew she didn't have a sixpence, she added, *dear Ewan, I'm missing you already, and I wish you could be here.*

But if that was true, why was she five hundred miles away from dear Ewan? Why did she want so much to be in bed with another man?

CHAPTER 14

WHEN the gas ran out, she went to bed. She couldn't sleep. She tossed and turned and fidgeted, unable to get comfortable on the flock-filled mattress.

All night long, cockroaches and beetles ran across the lino, while other, larger creatures rustled and scrabbled beneath the broken floorboards, and in the attics high above her head.

After living in India, Daisy was used to birds and rats and insects coming uninvited into people's houses, but the antics of their British counterparts still kept her awake. The actual bed was full of wildlife, too. She woke up from a fitful doze to find that she was being bitten to bits, and in the morning her fair skin was blotchy, red and itching. She thought, I must try not to scratch the bites.

When she met Jesse on the landing, he too looked as if he hadn't slept. 'I'm going to have a shave,' he said, dipping a chipped enamel mug into the bucket of cold water which someone had brought up. When they had mentioned washing, the landlady had told them that there would be "arrangements", and it seemed as if the half-full bucket was what she had arranged.

'*You* could try and do something with your hair,' continued Jesse. 'You should wash your fringe, at any rate. It's very greasy.'

'Yes, I know,' said Daisy, annoyed that he had noticed.

They'd spent most of Sunday just wandering around, getting

their bearings, looking for digs and gazing in awe at all the West End theatres, imagining their own names up in lights, and snacking off cheap food from vendors' stalls. But now, on Monday morning, Daisy posted Ewan's letter, and after a shared breakfast of bacon, eggs and sausages in a workmen's café, they walked to the West End again, where they bought a copy of *The Stage*.

But although they pored over the small ads, and then spent all that morning in two adjacent telephone kiosks making calls to agents, they got nowhere. Every part was filled, and every agent's books were closed. Nobody was interested in their rave reviews in Stoke on Trent, or their notices in Macclesfield. They were just two more provincial players, come to London to join thousands who were also unemployed.

In the afternoon, they traipsed round Soho, where management after management refused point blank to see them. Secretaries shooed them out of offices already full of hopefuls sitting on hard chairs. One or two agents had a list on which they could leave their names and details, so they did, but without much hope of being called in.

They didn't have a telephone, anyway.

Soon their feet were blistered, and by nightfall they were cold and starving. Daisy had a ten-bob note still, but they knew they shouldn't break into that, and after rummaging in all their pockets, they scraped together one and fivepence. As they made their way back home, they noticed girls of Daisy's age or younger, loitering in shop doorways, grinning desperately at passing men.

By Friday, they'd run out of faith, of optimism, and were down to Daisy's last half-crown. 'We'll have to get non-acting jobs,' said Jesse, as they shared a fourpenny bag of chips, warming their hands by cupping them around the greasy paper.

'But if we get jobs,' objected Daisy, 'what do we do if an agent finds us something? What about auditions, if we're working?'

'We work at night,' said Jesse.

'Doing what, exactly?' Daisy asked, rubbing at some flea-bites on her arm, desperate to have a good old scratch. 'If there were any jobs, there wouldn't be three million unemployed.'

'We get the sort of jobs nobody else will do,' said Jesse, smoothing out the paper which had contained the chips. 'Got a pencil, have you?'

The factory was in Deptford, two or three hours' walk away from Clapham, or an hour by bus with several changes. But they couldn't afford the bus.

They didn't have to ask directions. As they made their way up New Cross Road, their noses led them to it.

'It'll be a bit of a comedown for a girl like you,' said Jesse, as they walked up a dirty cobbled alley, and the truly awful smell grew stronger.

'What do you mean, a girl like me?'

'Someone who's been well brought up,' said Jesse. 'Somebody who's posh.'

'God, *I'm* not posh!' cried Daisy, thinking, if he only knew.

'Well, you sound it.' Jesse stopped for a moment. 'If we're to survive here, Daisy, we must both fit in. Your Cockney accent's terrible, so don't try to be a London girl, they'll know you're faking straight away. What about doing Dorset peasant again?'

'Yes, I suppose I could do peasant.' Daisy grinned. 'What about you, then, son of the preacher-man?'

'Oh, I'll do peasant, too.'

'Come from the country, 'ave you?' asked the foreman, as he looked them up and down.

'That's right, zur,' Jesse told him, tugging obsequiously at his forelock.

'The work 'ere isn't pleasant,' said the foreman.

'We're not bothered about it, zur, so long as we gets paid,' said

Jesse, sounding like a real West Country bumpkin, born and bred.

'It's night shifts, eight till eight – an hour off at midnight, and there's a meal provided,' said the foreman. 'So, with bonuses, a strong young lad like you could clear five quid a week, an' probably two or three for this young lady – if she pulls her finger out.'

'When can we start?' asked Jesse.

'I could take you on tonight. We got a government job on, see – five hundred thousand candles.' The foreman scratched his nose. 'Somebody 'igh up must think we're gonner 'ave another war.'

The tallow-rendering plant and candle factory attached to it were black-grimed buildings, dirty, tumble-down and full of rats – there were traps and metal boxes full of poison everywhere.

Inside, everything was grey and greasy. The atmosphere was thick with lazily dancing motes of fatty grime. As she bundled up her hair, pulled on a cap and tied the strings around her overall, Daisy felt the pinprick drops of grease float down and settle on her face. As she sat down at her bench, she noticed that the other women and girls all had a tired, defeated look about them, even though the shift was only starting.

But instead of the red and roughened hands which Daisy had assumed must be the lot of working women everywhere, all *their* hands were snowy-white, as smooth and soft as silk. So there was a glimmer of a silver lining on this particular cloud. . . .

The heavy work was done by men. They did all the humping of the sacks of animal fat, the skins and bones and fish-waste and industrial grease which, separated into solids and liquids by strong alkaline and thus turned into stearin, finally ended up as hard, white candles.

So began the days of drudgery. Jesse hated everything about it, and grumbled constantly, but Daisy couldn't blame him. Ewan had written back to her, telling her that the people at the Comrades were a grand bunch of folk, that he was doing fine. But when he added at the end *I miss you, too*, Daisy almost cried.

'How's your darling Fraser getting on?' asked Jesse, scowling as she read the letter on the bus back home.

'He's doing well, he says the other people are very nice, and that they're doing challenging new plays.'

'Challenging, eh?' sneered Jesse. 'He means they spout a load of left-wing drivel at half a dozen people every night, and they have no scenery.'

'You don't approve of communism, then?'

'It's a nice idea in theory, all that caring, sharing rigmarole. Up the workers, shoot the royal family dead. Nationalize the factories, house the bloody homeless in the mansions of Mayfair.'

Jesse yawned and rubbed his worker's eyes. 'But it won't catch on here. Most British people like to own things, and anyway the working-classes idolize the bloody monarchy.'

'You can eat the candles, acksherly,' the woman sitting next to Daisy said, as Daisy's empty stomach rumbled, as they tipped out moulds during one long, dull shift. 'That's why the gummunt wants 'em. When we 'as another war, 'an we're all sat in cellars, waitin' to be killed by poison-gas, we eats the candles.'

'Oh, I see,' said Daisy, not really tempted, even though she was always hungry now. She was really looking forward to the meal at midnight, even though it usually looked as if the food came straight out of the fat- and fish-waste sacks.

The work was boring and monotonous, and talking wasn't encouraged. As Daisy emptied moulds, discarded damaged or misshapen candles, sorted, packed up boxes, she often started nodding off to sleep. 'Oi, country bumpkin!' The supervisor made a habit of poking Daisy sharply in between the shoulder blades, a dozen times a night. 'You're 'ere to work, not kip!'

'You could always go back home to Dorset,' Jesse said, as they trudged their weary way back to their squalid rooms one yellow dawn, too poor to get the bus, to go to bed for a few hours, then get up and hoof it round the managements and agencies, then go on shift again.

'You mean, admit defeat?' Daisy shook her head. 'Anyway, I have it easy, in the moulding-rooms and on the packing. You've got the really nasty jobs, loading and unloading all those stinking sacks, or working in the boiling-rooms.'

'It's money,' said Jesse, yawning.

'We both stink,' said Daisy. 'It's so difficult, washing piecemeal with a bowl of lukewarm water and a flannel, up there in my room. If I could have anything in the world, I'd have a real bath with running water – full up to brim. I'd lie and soak for hours.'

'Let's do it, then.' Suddenly brightening up, Jesse took her hand and made her run along the street. 'Expense be blowed. Let's go to the Clapham public baths and get ourselves cleaned up.'

'We'll only get all greasy again tonight.'

'I can have a proper shave, and you can wash your hair,' Jesse went on, as if she hadn't spoken. 'Believe me, love, it needs it.'

'Beast,' said Daisy, but aware that he was right.

The following day, she bought a pair of scissors from a market-stall and gave herself a clumsy, hacked-off shingle. 'Less of it to get dirty,' she told Jesse, when he stared at her in horror.

'Actually, it suits you,' he decided, when he had calmed down, and she had let him tidy up the mess she'd made by chopping so haphazardly round the back. 'You've got a very well-shaped head – not many people have.'

Jesse was up one day, down the next. He kept Daisy's spirits up, but also criticized her, which she found inspiring and dispiriting by turns.

'You need some singing lessons,' he declared, after they'd spent all Sunday on a deserted stretch of Hampstead Heath, determined to use their time to best effect, practising a song-and-dance act which they hoped might wow any agent who would kindly condescend to meet them. 'You're still not breathing properly.'

'How would I pay for singing lessons, eh?'

'What about your parents, wouldn't they help you out?'

'They'd send me the money for the first train home. They think I'm still in Birmingham with Ewan and the company, being chaperoned by Mrs Curtis. Mum would have a purple fit if she knew that I was on the loose in wicked London, with the likes of you.'

'So what's wrong with the likes of me?' Jesse already had her in his arms, and now he pulled her closer, gazing deep into her eyes.

'You're a man,' said Daisy, 'and men get women into trouble – it's a well-known fact. They love them, then they leave them. Sometimes they don't bother with the loving bit, provided they can get their wicked way.'

'I'm not like that,' said Jesse.

'Oh, of course you're not. Jesse Trent's some kind of plaster saint.'

'Daisy, I adore you, I'd defend you with my life.'

'I hope *that* won't be necessary,' Daisy told him, laughing.

'Daisy, come to bed with me?' Daisy saw that Jesse's eyes were dark with longing. 'You don't know how it tortures me, knowing that you're lying there three feet away from me, hearing you breathing, imagining how it would feel to run my fingers through your hair. Or what's left of it.'

'You know I can't,' said Daisy.

'Why not, are you too holy?'

'I'm not holy, but I don't want a baby.'

'I'll make sure you don't have one.'

'Plenty of women have heard *that* before, but the world's still full of little mistakes and indiscretions.'

'Oh, Daisy,' Jesse sighed, 'don't be so mean to me! You're very cynical and worldly-wise.'

'One of us has to be – and anyway, I thought you were brought up to be religious?'

'I gave up all that guff when I left home.'

*

On the way home from work one morning, Daisy saw an ad in a shop window: *female vocalist wanted, mostly shift-work.*

'It'll be in a club up west, or in a part-time brothel,' Jesse said. 'They must be desperate if they're advertising out here in the suburbs. I'd better come along, hope I can get a job as a doorman, keep an eye on you.'

But it wasn't in a brothel. It was in a seedy dance-hall in Tulse Hill. Mostly afternoons, it would fit in well with Daisy's shift-work at the candle factory.

Daisy sang for old-age pensioners doing shuffling quicksteps, and for couples dancing in the prize-winning marathons that were currently all the rage – crooning, half-asleep herself, to the exhausted, desperate couples wanting to win a ten-pound prize for staying on their swollen feet the longest.

Jesse was getting desperate, he said – he couldn't find any acting work, he couldn't even get a lousy job like Daisy's singing shifts, and Daisy herself was being a cruel tease.

'It's a waste of money, renting two rooms when we need just the one,' he grumbled, as they walked to work one evening, saving on the bus fares.

'We can't take a room together, it would be immoral,' Daisy told him.

'That old witch in the basement wouldn't care, as long as the rent is paid,' growled Jesse, crossly. 'Well, I'll wait,' he added. 'You'll crack eventually.'

They decided to split up, to do the rounds of managements and agents independently, agreeing to pool resources. Both of them had almost given up hope, and Daisy was resigned to working in the factory and singing in squalid dancing-halls all her life, when she was called in for an audition for the chorus in a new revue, in a little theatre that was *almost* the West End. Jesse decided he would tag along.

When they saw the line of hopefuls stretching round the block, they looked at one another in dismay. 'Oh, sod it – let's go and have a drink,' said Jesse.

Daisy was very tempted. It was a hot afternoon for May, and she was tired and thirsty. But then she squared her shoulders. 'No, we came to London so we could be in a show,' she said. 'We can't give up now.'

She'd made a special effort with her appearance, too. When she'd got in from work, she'd washed her hair, then brushed it hard until it was a glossy golden helmet. She'd sponged Amy's skirt and jacket until they were as clean as she could get them. She'd used the last of the stub-end of lipstick that Julia had given her, several weeks ago. She'd polished up her dancing-shoes and wrapped them in brown paper, and now she was praying hard. 'You go if you want,' she said to Jesse. 'I'll stay here.'

'You won't have a partner if I go.'

'I don't *need* a partner for the stuff I plan to do. Anyway, there must be a hundred gentlemen in this queue. I'm sure one of them would dance with me.'

'Oh, very well, since you insist, I'll stay.' Jesse lit a cigarette and lounged against a billboard advertising current offerings. 'I'll bet they don't have finance, anyway. So all this is probably a total waste of time.'

The queue began to shuffle forward.

Jesse and Daisy did a double act, then a few minutes individually. They and twenty others were asked to stay behind, and a few hundred disappointed hopefuls shambled out, darting jealous glances as they went.

The producer addressed the people still on stage. The show was being done on a tight budget, he began. The cast would have to provide their costumes – top-hats, tails and patent dancing-shoes for all the men, evening dresses and white leather shoes for all the ladies. Daisy gulped – she didn't have an evening dress, had never owned an evening-dress, couldn't make an evening dress and certainly couldn't buy one.

But looking round the other people lined up for the chorus, Daisy realized that this was her big chance. She wouldn't get another. The others were all hungry enough to sell their little sisters into prostitution, if it meant being in a London show.

'We'll have to hire,' said Jesse, as they checked their savings.

'But you can't hire dancing-shoes,' said Daisy. 'Or, if you can, you wouldn't want to, because you'd get some foot-rotting disease. My mother wouldn't want me to dance in someone else's shoes.'

'All right, buy shoes, hire clothes, then,' Jesse said. Thanks to living on chips and gristle-pies, and walking to and from the factory unless it poured with rain, they had just enough to buy some shoes, hire evening clothes from a theatrical costumier's musty bargain basement, and feed themselves until they first got paid.

They gave their notice at the factory. 'Going back to Dorset?' grinned the foreman. 'I didn't think you'd stick it.'

'But why not?' asked Jesse, as they walked home from the pub, where they'd celebrated getting jobs in the revue and leaving the factory.

'Just – Jesse, I just can't,' said Daisy.

'You're a tease,' scowled Jesse.

'I am *not* a tease!' It was awful having Jesse looking at her like that. But it would be more awful if she had an illegitimate baby, if she had to go crawling home to Dorset in disgrace, like a girl in melodrama, her baby wrapped up in a tartan shawl. . . .

'I love you, Daisy Denham,' Jesse said. 'You're a wicked flirt, you know, but I'll always love you.'

143

Daisy looked at him. So was she in love? She didn't know.

When she next wrote to Ewan, telling him rehearsals for the revue were going well, as usual she left many things unsaid, but she did finish up with: *I often think of you.*

When he wrote back, he said: *I wish we weren't so far apart.*

'Well, she sounds an awful wicked flirt,' said Sadie Lawrence, briskly.

It was a rest day, and she'd taken Ewan to a crowded ice-cream parlour run by cheerful, garrulous Italians, and so full of music, smoke and noise that he could gulp and snivel about his girlfriend without attracting very much attention.

'No, she's lovely.' Ewan sniffed. 'You should meet her, Sadie – you'd adore her, everyone adores her, she's that sort of girl. But she wastes her talents. She's misguided.'

'How do you mean, misguided?'

'She's working in revue.'

'Oh,' said Sadie, and looked at him as if he'd said that Daisy walked the streets. 'She wouldn't fit in here then, would she, Ewan? We do only serious drama at the Comrades.'

'Yes, and that's what she should do, some proper, serious drama. She's a natural for Juliet, for Rosalind, for—'

'Ewan,' interrupted Sadie.

'What?'

'It's very tedious when you go for an ice-cream sundae with a man, and he keeps going on and on about some other woman.'

'Oh – I suppose you're right.' Ewan sat up at looked at Sadie, who was regarding him with dark-brown eyes which blazed from underneath severe dark eyebrows. She looked like some wee kelpie in that coat and tam o'shanter, he decided, and the thought of Sadie sitting on a tussock giving orders to a mob of pixies made him grin.

'That's better,' Sadie said, and smiled herself. 'Here, Ewan – you can have my cherries, I don't really like them.'

144

After only two weeks of rehearsals, nobody felt ready, but the management said the show must open. The company financing it, Hanson Enterprises Limited, apparently insisted. So the bills were printed, the show was advertised, and then the bookings started trickling in.

'It'll be all right,' said the producer, as he surveyed his ragged chorus line and as he smiled encouragingly at his off-key singers. He ran his finger round his collar, and Daisy saw his face was damp with sweat. 'Mr Daniel Hanson,' he continued, grimly, 'is not a man who likes to be let down. So do your best.'

To everyone's relief, the first night went extremely well. On the whole, the notices were good, and the producer said – in jest, they all supposed and hoped – that Mr Hanson wouldn't need to get his men to smash their kneecaps now.

But Jesse wasn't altogether pleased, because one critic on a daily paper singled Daisy out for special mention. *The soubrette with the lovely smile, forget-me-not-blue eyes and stunning figure, whose short solo in the second half was quite delightful, Miss Daisy Denham should go far*, the critic said – and hadn't mentioned *him*.

'Your turn next time,' said Daisy, at the end of one evening performance when Jesse was still rumbling on about it. Goodness, he was such a baby sometimes.

'I need a drink,' said Jesse, grumpily. But then he turned to look at a girl who was also in the chorus-line, a girl with dyed red hair who looked on the wrong side of thirty-five, but dressed and made up young. 'You all right, Belinda?'

'Smashing, Jesse,' said Belinda, flashing a bit of leg in his direction. 'You?'

'I'm fine.' Then Jesse turned his back on Daisy. 'Where are the others going for a drink tonight, d'you know?'

'The Old Nag's Head,' replied Belinda, tossing her head flirta-
tiously.

'See you there,' Jesse said, grinning.

'Excuse *me*?' said Daisy.

'Oh, but I thought you didn't drink,' said Jesse. But then he
turned back to her and gave her such a smile her heart turned over.
'Only kidding, sweetheart – you can tag along.'

Phoebe walked down the cobbled side-street, thinking about her
youth and wondering where the years had gone. The smell of the
dusty little theatre brought the whole thing back – those nights
during the war, the men and officers hanging round and looking
hopeful after every show, picking up the chorus-girls and taking
them off to pubs and clubs. One officer in particular, there'd
been . . .

The stage door was open now, and people were pouring out. A
blonde girl and a dark-haired man were coming down the stairs, he
was nibbling at her ear, and she was half-pushing him away, but
also laughing.

Phoebe had been studying the picture Rose had given her; she
had the girl's features hot-pressed on her brain, but what if she was
wrong?

She stepped into a pool of lamplight. ' 'Scuse me – are you Miss
Denham?' she began.

'Yes, I am,' said Daisy, smiling, delighted to have fan at the stage
door, wondering why the woman didn't seem to have a programme, if she wanted Daisy's autograph.

Phoebe had rehearsed this moment over and over and over in her
mind. She had her speech all ready. But now she forgot her lines,
and all she said was, 'Daisy, darlin', I'm your mum.'

CHAPTER 15

'EWAN, you must forget this girl,' said Sadie Lawrence, sternly. 'All your mooning around the place and all your day-dreaming – it makes the others laugh at you, you know. Romantic love's a base and bourgeois concept, anyway. It's totally discredited. It has no place in twentieth-century thinking.'

'I suppose not,' Ewan agreed, pushing his hand into his trouser pocket where Daisy's most recent letter lay crumpled up. A symbol of hope, he wondered, or of futility?

The Glasgow Comrades Company was rehearsing for the premier of a new drama set in Tsarist Russia, in which heroic workers battled against a brutal Tsarist boss. Ewan played a worker who stabbed and killed the boss. The worker's subsequent arrest, imprisonment, trial and gruesome execution were acted out on stage, in as much lurid detail as the producer thought the Lord Chamberlain's office would allow.

Mrs Fraser would have hated it, all those nasty people being horrid to her boy, all that unnecessary, ill-bred shouting, all that blood. Even Ewan thought his death scene did go on a bit.

But when they eventually opened, he got good notices in the left-wing press about his passion and commitment to the cause of workers' freedom. So he kept his reservations to himself. At least nobody expected him to speak as if came from Surrey. In fact, the producer had wanted all the workers to have strong Glaswegian accents, while all the villainous bosses and their lackeys sounded English to a man.

Sadie was a fully paid-up member of the British Communist Party, and her father had worked for thirty years in various Clydeside shipyards, but was currently unemployed. She spoke her lines with fervour and, as Ewan's wife, she raged and carried on like anything about the awful things done to her man, and by extension to workers everywhere.

'I'd always thought red hair looked better on a lassie, but on you it's bonny,' she told him smiling, after one performance in which Ewan had died especially noisily and energetically, cursing the capitalists and all their works, to great applause.

'Thank you.' These days, Ewan's wounded heart accepted any compliment as balm, and he smiled back at Sadie. 'It's nice of you to say so.'

'Hey, Fraser, coming for a beer?' Mungo, another tormented worker, clapped him on the back and grinned at him. 'We're going to the Thistle, but some of the others are going to the Lion. So which is it to be?'

'Oh, he's to come with us,' said Sadie. Even off stage, the company split naturally in two, heroic workers sticking together and drinking in the crudest pubs, while most of the capitalist running dogs frequented slightly posher, more expensive bars.

At chucking-out time at the Thistle, Sadie laid her hand on Ewan's arm and slid her fingers underneath his cuff, stroking his wrist. 'Poor Ewan, you look fed up, you need some loving,' she whispered, kindly. 'I think you should come home with me tonight.'

'But – er – won't your mother mind?' asked Ewan, who could imagine what his own would say.

'She's away at her sister's in Arbroath.'

'What about your father?'

'Man, do you want to sleep with me, or not?' Sadie pushed him out on to the pavement. 'We've some whisky in the house, so that'll give you courage.'

'But how did you find me?' Daisy asked, when the three of them had all got over the first shock, and were sitting comfortably in a restaurant in the Strand.

'It wasn't easy, darlin',' Phoebe said. 'I 'ad to trawl round all the ruddy digs in Birmin'ham before I found out where you'd stayed. Then, when they told me they thought you'd gone to London – well, I thought, a needle in an 'aystack!

'But then I pulled meself together, come down 'ere, an I 'ired a taxi by the day. I started goin' round the theatres askin' if they'd 'eard of you. I been 'ere a month, an' I was close to givin' up, I'll tell you!

'But then I saw this notice in the papers, all about your show, said it was good. The bloke had specially mentioned a Miss Denham in the chorus, and me old 'eart did a little flip. So then the doorman at my 'otel up west, he tells me yes, he knows the place. It's maybe a bit rough, he says, but they has try-outs there, an' sometimes stuff transfers to the West End. Daisy, you ain't told Rose you've come to London. She thinks you're still in Birmin'ham, you know.'

'Yes, I must write,' said Daisy, her eyes still fixed on Phoebe's face, realizing this must be the dark-haired woman who had haunted all her childhood dreams. She had a *real* mother now, and it was wonderful. She felt so happy. It was as if she had come home.

'Come on, love, drink up. We're celebratin', ain't we?' Phoebe motioned to a waiter to top up Daisy's glass. She gazed all round the restaurant. 'Dear old London, eh?' She sighed. 'God, it seems like only yesterday that I was just a kid – just startin' out meself. But the last time I was sittin 'ere was – oh, must've been more than fifteen years ago.'

'You used to come to *this* place, then?' asked Jesse, gazing at the polished woodwork, inlaid-marble panelling and gilded chandeliers.

'Yeah, a boyfriend used to bring me regular.' Phoebe lit a cigarette. 'I was on the stage meself, you know – in the varieties.' She launched into a long résumé of her many triumphs, boasting about the officers she had known, how they had wined and dined her and how marvellous it had been, all the parties, dances, the champagne. . . .

'Where are you staying, Mrs Rosenheim?' asked Jesse, when Phoebe at last took a break from showing off to drink some more champagne.

'I got a suite in a hotel, in Piccadilly.' Phoebe looked at Daisy. 'What about you, love – you got good digs?'

'Oh, yes – they're fine.' After all these tales of splendour, Daisy didn't want to admit that she was living in squalor, that there were mousetraps everywhere, and damp ran down the walls.

As the restaurant started closing, Jesse went out to the Strand to find a taxi. Phoebe took Daisy's hands, and looked deep into her blue eyes. 'You don't mind me comin' to see you, darlin'?' she asked, anxiously. 'Only you ain't said much.'

'I'm still trying to take it in.' Daisy gazed at this stranger who said she was her mother, but who was far more exciting, beautiful and glamorous than any mother Daisy had ever known.

'Well, we'll be better acquainted soon,' said Phoebe, smiling. 'When I gets you back to the States, an' takes you all around, we're gonna have such fun!'

'You want me to go to America with you?'

'Oh, love, of course I do.' Phoebe stroked Daisy's face with one soft hand. 'I just can't tell you 'ow I've dreamed about this moment, when I'd be reunited with my darlin' little girl. I don't ever want to let you go.'

*

'Well, that was exciting,' Jesse said, as he and Daisy sat on the last bus, alone on the top deck. 'You're full of surprises, aren't you?'

'I didn't know she was coming to see me!' Daisy wished Jesse would shut up, would let her think things through, would let her decide what she should do.

'She was nice.' Jesse took Daisy's hand and started playing with her fingers. 'She's really attractive, too. It's obvious where you get your looks.'

'But I don't look anything like her, do I?' Daisy watched Jesse's fingers intertwining with her own. 'She's very dark, I'm fair.'

'You're both beautiful.' Jesse leaned towards her, kissed her, leaned back smiling, knowing she hadn't had enough, knowing she wanted to be kissed again.

Daisy knew it, too.

She'd drunk a little wine – far less than Jesse, and nothing like as much as Phoebe. But she had known she shouldn't, because she wasn't used to drinking any. Now, she felt light-headed, tired but relaxed, and also – much to her embarrassment – she knew she was hungry for a man. . . .

She looked at Jesse. He was so attractive, he was kind, he said he loved her, and perhaps he even meant it? Why shouldn't she sleep with him?

Jesse stroked her forehead, teasing strands of hair away, printing little butterfly kisses all along her jaw-line. 'Daisy,' he whispered, softly.

'Yes, all right.' She turned to him. 'But, Jesse – you will be careful?'

'I'll be careful.'

Daisy didn't quite know what she thought would happen next. She only knew she wanted Jesse. If she went to bed with him, if she fell asleep beside him, she would wake up different. She'd no longer be a silly, blushing child. She'd be a woman.

When he undressed, she saw the scars across his back, the marks from all those beatings his father must have given him. Poor Jesse, she thought tenderly, he's had such a rotten deal in life. Now he deserves some love.

She tried to feel some passion. She tried to let herself be swept away. But it didn't work out like that, and she found she was almost dozing off as Jesse stroked her, kneaded her, as he ran his hands over her body, like a cowman with a cow.

When it actually happened, it was just a bit uncomfortable. Contrary to what the girls from school had managed to elicit from their married sisters, it hadn't hurt at all. But neither had she been in ecstasy.

When Jesse had finished and was lying on his side, looking very pleased with his performance and idly plaiting his fingers in her hair, she had to stop herself from saying, 'Well – was that it?'

'So was that wonderful, my darling?' demanded Jesse, looking as if he expected her to clap.

'Yes, it was lovely,' Daisy lied, anxious to spare his feelings. 'But you were careful, weren't you?'

'What?' frowned Jesse, suddenly looking miffed. 'Oh, for God's sake, sweetheart, don't go on so! Listen, I was *extra* bloody careful!' Scowling, he turned over on his side, and soon he was asleep.

Ewan woke up in a single bed under a skylight in a Glasgow tenement, somehow knowing where he was, but having no idea how he'd got there. Then he became aware of someone breathing close beside him, and suddenly it all came hurtling back.

He groaned and sat up carefully, feeling sick, hoping he wouldn't actually throw up. He'd drunk too much, for sure, and how he was going to do a matinée this afternoon, he didn't know.

Sadie woke up now, and twisted round to look at him. 'Good morning, lover,' she began, and grinned. 'So how are you today?'

'Sadie, I'm sorry.' Ewan blinked and shut his eyes, for the harsh

Glasgow dawn was blinding him. 'I took advantage of you, and I shouldn't have done it.'

'You mean, you tried to take advantage!' Sadie giggled. 'You had too much to drink. But you look much more sober now.' She rubbed her foot against his leg. 'So what about it, want to try again?'

Ewan could feel the softness of her, smell the musky scent of her, feel himself responding, even though he didn't think it was advisable, not when he was so in love with Daisy.

'Yes,' he said, 'let's try again.'

Daisy wrote to Rose, explaining about the move to London, saying she'd been really busy, telling Rose that she was with a Mr Daniel Hanson's company, and Mr Hanson was a very important, powerful impresario – had Rose heard of him? She sent Rose all her notices – three or four by now – and a programme with her name in it.

Phoebe had been to see the show at every opportunity, always sitting in the front-row stalls. When Daisy told her who was financing it, Phoebe had sucked her teeth and said, 'Oh yes, Mr Daniel Hanson, eh?' She knew him of old, she said, from when she'd worked in the varieties herself.

'We hardly ever see him, though,' said Daisy, when she met Phoebe in a West End café, after a matinée one afternoon.

'Yeah, an' you want to keep it that way, love,' said Phoebe, darkly.

'Why, isn't he very nice?'

'Mr Daniel Hanson is a bugger, 'scuse my French. I walked out with 'im once, durin' the war years.' Phoebe lit a cigarette, inhaled. 'When I got caught with you, 'e threatened to make me sorry I'd been born. 'E wasn't your dad, you see – thank God for that – an' 'e didn't want any other fella interferin' with 'is girl.

' 'E ran vice-rings, Dan did, 'e 'ad people's legs broke if they

153

didn't do what he said, or if they upset 'im. The police was in 'is pocket. They still are, I dare say.'

Phoebe shook her head, but then smiled brightly. 'Rest day tomorrow, ain't it? I thought we could go up Oxford Street, an' buy you somethin' nice. The boyfriend can come along as well, that's if 'e's got nothin' else to do. I likes to 'ave a bloke to carry all me bags, especially if he's kinda cute like yours! Now, Daisy – 'ave you thought any more about that stuff I said?'

'You mean, go to America with you?'

'Yeah, it's time we got to know each other better, don't you reckon?' Phoebe poured out tea and snapped her fingers to the waitress for more cakes. 'You're so talented, you could do so well on Broadway. I can already see your name in lights! My Nathan, he could help you. He's a big shot now. He's got connections.'

'In the theatre?'

'Everywhere!' Phoebe spread her hands. 'America's not like Britain, where you has to know your place. It's the land of opportunity. Look at me and Nathan – we come to New York City without a penny to our names, but we worked an' worked an' worked, an' now we're doin swell.'

'I'd miss my parents, though.'

'Darlin', you're forgettin', *I'm* your mother.' Phoebe's dark eyes narrowed, but then she smiled graciously. 'Rose and Edgar and the kids – yeah, they could visit. We'd be glad to see 'em, show 'em a bit of life.'

'I'll think about it,' Daisy promised, tempted.

'Britain's all washed up,' continued Phoebe. 'It's a mess, just look around you, dirt and gloom and misery, not like in the States.'

'I didn't think things were going so well there, these days,' Daisy said.

'Oh, everything's just fine!' Phoebe covered Daisy's hand with hers, gave it a gentle squeeze. 'It's the land of opportunity, the good old USA. I was a kid from the East End, I 'ad no education, but I knows 'ow to graft. So now I wears fur coats, I got a business, I 'as a dozen girls workin' for me. I couldn've done that 'ere.

'Daisy, I knows people, *lots* of people, not little fish like Daniel bloody Hanson. I knows the ones who matter.'

'Phoebe—'

'Mum,' said Phoebe. 'I'd like you to call me mum, my darlin' – or maybe mommy, eh?'

'As I said, I'll have to think about it.'

'Well, don't you take too long, my love.' Phoebe lit a Turkish cigarette. 'I'm goin' 'ome next Saturday. I want you to come with me, an' before you says it, yeah, I know – you're very fond of Jesse. But 'e could tag along. I'll even pay 'is fare. Your understudies'll be glad to take your places in the show.'

'But we have contracts—'

'Oh, sweet'eart, tear 'em up,' said Phoebe, grandly. 'Now, about tomorrow, where we gonna meet? At my 'otel?'

The following morning, Jesse said he didn't feel like traipsing round round the shops. He'd pulled a tendon in his foot, he added, and it was rather painful. Maybe he should rest it. 'You go, and have real swell time,' he grinned.

'Well, all right. I'll bring you something nice,' said Daisy, buttoning up her jacket, smoothing the lapels, and blessing Amy for her generosity.

'Something expensive,' Jesse said. 'Some gentleman's cologne, from some exclusive little shop in Regent Street. The old girl can afford it.'

'I'll see what I can do.'

'Gorblimey, Daisy, where d'you get your clothes?' demanded Phoebe. She tweaked the collar of Daisy's jacket, testing the quality of the fabric, finding it wasn't up to her exacting expectations. 'We'd better get you somethin' decent, if you're comin' 'ome with me.'

155

So Daisy and Phoebe hit the West End shops, and spent a fortune. They didn't have time for lunch, but by three o'clock they were so tired that they got a taxi back to Piccadilly, and went to have afternoon tea at Fortnum's where, as Phoebe said, they did a decent cup of char.

'I been to see you nearly twenty times,' said Phoebe, tucking her arm through Daisy's as they made their way upstairs. 'You gets better an' better every day.'

'Thank you,' Daisy said, wishing that Phoebe wouldn't cling like this, but not wanting to hurt her mother's feelings by seeming to shake her off.

'But,' continued Phoebe artlessly, 'I bet Rose an' Edgar been to see you *far* more times than I 'ave?'

'No, actually, they haven't,' Daisy said. 'It's the farm, you see. They can't afford to hire any help, so they don't have the time to get away.'

'Daisy, if my little girl was on the London stage, an' if I was anythin' like a proper mother ought to be, I'd *make* the bloody time to get away!' Phoebe nodded to a waiter, who came up smartly and led them to a window table. He pulled out both their chairs and got them comfortably seated before beckoning a waitress to make sure they had everything they needed in the way of napkins, finger bowls and cutlery.

'But then that's Rose all over,' Phoebe added, drawing off her fine kid gloves. 'She gets obsessed with things, does Rose. My sister always said so. Rose 'as got a one-track mind. Right now, it's 'er flippin' chickens is occupyin' 'er time, an' she ain't got a moment for anythin' or anybody else – not even for you, my darlin' girl. But never mind, my lovely daughter, your *real* mommy loves you, an' she wants to see your show.

'So, angel, what d'you want today? Some little sandwiches, and some of them French fancies what that fat woman's eatin' over there? They looks tasty, don't they? Them, an' 'alf a dozen little scones, with Devon clotted cream?'

'Mmm, delicious,' Daisy said, slipping off her jacket. She wished that Phoebe would shut up for just one minute. Or at any rate not talk about poor Rose in that nasty, supercilious way.

'That's what we'll 'ave, then.' Phoebe summoned the waiter, gave her order, and sent him on his way. 'You thought any more about goin' to the States with me?' she demanded, as the waitress set out fine bone china and lit the small spirit-stove which would warm their scones. 'Just for an 'oliday at first. But if you like it, you could settle down permanent with me, in my apartment.'

'What about Mr Rosenheim?' asked Daisy.

'What about 'im?'

'Well, I'm not his daughter.'

'But you're mine, an' he loves me, an' so he'd make you welcome.' Phoebe smiled. 'He's lovely, is my Nathan. You'd like him, he'd like you.'

'I'm sure I'd like him, Phoebe, but you haven't said very much about him.'

'Mommy,' corrected Phoebe.

'Where did you meet him?' Daisy asked.

'My Nathan?' Phoebe grinned. 'I've known 'im all my life. Nathan was the boy next door, back in the old East End. I was always goin' to marry 'im.'

'But he'd make *me* welcome?'

'Daisy, sweet'eart, 'e can't wait to meet you, 'e's told me so 'imself. So, darlin', what d'you say?'

'Give me another day or two to think,' said Daisy, glad to see the waiter coming over, pushing a little gilded trolley laden with plates of delicate little sandwiches and cakes, and all the other things they'd have for tea.

Phoebe merely fiddled with her sandwiches and scones, but she drank several cups of tea. 'I 'ave to watch me figure,' she explained. 'I ain't gonna dance it off, like you. Go on, 'ave a fancy.'

'I don't eat much sweet stuff, it gives me spots,' Daisy said apologetically. She'd eaten only half a fancy, and for some reason had gone off the scones.

'You ain't got any spots, you silly girl. So come on, eat up,' said Phoebe, sharply. 'I ain't payin' out good money for nothin'.' But then she blushed, and shook her head. 'I 'spect you've wondered about me all your life,' she added, picking up the silver sugar-tongs.

'No, I didn't find out about you till a year ago,' admitted Daisy. 'Mum – sorry, I mean Rose – she told me when I was fifteen.'

'Oh.' Phoebe looked both embarrassed and annoyed. 'So up until then, you thought that you was Rose and Edgar's kid?'

'Well, naturally.'

'They been good to you?'

'Yes, they've been wonderful.' As Daisy said it, she realized she meant it, and she felt a pang of longing for the people who would always be her mum and dad.

'They tell you about your *real* dad?' asked Phoebe.

'No, and I didn't ask them,' Daisy said, and shrugged. 'I thought perhaps they didn't know.'

'Oh, they knows all right.' Phoebe crushed a sugar-cube with more than casual violence. 'You know the bloke what lives at Easton Hall, near Rose and Edgar's place?'

'Yes, Sir Michael Easton. But I don't actually know him. He doesn't have anything to do with us.'

'I wonder why,' said Phoebe savagely. 'Listen, 'ere's the facts. I knew 'im in the war years, when I was on the 'alls, an' he was a regular stage-door Johnny. All us girls was very sweet on 'im, on account of 'e was very 'andsome and an' generous with 'is cash. So anyway, we 'ad a little fling, and you was the result.'

'I – I don't believe you!' Daisy stared in horror. 'How could *you* have met Sir Michael Easton, and if I'm his daughter, why doesn't he want *me*? Why don't I live with him?'

'Calm down, Daisy, darlin', keep your voice down.' Phoebe

THE LONG WAY HOME

touched her daughter's hand, but Daisy jerked it back, as if her mother's were red-hot. 'In the war years, people got about a bit. Rose was a nurse in London, as I 'spect you know, an' she was friendly with my sister.

'Mike was sweet on Rose, an' he come up to London once to see 'er. Me and my boyfriend walked into this caff, and there she was with 'im. She was in 'er nurse's uniform, an' he was an officer – God, 'e looked so gorgeous! We was introduced—'

'So it all went on from there.' Daisy glared at Phoebe, blue eyes glittering. 'Sir Michael wanted to marry Mum, you know.'

'Yeah, I did know that. But Rose, she didn't want to marry 'im, she told me so.' Phoebe looked at Daisy. 'Darlin', she's very 'appy with 'er Edgar, she told me that 'erself.'

'You spoiled it all for Mum!' cried Daisy, glaring. 'You deliberately wrecked her life!'

'No, Daisy, you don't understand, I—'

'It's all your fault – the mess they're in at home, the fact we haven't got any money—'

'Daisy, just 'ang on just a minute,' interrupted Phoebe. 'God, I shouldn't have told you so abrupt—'

'No, I'm glad you told me!' Daisy stood up, blue eyes blazing. 'I should have been told all sorts of things, years and years ago! You've all lied to me!'

Daisy pushed her chair away, snatched up her old tweed jacket. 'You abandoned me!' she cried, as the entire café turned to stare. 'If Rose and Edgar hadn't adopted me, I'd have ended up in some disgusting East End orphanage, along with all the other nameless bastards. All the time I was growing up, you never had any contact with me, never wanted to know about me, never even sent a birthday card.

'But then, all of a sudden, you walk back into my life, buy me lots of expensive junk, ask me to call you mommy and want me to go home with you. Well, forget it, Phoebe, it's not going to happen.

I'm going now. I never want to set eyes on you again.'

'Darlin', don't forget your bags!' cried Phoebe, as Daisy strode off across the deep-pile carpet.

But Daisy kept on walking.

CHAPTER 16

DAISY arrived back at her digs in Clapham hot and tired. She'd walked home all the way, and the day was far too hot for Amy's smart tweed suit. She was still furious with Phoebe, but more furious with herself for being such a fool, for being taken in so easily, so willing to be seduced by Phoebe's gaudy, tawdry charm.

As she climbed the stairs up to her room, she began to feel a little calmer. If Jesse's foot was feeling better, she decided, they could go down to the Lamb and Flag, then she could tell him all about it. Or, if he was still resting up, they could stay at home, and she could make some supper on the gas-ring on the landing. She'd go and get some ham or something from the corner shop – they'd give her tick – and then they could have ham-fritters and fried potatoes in his room.

She tapped on Jesse's door. She heard a muffled giggle, and Jesse saying, 'sssh,' and then 'hang on a minute!' But Daisy was in no mood to mess about. Opening the door, she marched straight in.

Jesse was lying face down on the bed, his wrists tied to the head-rail. Belinda from the chorus line was lying next to him, wearing a black-silk petticoat, smoking a Sobranie, a birch-switch in her hand. Jesse's back was hatched with streaks of blood.

Daisy stared in horror.

Whatever were they doing?

Why was Jesse letting Belinda hurt him?

What was going on?

But then it all clicked into place. The whole room stank of sex and alcohol. It smelled so rank and foxy that she gagged, and felt the bile rise in her throat.

She felt the ground cave in beneath her feet a second time that day. She felt so stupid, so ashamed, so totally ridiculous that she could have cried. She turned and fled, ran back down the stairs and out of the front door, gasping for what passed in London for fresh air.

She was packing in her room when Jesse came to talk to her, clad only in a velvet dressing-gown he'd stolen from some costume hamper, smelling like a brewery, his black hair ruffed up like raven's feathers.

'It wasn't what it looked like,' he began.

'Don't talk to me,' snapped Daisy.

'Darling, you must understand that sometimes I have needs.' Jesse sat down on Daisy's bed and tried to take her hand.

She slapped him off.

'You're so young, so innocent,' he continued, ploughing on. 'You're still on the nursery slopes of sex. So I couldn't have asked you to do that. But whatsername's an instrument, that's all. She doesn't mean a thing to me.'

'Oh?' Daisy clicked the locks shut. 'But while you were with whatsername, *I* didn't mean a thing.'

'Daisy, you mean everything to me!'

'I should have listened to Amy,' muttered Daisy, more to herself than Jesse. 'Amy and Julia, they both had your number from the start. God, I was so horrible to Ewan—'

'Oh, that's right, drag your precious Och the Noo in,' Jesse sneered. 'That's what you women always do. The man you love upsets you, so you start droning on about some hopeless, deadbeat loser who used to drive you mad—'

'Don't you dare slander Ewan!' Daisy cried. 'One day, he'll be a star. You wait and see!'

'I'll hold my breath,' yawned Jesse, raking a languid hand through his becomingly tousled hair.

'God, you're such a poser, such a fraud!' Daisy glared at him. 'Listen, Jesse Trent. I don't care what you do, what needs you have. I'm old enough to realize that people must like different things in bed. But you lied to me. All that rubbish about your father, all the sympathy you milked from me, it was all a load of fabrication, wasn't it?'

'Perhaps I did embroider just a little. But—'

'What does your father *really* do?'

'He's a delivery man,' admitted Jesse. 'He and my mother live in Dunstable. Dad wanted me to be a bank-clerk, shop-assistant, something boring and respectable. I wanted to be an actor. So I left.'

'Do you ever see your family?'

'No, I sort of borrowed some money the last time I was there.' Jesse shrugged. 'It would be rather awkward to go back.'

'You mean you stole their savings. You really are a rogue and vagabond.' Daisy picked her case up, but Jesse grabbed her wrist.

'Darling, where are you going?'

'Back to Dorset,' she replied.

'You're going *home*, you mean?'

'Yes, Mr Double-Dealer, I'm going home to Charton with my tail between my legs. I'm going crawling back to Mum and Dad.' Daisy shook him off and stared him out, her blue eyes flashing. 'You want to make something of it?'

'But what about Mr Hanson? He gave us our first break in London, and everybody says it's very dangerous to cross him. What about his show?'

163

'Sod the show,' said Daisy. 'Sod Mr Hanson, sod his bloody show, and sod you, too.' She put her case down, rummaged in her handbag, and eventually found the bottle of cologne she'd bought with her own money, not with Phoebe's. 'Jesse?'

'Yes?'

'This is for you, so make the most of it.' Daisy dropped the heavy crystal bottle on his foot, picked up her case and ran downstairs, leaving Jesse cursing on the landing.

The walk from Charton station to the bailiff's cottage was less than half a mile. But it was by far the longest journey Daisy had ever made, and even after sitting on a train for several hours, she was still all churned up inside.

Why hadn't Rose replied to the letter Daisy had sent from London? Rose usually replied to Daisy's letters by return of post. Oh God, thought Daisy, maybe Rose was planning to say, 'Well, Daisy – you've found your natural mother, Edgar and I have done our duty, so now off you go.' It would serve her right, she thought. She'd been such an ungrateful little cow. She didn't deserve to be their daughter.

Phoebe's easy assumption that Daisy would just abandon Rose and Edgar, and swan off to America, really rankled. Especially as Daisy had to admit that she'd been tempted by a vision of her name in lights on Broadway, and had for a few seconds believed that Phoebe's husband was some kind of big shot who'd arrange it.

As for Jesse – she couldn't imagine why she'd ever thought he was attractive, ever thought she was in love with him. As she walked up the path to the bailiff's cottage, the smell of bridges burned down to their foundations filled the soft, night air.

She hadn't realized it was quite so late. The Dorset sky was still a bluish-reddish-orange-purple, promising a perfect day tomorrow, and the moon was still a pale ghost, but it must be well past ten o'clock. The cottage lights were out, and she supposed they must all be in bed. Of course, they had to get up very early for the milking.

She hadn't got her key, so she knocked softly on the door, and eventually Rose came down to open it. 'Mum?' said Daisy fearfully, seeing at once from Rose's face that something must be wrong.

'Oh, Daisy, love! I'm so glad you could come!' Rose threw her arms round Daisy, hugged her tight, and Daisy could feel tears on her cheek, although she knew *she* wasn't crying. 'But we couldn't find you,' Rose continued, choking back a sob. 'You didn't put an address on your last letter, and the theatre people wouldn't tell us where you lived. So how did you know?'

'How did I know what?' Daisy's neck-hairs prickled, and she felt a cold snake of terror go slithering down her spine. 'Mum?' she whispered, pulling away and giving Rose a little shake. 'Tell me! What's the matter?'

But Rose was crying now, wringing her hands, and couldn't seem to speak. So Daisy had to lead her back inside, sit her down at the kitchen table, put the kettle on and make some tea.

'Mum?' said Daisy softly, as she set out cups and saucers.

'It's your father.' Rose had managed to choke it out at last. 'He – well, I don't know what's the matter, but it seems the life's gone out of him. He's in hospital in Dorchester. They've done lots of tests, but they still don't know what's wrong with him. Oh, love, he's been so ill—'

'But he's still alive?' demanded Daisy, urgently. 'Mum, it's not *that* serious? My dad's not going to die?'

'I hope not, but. . . .'

Rose shrugged and looked so helpless and so little that Daisy could have wept. 'What about the boys?' she asked.

'Oh, the twins are fine. They've been such bricks!' Rose smiled through her tears, then shook her head. 'I'm sorry, love,' she whispered. 'It was the shock of seeing you, standing on the doorstep at this time of night. It was as if I'd sort of summoned you, and you had come home. But we should go to bed. I'll have to be up at five tomorrow morning. Come on, I'll make your bed up.'

'I'll do that,' said Daisy. 'You go back to sleep.'

'I'd like to have your company for a few minutes more.' Rose brushed her hand across her tired eyes. 'I can't sleep, anyway.'

Daisy went to bed, but didn't sleep. All night she heard Rose pacing up and down, the scrape of matches as Rose lit cigarettes, the clatter as she put the kettle on. When she got up, bleary-eyed and sluggish at five the following morning, she found that Robert and Stephen were as glad to see her as their mother had been last night.

They'd changed, thought Daisy. The brats were growing up. They were still two scruffy-looking kids, but they were doing all the milking, looking after their mother and the farm, and taking the responsibility that Daisy knew she should have taken. She shouldn't have gone gallivanting off, and showing her legs to anyone with a bob or two to spare.

'Edgar's just been working much too hard.' Rose and Daisy stood at the kitchen table, mixing mash for Rose's chickens, while the twins were seeing to the cows before they went to school. 'Your father might look hale and hearty, but he's not strong, you know. He was wounded several times during the war, then he got shot in India, and he's never quite got over that.'

Rose poured the mash into two buckets. 'After the India business, they said they couldn't keep him in the army. He wasn't fit enough. He never complains to me, but I can often see that he's in pain.'

'How often do you visit him?' Daisy asked.

'Every weekday afternoon,' said Rose, 'and twice on Saturdays and Sundays, if I can get away. I usually catch the bus to Dorchester. Yes, the bus takes ages, but it's sixpence cheaper than the train.' Rose glanced up. 'Darling, I'm rattling on about myself, but how are you, and how did you get on with Phoebe?'

'Oh, we met for lunch a couple of times, we had some chats,' said Daisy, blushing at the memory of the scene she'd made in Fortnum's.

'But you *did* get on?'

'Well, we didn't *not* get on.' Daisy picked her bucket up, and shrugged. 'But we didn't have very much in common. I probably won't be seeing her again.'

Rose and Daisy got the bus to Dorchester that same afternoon. As she walked into the public ward, Daisy saw at once that Edgar must be very ill. As she went up to him, she could see grey streaks in his black hair, which she was sure had not been there last year, and he was getting wrinkles round his eyes.

He was very thin and haggard, and his skin looked yellow. But he was obviously delighted to see Daisy. He wanted to know about her show in London, said how thrilled he'd been to see her brilliant notices from all around the country, said how proud he was to have a daughter who was such a star.

'I'll stay in Charton until you're on your feet again,' she promised, as – all too soon – the sister rang the bell and started shooing visitors out, as if they were so many wayward hens.

'Oh, I'll soon be better, there's nothing really wrong with me,' said Edgar, as she bent to kiss him. 'It's such a tonic to see you, love,' he added. 'You can't think how we've missed you.'

'I've missed you too, Dad,' Daisy told him. 'Now, you get well again.'

'I'm just shirking.' Edgar grinned at Rose. 'Your mother panicked. She called the quack in, had them cart me off to this place – eh, my darling?'

'We'll see you tomorrow,' Rose said softly, and she even managed a brave smile. But Daisy saw the fear in her eyes, and suddenly knew how it would feel to lose someone you loved.

The doctors took more of Edgar's blood, shone lights into his eyes, did lots of other tests, and eventually agreed that there was nothing wrong with him. Or nothing that they could fix, at any rate. Luckily, he didn't seem to have tuberculosis, diabetes, or anything like that.

He was just exhausted, they told Rose. He needed lots of rest. So he was discharged from hospital into his wife's and daughter's care, told to stay in bed in the mornings, eat a lot of meat and fish and eggs, drink a daily pint or two of stout, and build his strength again.

Daisy's wellingtons stood in the porch by Edgar's, hers all caked with mud and muck, while his stayed clean and dry. She worked so hard she fell into bed exhausted at nine o'clock each night, and then got up at five the following morning for another gruelling day.

She watched the calendar, fingers twisted and hoping for the best, aware that it would serve her right if she'd been caught, if she were fated to join the wretched club of idiot women who believed the lies men always told.

She thought of still-warm parcels shoved in dustbins – no, she couldn't do that, she didn't know how, and it would be wicked, anyway. She thought of all the gossip there'd be in the village when it started showing. She thought of Rose's disappointment that Daisy had proved to be her mother's daughter in every single way. Listen, God, she thought, my mum and dad have got enough to cope with, they don't need this, as well.

'Why didn't you tell me about Sir Michael Easton?' she asked Rose, as they trudged home from Charton, loaded down with shopping, one June day.

Daisy couldn't really understand why they didn't have groceries delivered, like everybody else. But Rose wouldn't have it because, she said, if you sent in an order, the tradesmen sent you any old thing. She wasn't paying out good money for flour with weevils in it, sugar that was damp, or rusty tins of pilchards that had been in Mr Gorton's shop since Adam was a boy. She preferred to choose, get *her* stuff fresh. She wouldn't have an account or buy on credit. She said she preferred to pay her way.

'Mum?' persisted Daisy.

'What would have been the point?' Rose put one of her oilcloth shopping-bags down for a moment, and flexed her aching fingers. 'He's never admitted he's your father. Darling, I'm not being unkind to Phoebe, don't think that – but we have no proof. It's just her word against his, and he's always denied it.'

'Perhaps I ought to meet him.'

'Well, of course that's up to you,' said Rose.

'What's he like?' persisted Daisy. 'I mean, perhaps he wasn't very nice when he was young. But people change.'

'I haven't seen Mike to speak to for fifteen years or more,' said Rose, picking up her shopping-bag again. 'So really, darling, I honestly couldn't say what sort of person he is now.'

CHAPTER 17

As she walked down the gangplank, scanning the crowds for one beloved face, Phoebe reflected sadly that she hadn't intended it to be like this at all. The wires and letters she had sent from England must have given everyone she knew in New York City quite the wrong impression.

She hadn't had the time or the emotional energy to send the last instalment of the story. So perhaps there'd be a feast prepared. They might have killed a fatted calf, or at any rate bought up the contents of the local delicatessen. They'd be ready to welcome Phoebe and her long-lost daughter to the Lower East Side.

It was going to be awful.

She wiped away a tear or two, and scanned the crowds again.

But then, as she was almost beginning to think he hadn't come, and her cup of bitterness was full to overflowing, she saw Nathan stumbling through the throng, pushing through the hawkers, brass-band-players, general gawpers and all the other people who'd turned up to greet the ocean-going liner. Then she was in his arms, and she was sobbing with happiness, despair and a half a dozen other mixed emotions.

'You on your own?' she asked him, when they'd kissed and she had hugged him back and had a look at him, when she was satisfied that he'd been eating properly in her absence, and was well.

170

'Yes, my dear,' said Nathan. 'I thought it would be better than having a great gaggle of people standing on the quay, all jostling and pushing and staring at the girl. The boys all sizing Daisy up, the women deciding whom she ought to marry, and all that sort of thing.

'But Vinnie and her cousins have been in with brooms and dusters, the whole apartment is immaculate, and her bedroom's ready. There's a new dressing-table and a new quilt on the bed, and the room's been painted pale cream, just like you told me. Vinnie's made the whole place look a treat.'

Getting out a clean, white handkerchief, Nathan wiped Phoebe's tears away and smiled encouragingly. 'So, this daughter of yours, where is she, then?'

'She – she ain't coming, Nathan.' Phoebe began to cry again. 'It all went wrong. My Daisy, she don't want to be my daughter, 'cos she 'ates me.'

'Oh, Phoebe!' Nathan pulled her close to him, let her bury her face against his shoulder while she sobbed. 'Oh, my darling, after all you said! I thought it was all going so well! Phoebe, I'm so sorry!'

'Yeah, well, can't be 'elped,' choked Phoebe.

'Come on, love,' said Nathan, and started pushing through the crowd. 'Let's get you home again.'

They went home in a cab, Phoebe's head on Nathan's comfortingly familiar shoulder, his arm around her waist.

'It wasn't such a great success, then?' Nathan asked her sympathetically, when they were on their own in their apartment.

'Yeah, you could say that.' Phoebe sat on the sofa, kicked off her high-heeled shoes and put her feet up. She closed her eyes and started massaging her aching forehead.

But Nathan soon took over, soothing away her headache, just as he always managed to soothe away a little of any pain that racked her heart.

171

'At first, I thought it was all goin' so well,' said Phoebe, wretchedly. 'Rose was 'appy enough for me to see my little girl, an' when we finally met up, Daisy was sweet to me. But when I told her all about when she'd been born – I thought I was doin' right to be honest, Nathan, but it seems I should've kept me trap shut – Daisy got all upset, an' said I'd ruined Rose's life.'

'Poor Phoebe.' Nathan's gentle fingers stroked her temples, and she lay back against him, wondering what she'd ever do without him. 'About you, though, my dear – any news?'

'No,' said Phoebe. 'But I'm not going to 'ave another kid. I feel it in me bones.' She sighed and shook her sleek, dark head. 'Nathan, I was a fool to think she'd like me, an' want me to be 'er mother. It's not who actually 'ad you, it's who brings you up that really counts. I should have known that, shouldn't I? Bein' brought up by a foster mother meself.'

'So why don't *we* adopt?' Nathan stopped his massaging, and gently turned his wife around to face him. 'These days, things are very bad in Europe, and they're going to get worse. Children as young as eight are coming here from Poland and from Russia all alone. The agencies and charities can't cope with all the orphans in New York. Phoebe, maybe we could do some good.'

'I'll think about it,' Phoebe said.

'I'm so glad you're back.'

'So am I, my darlin', so am I.' Phoebe managed a little smile. 'I shouldn't be so flippin' greedy, should I? It's not every girl that's got a husband who's as good as you, her own little business, an' a lovely home.'

'What's Daisy like?' asked Nathan.

'She's lively, smart, she's got a gob on her, an' she's very pretty,' Phoebe said. 'I've got a photo somewhere in my luggage, I'll show you when I find it. But anyway, she's got a lovely figure, she's a blonde, she's got them sort of sparkling blue eyes. In colourin', she's the dead spit of 'er dad. But she don't even know 'im, an' I don't think she'd *want* to know 'im, either.

' 'Course, she thinks of Edgar as 'er father, an' Rose is always gonna be 'er mum,' said Phoebe, sighing again. 'So, although I'll always be the woman who gave birth to 'er, Daisy's never gonna be my child.'

Daisy had decided she didn't really want to meet Sir Michael. She wasn't disposed to like him, not after what he'd done. She had the world's best father, anyway.

She gave a cow a shove and edged it through the doorway into the milking parlour. Robert had the churns all ready, sterilized and shining. The twins had found a wind-up gramophone in the ruins of Melbury House, and now Stephen put a record on.

'What's all this in aid of, eh?' asked Daisy, as old-fashioned pre-war music filled the parlour with its decorous strains.

'The cows like music,' Stephen said.

'They know we have to milk them, but they don't really like it, that's why they kick and fidget,' added Robert.

'But they calm down if you play them music, and they give more milk,' continued Stephen.

'Yes, they do,' said Robert, and he grinned at Daisy's frown. 'Dad didn't believe us when we told him first. But now he says there must be something in it. Ruby's and Clover's yields have nearly doubled since they discovered ragtime.'

'They're not pets, you know,' said Daisy, sternly. 'You shouldn't get so fond of them. Sooner or later they'll be off to market, or to the slaughterhouse.'

'Yes, and that's another thing,' said Robert. 'We think that when they're for the chop, we should have a man come over here to do the job, not send them somewhere else to die, it isn't fair on them. Dad says he'll think about it.'

'Daze, have you seen the rabbit farm since you came back from London?' Stephen asked.

'No, I haven't had time.'

'It's going great guns now, you'll be impressed.'

After they'd finished milking, the twins took Daisy to visit their own enterprise, and she saw it was more than rabbits now. Guinea-pigs and piebald mice and fancy rats all had quarters in the stable-block.

'Still selling livestock to your friends at school?' she asked, amused.

'Yes, and to a lot of other schools,' said Robert proudly. 'Form-room pets are all the rage now, Daze. Rats are very popular because they're very intelligent, you know.'

'So I understand.' Daisy wished the twins had not reminded her of Archie, Ewan's pet, and thus of Ewan, too. She hadn't written to him for weeks, and he wouldn't know where she had gone.

What was he doing, she wondered, was he still in Glasgow? Did he ever think of her, and was his opinion of her even lower than hers was of herself?

She worked very hard, so hard that she had little time to think, remember or regret.

But in her heart of hearts, she knew that she was playing at being a farmer. It wasn't her real life. Real life was on the stage, when she could be herself, but lots of other people, too. She realized she was someone for whom just one reality would never be enough. She almost understood why Jesse needed to reinvent himself, to tell so many lies.

'You mustn't work too hard, my dear,' said Rose, when Daisy came in from the milking-parlour one June evening and promptly set about making mash for hens.

'But I must keep busy,' Daisy said, wondering if gin and exercise – jumping off tables, wasn't it, and riding hard to hounds? – might do the trick. Then she felt very wicked for wanting to destroy a little life. If indeed there was a little life.

When at last she went to bed, she didn't want to dream. But she found she often dreamed of Ewan, of the smile that lit his face whenever he had looked at her, and which she'd thought was foolish at the time.

But *she* was the foolish one. She understood that now. She'd been so mean to Ewan, belittled his affection, gone chasing after Jesse and followed him to London, and look where that had got her – up the duff, as Amy would have put it.

What was she going to do?

When should she tell Rose?

What would Edgar say?

Edgar was getting better and better. He wasn't fit enough for any physical work, not yet. But he was walking round the farm and criticizing, which was good. When he'd been so ill, he hadn't cared what anyone did, if the cows had not been milked, or if the hens stopped laying.

Mr Hobson came to do the heavy work that the twins and Daisy couldn't manage, bossing her and the boys around, but in a genial, tolerant kind of way. But the revived, revitalized Edgar was a martinet, dressing them down when something wasn't perfect, telling them off for cutting any corners, until Rose reminded him that he wasn't in the army any more. It was both good and bad to have the master fit again.

Daisy wondered if she'd ever have the courage to own up. She knew Edgar wouldn't turn her out, he wouldn't lecture her, or anything like that. But he'd be so upset on her behalf, then he'd be angry. She feared for Jesse's life.

Daisy and Rose took turns to get the bus to Dorchester, to buy the things they couldn't get in Charton. Daisy enjoyed the ride, which was a rare chance to put her feet up and relax. In Dorchester, she could look round the shops, and buy *Variety*.

It was her turn to go to town this week.

She did her shopping, gazed in dress-shop windows at clothes she couldn't afford buy, then bought some flowers for Rose, some toffee that everybody liked, and a copy of *Variety*.

There was an article on experimental drama. It all sounded very heavy, intellectual stuff. Surely there couldn't be an audience for that sort of thing? Surely people went to see a show expecting to be entertained, not bored or mystified?

Ewan had gone to Glasgow to act in plays like that. But lying on the stage and howling, or spending an hour staring at the audience and having them stare back – that wasn't like the Ewan she had known and, too late, had loved.

As the bus pulled into Charton, Daisy put away the magazine. But as she shoved it into her shopping-bag, on the back page she spotted a short item that soon made her pull it out again. A new rep in Leeds was due to welcome Ewan Fraser, Sadie Lawrence and Mungo Campbell, all from the Comrades Theatre Company, Glasgow, for the autumn season.

Leeds, mused Daisy, thinking hard. If I went to Leeds, perhaps I could sort something out. I don't know what, but surely there wouldn't be any harm in writing to the manager in Leeds. If this is a brand-new company, they might still be casting. Or they might need an ASM, at any rate.

When she got home, she wrote a letter.

'Mum, I've got an audition,' Daisy said, a fortnight later.

'Really?' Rose was doing something at the kitchen sink. 'I thought you'd got that theatre business right out of your system. I hoped you'd be staying here in Charton, until we find a man to marry you.'

'Mum!' cried Daisy, horrified.

Rose turned round and smiled. 'Just joking, dear. Your dad and I were saying the other night, it's time you were getting itchy feet again.'

'Oh,' said Daisy, annoyed to be so easily understood. 'But you wouldn't mind if I did a season now and then?'

'It's what you want to do, and people should be allowed to chase their dreams.' Rose sat down at the kitchen table. 'Edgar's better now, and we did quite well this summer, mainly thanks to you. We can just about afford to hire a part-time cowman, maybe to share him with another farmer. The twins are doing more and more now, bless their little hearts. You go for your audition, and good luck.'

A few days later, Daisy sat on the train to Leeds, wondering if this new adventure was a big mistake. Well, she thought, it wouldn't show for a while, and if she actually got a job, she'd earn some money.

She'd also get a chance to make it up to Ewan, to say she was sorry for being such a bitch. She was so looking forward to seeing him again, the thought of it buoyed her up and made her smile, even though she was in such a mess.

When she had the baby, maybe Ewan – but no, she mustn't race ahead.

She grimaced at her reflection in the window. In a few short hours she'd be in Leeds, where she'd be eating yet more humble-pie.

CHAPTER 18

WHEN Daisy arrived in Leeds, she took her case to the left-luggage office and paid the woman one of her precious shillings to leave it there. It didn't do to turn up at auditions looking too optimistic. Anyway, her suitcase weighed a ton, and she didn't think she ought to be lugging heavy loads through city streets in her condition.

If they didn't want her, she decided, she wouldn't hang around. She wouldn't let on that she knew Ewan, or ask where she could find him, or anything like that. She'd simply get the next train home, sitting up all night if necessary. She couldn't afford a sleeper.

She wondered how many other people the manager was seeing. Whether she had any chance. Or whether she was just chasing wild geese. Or wild Ewans.

Mr Taylor had arranged to meet her in a Victorian pub in Leeds town centre. She'd never gone into a pub alone before, and as she walked across the room, she was aware of being sized up in a way that wasn't entirely pleasant. Surely it didn't show, not yet? After enquiring at the bar, she was relieved to find that the manager was already there.

He turned out to be a youngish man – mid-thirties, she'd have guessed. One of the newer breed of actor, manager and producer, he wasn't an Alfred Curtis look-alike, straight from a Dickens novel. This Mr A. S. Taylor had an open, shrewd and honest face, wore ordinary clothes and knew a barber. There was nothing of the theatre about him, at least not on display.

'Why did you leave your last job?' he began, as the white-aproned waiter placed the manager's pint of best and Daisy's half of shandy on the table, as Mr Taylor scanned her letter. 'Let me see – you were with Daniel Hanson's company, weren't you?'

'Yes, that's right, in London.'

'But you just walked out?' The manager glanced up and shook his head, a wry grin on his face. 'I've never heard of anyone walking out on *him* before!'

'We had a serious illness in the family, and they needed me at home.'

'The show must still go on, you know,' the manager said, impressively. 'This family illness – everything's resolved now, I presume, and you're fit yourself?'

'Yes, absolutely,' Daisy assured him, crossing her fingers underneath the table, willing him to take her on and pay her decent money, so she could send some home.

'Well, that's good to hear,' he said, 'because I'd work you hard.'

Mr Taylor had Daisy's cuttings spread across table, and she thought, at least I've had reviews, and that must count for something, even if most of them are for *Blighted Blossoms*, and only three for the revue.

'The *Daily Telegraph* picked you out for a special mention, yes?' the manager murmured. 'But we're not doing any musical comedy, you know, if that's your thing?'

'I want to do straight acting now,' said Daisy. 'I – I've prepared some pieces, if you'd like to hear them?'

'You mean, you'd do them here, in the pub?' The manager grinned, considering her, appraising her and screwing up his face. 'Very well, Miss Denham,' he said, at last, 'I'll take you on. But you'll have to sign a binding contract. You won't walk out on *me*.'

'Of course I won't,' said Daisy.

'You'd better not, I'll set the dogs on you. We're running this company on a bloody shoestring as it is.' But then the manager smiled. 'OK, read-through tomorrow, ten o'clock in the upstairs room here, right? I'll let you have a list of digs.'

'Mr Taylor, may I ask you something?'

'Yes, of course.'

'I saw in *Variety*, that you'd engaged some people from the Comrades Theatre, Glasgow.' As she thought of Ewan, Daisy felt her face grow hot. 'Er – did their company fold?'

'Their audiences were falling off, and their management had to cut their losses.' Mr Taylor shrugged. 'It's not surprising, really. They were doing gloomy, left-wing drama for half-empty houses. But there are some fine young players among them. Very enthusiastic, keen to learn. So I was glad to snap them up.'

The manager allowed himself a wry, world-weary smile. 'Good communists they might be, all burning with the fire of revolution, but empty bellies have no ears, and starvation's not an appealing prospect, in whatever cause. So three of them were happy to take my filthy capitalist shilling. Miss Denham, do you happen to have a pen?'

Daisy walked back to the station, got her case, then spent another sixpence on her bus-fare to the lodging-house that Mr Taylor said was sure to have a vacancy. When she saw her room, she realized why. It made the place in Clapham look like a palace. She wondered just how ruinous houses had to get, before they actually started falling down.

As well as all the usual insect life, the house was home to dozens of rats and mice, and two very lazy, clearly ineffectual ginger cats. But it was cheap, the landlady was friendly, and the food at supper turned out to be plentiful, if stolid: lots of mashed potato with greyish, lumpy sausages, then prunes and tapioca, all washed down with dark brown builders' brew.

So, she decided, 14 Milton Mansions would have to do for now.

Anxious to make a good impression, she was the first to arrive the following morning. 'Just go on up, my love,' the barman said, when she rang the bell and said she was with Mr Taylor's show.

As she climbed the creaking stairs to the rehearsal room, her heart was hammering and her palms were damp. What would Ewan say, what would he do, was this a big mistake? She'd been so keen to see him that she hadn't really thought it through. What if he just nodded, or if he even scowled? Or if he cut her dead and turned away?

But it was too late to run. She'd signed the contract with its penalty clauses, so she simply couldn't afford to leave. She had to see at least this season through.

The dusty, yeasty scent of the rehearsal-room above the dingy pub brought a flood of memories rushing back, and she inhaled deeply, savouring the smell and letting herself think back to those first rehearsals with Mr and Mrs Curtis, who had been so kind to her and given her a chance, even though they'd paid her almost nothing, even though they'd turned out to be crooks.

She stared out of the dirty window at the busy street below, remembering Amy striking attitudes, and Julia with her everlasting lipstick. She thought of Frank and George in their silk socks and natty little cravats, their make-up carried in boxes that had once contained Havanas, so they wouldn't look like deviants, and get attacked by thugs. She thought of Jesse, dark and dangerous as a panther, prowling round the stage, of Ewan in a panic because he couldn't find his violin. . . .

Then, suddenly the door behind her opened, Daisy turned, and he was there.

He'd grown a little taller, and he moved more gracefully as he came into the room. But he was still the same old Ewan Fraser, red-haired, green-eyed and handsome. Now those green eyes positively glowed, with what she hoped was pleasure to see her standing there.

'Er – hello, Ewan,' she began.

'Daisy!' Ewan stared for a moment longer, blinking as if he couldn't believe his eyes. But then he smiled, a warm and welcoming, thrilled-to-see-you smile, and she knew it was going to be all right. 'I didn't recognize you for a moment,' he continued. 'It's because you've had your hair cut. Oh, it's *wonderful* to see you!'

'It's lovely to see *you*!' cried Daisy, beaming.

Then she held out her arms to him, in her mind already in his embrace. Ewan came towards her, arms outstretched. . . .

'Och, darling Ewan, *there* you are!' A small, dark, pretty girl came bursting in, ran up to Ewan and linked her arm through his, rubbing her cheek against his shoulder, leaving Daisy in no doubt that these two must be lovers.

Then she smiled at Daisy, narrowing her hazel eyes. 'You must be the new girl, come from Dorset, I believe? I just saw Sandy in the paper shop. He told me he engaged you yesterday.'

Daisy choked back her shock and disappointment. 'Y-yes, that's right, I'm Daisy Denham,' she managed to reply.

'I'm Sadie Lawrence. You and Ewan used to know each other, I understand?' Sadie's grip on Ewan's arm grew tighter, and as Daisy watched her fingers digging into Ewan's sleeve, the knife of jealousy in her heart began to twist in earnest.

'You were in a musical, weren't you?' Sadie continued, in a tone suggesting that being in a musical wasn't far removed in general iniquity from kicking helpless kittens.

'I was in revue, but I've done serious drama, I—'

'Och, yes indeed, I'm sure you have, you'll be an all-round entertainer,' Sadie said sarcastically, pursing her lips in scorn and disbelief. 'Ewan, we have ten minutes before the read-through, and there's something we need to have a little talk about. In private,' she added, tugging at Ewan's arm and dragging him towards the fire-escape.

Ewan shrugged at Daisy, smiled again, but then allowed himself to be led away.

Two more members of the company now came up the stairs, followed by three more, all chattering and laughing. Sandy Taylor followed them, brought them all to order, then introduced the newcomer, giving a brief résumé of Daisy's career so far.

Daisy couldn't help but notice that Daniel Hanson's name provoked a shudder in a couple of the players. Phoebe had muttered darkly about him, too. Maybe she'd had a lucky escape from him?

Then scripts were handed round, and soon the read-through was well under way.

'Miss Denham, are you all right?' asked Sandy, when they broke for lunch.

'Yes, I'm fine,' lied Daisy. 'Why d'you ask?'

'You're looking very pale.'

'I'm always pale,' said Daisy, smiling hard.

Daisy felt rather sick and ill all day. She started wondering if this was the famous morning-sickness. If it was, could you have morning-sickness all through the afternoon? She had awful stomach cramp, as well – the kind of griping, twisting agony that made her want to retch. Maybe she was in for months of this?

Then, that evening, when she went to bed, she found she wasn't pregnant after all.

But instead of feeling the relief she *should* have felt, Daisy felt bereaved. A baby would have loved her, and been someone to love, and Daisy needed loving. Ever since she'd known she would be meeting Ewan once again, she'd fantasized about them starting again from where they had left off. Maybe, she had wondered, even though the baby wouldn't actually be his child, they could be a little family. . . .

But it seemed that Ewan hadn't wasted any time moping around and being broken-hearted, as she'd feared. She needn't have felt guilty about going off to London, after all.

She cried herself to sleep that night.

After a week's rehearsals, they had three plays up and running, and two more almost ready. In a company where everyone was young, lines were committed to memory very quickly, and professional arrogance was in relatively short supply. Everyone needed this to work, and knew it. They needed to do well.

Sadie made it obvious to all she wasn't keen on Daisy, didn't want to be her friend. As time went on, Sadie's animosity burned Daisy like hot blasts from a volcano. Daisy hoped and prayed she'd never need to ask the other girl for a loan of make-up, pins or stockings.

But she was relieved to find that Sadie was a pro. She didn't upstage Daisy, didn't try to make her fluff her lines, didn't let her very obvious personal dislike affect the plays. But Daisy was aware of the cold malice in Sadie's hazel eyes.

They got into the theatre. The scenery – such as it was – had all been put in place. The lighting-man was sober. The first play would be opening to the public that same night.

'Mungo's very good,' said Daisy, as she and Ewan stood in the wings while Sadie and Mungo Campbell, the other actor from the Glasgow Comrades who had taken Sandy's shilling, ran through a scene together.

'He doesn't have to kiss her *quite* so hard,' said Ewan sourly, frowning even harder.

'Yes, he does – he's desperately in love with her, they're planning to elope.' Daisy touched Ewan's arm and smiled at him. 'But only in the play. Off stage, anyone can see that she's in love with you.'

'Yes, I know. She's lovely.' Ewan smiled. 'She saved my life, you know. She gave me back my self-respect. I'm very lucky.'

'I'm so pleased for you.'

'Thank you.' Ewan kept his gaze on Sadie. 'When you went off to London, I didn't understand. I won't pretend it didn't hurt, to see you go with Trent. But now I realize – everyone moves on.'

'Indeed they do,' said Daisy.

She saw she'd lost him, and her heart was sore.

CHAPTER 19

ALTHOUGH there were days when Daisy wished she was anywhere but Leeds, when Ewan and Sadie seemed to be a living, breathing, mortifying example of the perfect loving couple, she knew she had to stick it out.

She and Ewan were thrown together all the time. In two plays they were cast as actual lovers, and Daisy had to remind herself that when he looked at her with joy or longing in his eyes, he was a player, he was acting. But it was so difficult to see him, touch him, kiss him, flirt with him, and know it was a sham, that Ewan didn't feel anything at all.

Every passionate kiss was in reality chaste and cold. Sometimes, Ewan didn't kiss at all, just brushed her mouth with his, and he was always more than ready to pull away.

On rest days, when the company went off on expeditions, going by bus or train to other towns, or out on to the moors, she and Ewan were often on their own, especially on the moors. Sadie was no hiker, and she preferred sitting in a pub to getting chilled and windswept up on Ilkley Moor. But Ewan, Daisy and Mungo Campbell all loved being out in the fresh air.

'You're looking puffed,' said Ewan, one afternoon when he and Daisy and three other men had gone off for a ramble, leaving Sandy Taylor and Sadie stewing in the saloon bar of a countryside hotel.

'I'll be all right.' But Daisy had ricked her ankle earlier on, and now she couldn't keep up with Mungo Campbell, or the other men. She sat down in the shelter of a rock, pulled off her boot and checked her ankle, which was looking pink and puffy. 'But maybe I'll sit here a bit and read, and you can pick me up when you come back.'

'Aye, come on, Fraser,' Mungo said. 'Away, and leave the lassie with her book.'

'She could make a fire for us, perhaps,' said one of the other men.

'Aye, get the kettle on, she could, for when we come back down.' Rummaging in his battered army-issue khaki backpack, Mungo produced a workman's jerry-can, a twist of tea-leaves, a copy of the *Daily Worker* and a lemonade-bottle full of water.

'I'll stay with Daisy, if she doesn't mind.' Ewan sat down too, and yawned. 'I wouldn't mind a nap.'

'You've been having too much sex, man,' Mungo told him, scornfully. 'Wee Sadie's worn you out. Very well then, keep the lassie company. But if you make a brew-up, mind you don't use all the water.'

As Mungo and his friends strode off, Daisy looked at Ewan. 'You didn't have to stay,' she said, feeling her cheeks grow scarlet.

'I know I didn't. But you've hurt your ankle, you look tired, and it didn't seem very kind to leave you.' Ewan glanced at Daisy's swollen ankle. 'You need a cold compress. Otherwise, you'll never get your boot back on, and then what will you do?'

'Mungo said not to waste the water,' Daisy murmured, looking at her foot.

'Oh, bugger Mungo.' Ewan got out his handkerchief and poured cold water over it, then he wrapped it carefully round Daisy's damaged ankle, and she tingled at his touch. 'In ten minutes or so, when it feels numb, you must put your boot back on. Lace it up as tight as you can bear it, and then you'll be all right.'

'Thank you,' Daisy said politely, picking up her book. 'I'll be all right now,' she added, primly. 'So you can go to sleep.'

But Ewan lounged there, looking up at her, pulling at a clump of rusty-looking heather. 'Daisy,' he began, 'I hope it hasn't made things too awkward for you, having to act with me.'

'Of course it isn't awkward,' Daisy murmured, her eyes fixed on her book. 'It's very nice to see you, and to have a chance to act with you again.'

'It's lovely to see *you*.' Ewan smiled, and Daisy's heart did cartwheels. 'When I walked into that room above the Wakefield Arms, and saw you standing there, it was like Christmas and my birthday all rolled into one.'

'Ewan, don't,' said Daisy.

'Ewan, don't what?' asked Ewan.

'Be so nice to me.' Daisy forced herself to look at him. 'I was really horrible to you. I belittled and embarrassed you. I flirted with that awful man, then I went off with him, although I knew you'd be upset. I'm sorry, Ewan. I'm delighted that you're happy again with Sadie.'

'Yes, she's a lovely girl.' Ewan tugged more heather, twisting it around his fingers. 'Daisy?'

'Yes?'

'Oh, nothing.' Ewan looked across the moor, towards the distant hills. 'You and Trent – it didn't work out, then?'

'There was nothing to work out,' said Daisy. 'When we went to London, we were trying to find some work, that's all.'

'But you liked the sod?'

'I . . . really, Ewan, this is nothing to do with you.'

'He seduced you, didn't he?' Ewan kept his gaze fixed on the hills. 'He talked you into bed, then left you high and dry, the bastard.'

At the word *bastard*, Daisy flushed, but didn't say anything.

'I'm sorry, that was out of order,' Ewan said, eventually.

'It's more or less what happened, except that *I* left *him*.' Daisy

THE LONG WAY HOME

shrugged. 'I was stupid. I thought I was in love, but I was chasing rainbows.'

'But you're over him?'

'Oh, I'm *definitely* over him!'

'I won't pretend I liked him, but I'm sorry things went wrong for you.' Ewan turned to face her, took her hand, looked earnestly into her eyes. 'Listen,' he said, 'I know we've had some rather awkward moments, you and I. But whatever happens, I'll always be your friend.'

'I – thank you, Ewan.' Daisy looked at his hand on hers, and she was sorely tempted to pull him close, to kiss him properly. To tell him she was sorrier than he'd ever know, was heartbroken because she knew she'd lost him.

'Do you love Sadie very much?' she asked, not really knowing why she was so very intent on torturing herself.

'Aye, she's my little ray of sunshine.' Ewan grinned. 'She can be a minx, and sometimes she's contrary. But women all tend to be a bit contrary, now and then. Sadie and I agree on the important things in life. Yes, I like her fine.'

'Why don't you have your nap now?' Daisy said.

'I will, if you don't mind.' Ewan lay back on the heather, folded his hands across his chest and soon fell fast asleep. Daisy sat and stared down at her book, but didn't read a thing.

When Mungo and the others came back, she had a fire going, and the water boiling merrily.

'I see you've worn young Fraser out,' said Mungo. 'I dunno what all you women see in him.'

The season was turning out to be a very mild success, just covering its expenses, paying the actors' and producer's salaries, and making just the tiniest of profits week by week. But this was as much as Sandy had dared hope, he told the company, in these increasingly wretched days of unemployment, heartache and despair.

189

'We live in mean and grubby times,' he said, and Daisy knew exactly what he meant. Life was grey and thwarted – or hers was, anyway.

Anxious to avoid the happy couple, she took to spending much of her free time in the local spit-and-sawdust pub with Sandy and Mungo Campbell. Sitting in the bar and getting kippered by all the fetid smoke from workmen's pipes, she and Mungo listened to Sandy's stories about the many older, married women he had loved and lost.

'You're like the Prince of Wales,' said Daisy, patting his hand and trying to sound more sympathetic than she really felt, for she was privately a bit disgusted by men who fancied tough old hens like Bertie's Mrs Simpson.

'Yes, but if I *were* the Prince of Wales, I'd only have to tap the bloody husband on the shoulder, and the bugger would move over – not square up to me,' said Sandy, scowling down into his pint of best.

'Away, man – you're a pervert, you want tae fuck your mother,' Mungo told him, scornfully. 'The lassie should be younger than the laddie every time. It's a law of nature. Me, *I'd* never dip a fat old sheep, if I could get a lamb.'

'Campbell, you're never going to dip the lamb *you've* got your eye on,' retorted Sandy. 'We've all noticed the way you look at Sadie. If I were Fraser, I would stick one on you.'

'Fraser wouldnae even try it,' Mungo growled belligerently. 'He knows I'd lay him out.' He flexed his raw, red, worker's hands, and cracked his knuckles one by one. 'But the de'il only knows what a lass like Sadie sees in *him*. I'd have thought she'd want a *real* man.'

Unlike Ewan and Sadie, who seemed to have put their left-wing sympathies into storage while they were in Leeds, Mungo still spoke the language and wore the uniform – the collarless shirt and corduroys, the flannel neckcloth and big boots – of the ordinary working man. He played his parts in all the rather anodyne, lower-middle-class dramas that they were putting on in Leeds somewhat sarcastically.

But Daisy couldn't blame him when her own heart wasn't in it, either. As she trotted through her various roles of dutiful daughter, innocent *ingénue* and kindly sister, night after boring night, getting polite applause and equally polite, respectful notices in the local press, she wondered why she was doing this at all.

That silly melodrama *Blighted Blossoms* had had a lot more bite. The revue had been a lot more fun. Besides, they really needed her at home. Rose's letters had that tone of bright and brittle optimism which Daisy knew meant things were going badly.

We miss you, love,' wrote Rose. *I'm glad to know you're happy, and that things are working out in Leeds. We'd love to come and see you, as you know. But right now it's impossible for your dad or me to get away. I'm sure you understand.*

The chickens are doing well. I have an arrangement with the local egg-man now; he comes to collect the baskets every Saturday and Wednesday, and I'm earning enough to pay most of the vet's bills, and the boys' school fees.

The twins both send their love, and say they'd like some picture postcards, if you can spare the time to send them some.

Sadie and Ewan carried on being deliriously in love. She positively glowed with happiness, and every smile she gave her lover scraped another graze on Daisy's heart.

Ewan wasn't physically any bigger than when she'd met him in the rehearsal room above the pub, but in the past few months he'd sort of grown. He wasn't an awkward boy, he was a man. More to the point, he had the relaxed and easy confidence of a *happy* man.

He didn't yell at the audience any more. Instead, he played to them, took them into his confidence, and they loved him just like Sadie did. Each night, he got the most applause, and Mungo

191

Campbell's scowls grew even grimmer.

Daisy tried to be brisk and friendly when she spoke to Ewan, but it was very hard. She watched in silent misery as he touched Sadie's shoulder, stroked her hair, lavished upon her all the light caresses that lovers do.

She'd been such a fool. She'd thrown a good man's love away.

The day the season finished and the company got out, a letter came from Rose.

The twins are in trouble yet again, she wrote. But it's serious this time. They were caught on Michael Easton's land, the police became involved, and the boys were charged with trespass and malicious damage.

As you can imagine, Edgar isn't very pleased. Of course, the twins are guilty, and so there's no defence. Edgar knows we can't afford the sort of fine the magistrate, who's very thick with Mike, will almost certainly hand down. But if we don't pay, the twins could end up being birched, or sent away. I don't quite know what we shall do.

Daisy sighed. Poor Rose and Edgar, good as gold themselves, they'd somehow raised a trio of juvenile delinquents.

She checked her bank-book. In the past few months, she'd saved a mere three pounds, which almost certainly wouldn't be enough to pay a fine. Anyway, she had to settle up with her landlady, then get herself back home. . . .

Sandy Taylor had got a company together for a summer season in Southend, taking almost everyone from Leeds along with him. But Ewan, Sadie and Mungo were going back to Scotland, to try to interest managements in drama studio versions of some Shakespeare plays – *Julius Caesar, Romeo and Juliet,* and *Macbeth*

– which Ewan had adapted for three players, so they would be cheap to do.

'Bloody good luck to them,' said Sandy Taylor. 'Fraser will have his work cut out, though – Scots don't usually go for men in togas, or in tights. But our Mr Campbell will make a good Mercutio, the sarcastic, touchy bastard.'

Daisy's heart contracted at the thought of Sadie playing Ewan's Juliet.

'What about you, Daisy Denham, won't you reconsider coming with us to the seaside?' went on Sandy, for Daisy had told him she would not be going to Southend because they needed her at home. 'You can't keep chopping and changing, love, being an actress one year, and mucking out pigs down on the farm the next. It's hard to get anywhere in this damned profession, as you know. It's harder still if you don't take it seriously.'

'I do take it seriously,' said Daisy, imagining Rose's worried face and wishing she were home.

'But do you have that kernel of ambition that everybody needs, even when they have a wealth of talent?' persisted Sandy 'Do you have the necessary hunger? When you're on stage, you're fine – I've no complaints. You have the makings of an actress, and maybe you could even be a great one, who can tell? But do you *want* it? Do you have the hunger?'

'Sandy, I'm a two-bit entertainer, not Dame Ellen Terry. I play juveniles and people's sisters in provincial plays.'

'But you could be a star.'

'I somehow doubt it,' Daisy murmured, feeling she was being torn in two.

She got the next train home. But as she sat in the third-class carriage, trying to read the paper and take an interest in the real world, she wished she were going to Southend.

Charton looked the very same as when she'd seen it last. Golden in the sunshine, as it must have looked for a hundred, two, five hundred years.

Rose was not at home. Edgar was presumably working in the kitchen garden, or out in the fields with the cows. So Daisy left her case in the cottage porch, then went to find the twins.

'Honestly,' she cried, when she found her brothers in the stables, giving their menagerie their supper, 'I can't turn my back for fifteen minutes without you wretched children getting into trouble. What were you *doing*, you little clots?'

'Letting innocent animals out of traps,' retorted Stephen, cradling a rabbit which he was stroking tenderly. 'Surely you don't think *that* was wrong? Daze, we released three foxes, a young badger—'

'But you got *caught*, you idiots!' Daisy glared at them. 'As if Mum and Dad don't have enough to worry about—'

'Oh, look who's talking now!' Robert glared back at Daisy. 'Not so very long ago, *you* were running off to Scotland with that ginger chap from Easton Hall. Then you went off to London without telling anyone.'

'You hardly wrote to them at all when you were up in Leeds,' continued Stephen, righteously. 'If Mum and Dad have more grey hairs than when you saw them last, it's *you* as well as us who put them there!'

Daisy let that pass. 'What have you done with all the injured foxes and other things you found?' she asked. 'I hope you didn't let them go and limp into the undergrowth, to die a really slow and painful death?'

'Of course not, stupid,' Robert said. 'We put them all in baskets, then we brought them home. They're here in the stables.'

'Oh, and I just bet that thrills the rabbits.'

'They're in a different *part* of the stables, idiot – in our infirmary.' Stephen looked at Daisy as if she were a fool. 'We can't afford a vet, of course, but we got some books out of the library to find out how to treat them.'

'We made them muzzles so they couldn't bite us. We cleaned up all their wounds,' continued Robert, 'made splints for all their broken bones, and collars out of cardboard so they couldn't chew their dressings off.'

'So now they're all doing really well – that's except for one poor stoat, who died.'

'The baby badger with the broken leg is getting better, he can walk again.'

'We're going to release him on our land.'

'Dad says we may.'

'What about the foxes – feeding them on Mum's best chicken, are you?' Daisy asked the boys, sarcastically.

'No, of course not, they're having to make do with scraps and worms.'

'That bugger Easton is a bloody sadist, Daze. Everybody in the village says so,' muttered Robert grimly. 'Don't look at me like that, I know it's swearing.'

'They say he was a coward in the war,' continued Stephen.

'Daze, there's no *need* for all those iron traps in all the woods,' insisted Robert. 'Sir Michael Sadist just likes hurting things.'

'The kind of traps his keeper uses are illegal these days,' Stephen said. 'We went and looked it up. We're going to tell the magistrate about it when we go to court, and then Sir Michael will be fined.'

'You wish,' said Daisy.

'But Daze, he breaks the law!'

'Listen, you little idiots,' cried Daisy, 'don't you understand? In this part of Dorset, Michael Easton *is* the law!'

She looked from one twin to another, suddenly furious with Michael Easton, who had too much power for his own good. 'Right,' she said, 'I'm going to see him.'

'Who?'

'That bugger Easton.' Daisy put her hat straight, squared her shoulders. 'I should have done it long ago. I'm going to see him *now*.'

'Daze, you can't!' cried Robert. 'Dad said that from now on, no one in our family must go on Easton's land, or speak to him, or see him, or—'

'Well, Dad's not here right now.'

Still in her best high heels, her last pair of silk stockings and the smart tweed travelling-costume Amy had given her as a parting present, Daisy set off along the gated road, which was the quickest way to Easton Hall – far quicker than the cliff path, even though going this way meant she was trespassing on Easton land.

By the time she panted up the drive which led to Easton Hall, she was sweating heavily from exertion, as well as hot with rage.

CHAPTER 20

Aᴛᴇʀ she'd rung the bell, after the family butler had looked her up and down with cool disdain, after she'd eventually been invited her to state her name and business, Daisy was kept waiting on the steps of Easton Hall for almost half an hour.

The maid who eventually admitted Daisy didn't speak. She didn't offer to take her jacket, and didn't offer her any refreshment, even a glass of water, which Daisy desperately needed, but for which she was too proud to ask.

The Easton family was clearly stinking rich. The place was furnished in the latest style, and the mingled scents of beeswax, Spanish leather and artificial jasmine filled the air. There were hothouse flowers in huge arrangements on almost all flat surfaces, massed explosions of purple, red and gold, even though the grounds of Easton Hall were full of daffodils and tulips, and all the lovely, gentle colours of an English spring.

Daisy was led along a beautifully decorated hallway, hung with family portraits and carpeted with the softest, silkiest, cream-white Berber rugs. Then she was shown into a fussy drawing-room, full of expensive, nasty modern china, which she at once decided must be Lady Easton's taste.

There, she cooled her heels and fanned her face, telling herself she must stay calm, and that there was nothing to be gained from telling Sir Michael Easton what she really thought of him.

She hadn't meant her very first meeting with her natural father to be quite like this. In fact, as she'd huffed and puffed her way along the gated road to Easton Hall, she had quite forgotten that Sir Michael was supposed to be her father. She'd come to Easton Hall for just one reason, to make him drop the charge against the twins.

At last the door of the drawing-room opened, and a tall man came in. She found herself face to face with Michael Easton. Or so she supposed, since she had asked to speak to him. This man was smartly barbered, neatly shaven, and immaculately suited in the height of fashion. So he couldn't have been a servant, anyway. . . .

'You're Miss Denham?' he said, coldly.

'Yes, and I imagine you must be Sir Michael?'

'What do you want of me, Miss Denham?'

He was quite good-looking – she thought that straight away, even though she was disposed to hate him. She also realized that they looked like one another, for they had the same blue eyes, the same corn-coloured hair, the same straight noses, same long lashes, same slightly darker, arching brows. But their mouths were different – his lips were thin and mean, while hers were full and generous, like Phoebe's.

'I won't pretend this visit is a pleasure,' said Sir Michael. 'But you might as well sit down.'

So Daisy sat.

'What do you want?' Sir Michael asked again.

'My father has had a summons,' Daisy said. 'I would like you to revoke it, to let the matter drop.'

'Why should I do that?' Sir Michael's thin lips twisted. 'Those brats were trespassing, committing wilful damage on my land. They should be taught a lesson.'

'Yes, but by their father, not by you,' said Daisy, telling herself that she must keep her temper.

'Denham never taught anyone a single thing worth knowing. It's clear he can't control his wretched children. So someone else will have to do it for him,' said Sir Michael. 'I'm afraid the summons stands.'

'But my father hasn't any money, and he can't afford to pay a fine!' objected Daisy.

'Then of course the children will be birched, or sent to a reformatory where they will be taught respect for other people's property.'

'But they're only kids!' Daisy stood up and faced him, met his calm, superior blue stare. 'Sir Michael, we admit it, they were walking in your woods. They found some animals caught in traps, and set them free. If they damaged any of your traps, I'm sure my father would be more than happy to replace them, or to pay for them to be repaired.'

'I thought you said that Denham had no money?'

'Oh, very well, I'll pay myself, if you'll withdraw the charges.'

'Miss Denham, you don't understand. Your brothers are delinquents. They deserve a flogging, and I intend to see they get one.'

Daisy couldn't believe what she was hearing. Already half-ashamed of herself for offering to pay to have the cruel traps repaired, she glared at him 'Then what they say about you in the village must be right,' she muttered, as she turned to go.

'What *do* they say, Miss – what do you call yourself these days – Miss Denham?' asked Sir Michael, so calmly and sarcastically that Daisy was incensed.

'That you're a sadist and a coward,' she replied, as she made her way towards the door.

She didn't reach it. 'No one speaks to me like that,' Sir Michael told her coldly in a voice of steel and ice, as he placed himself between his visitor and the door.

'Well, I just did,' said Daisy.

'Miss Denham, listen to me carefully.' Sir Michael's fine blue eyes flashed angry fire. 'I have some standing in this county. I expect my inferiors to treat me with respect. I see your adoptive parents brought you up to be a hoyden, so perhaps it's not your fault, but you won't leave this room till you apologize.'

'Then I'll have to stay.' Daisy sat down again, folded her arms across her chest and glowered up at him.

'Please don't be so childish.' Michael Easton sighed. 'I don't know what else you might have heard about me, but—'

'Believe me, I've heard plenty!' Daisy held up one hand and started ticking off a list. 'Seducer, liar, law-breaker, arsonist and—'

'*Arsonist?*' A vein throbbed dangerously in Michael Easton's temple. 'Be careful, Daisy,' he said softly. 'What you say is slander. You could end up in a court of law yourself.'

'So you didn't set our house on fire?'

'Of course I didn't!' Michael Easton laughed. 'That ruin was a fire-trap. It was just a matter of time before the wretched place went up in smoke. It was probably an oil-lamp, or a candle falling over, and—'

'Why do you hate my parents?' interrupted Daisy.

'I don't hate them.'

'Yes, you do.' Daisy met his stare. 'You wanted to marry Mum, she wouldn't have you, and you've never forgiven her for it, have you?'

'You don't know what you're talking about,' Sir Michael said abruptly, but in a slightly less abrasive tone than he had used before. 'You're just a child, with a child's foolish notions, and you wish—'

'I wish you'd leave my family alone! Just let us all get on with trying to make a sort of living.' Daisy held his gaze, her own beseeching. 'Please, can't you forget about this summons? So, a couple of children go walking in your woods. They get upset when they find wild animals caught in traps. But how does that hurt you?'

'*Your* family.' Sir Michael shook his head. 'I know what the village gossips say, and looking at you today, I can see there is a kind of accidental likeness. . . .'

Daisy didn't want to think about it. 'Whatever our relationship,' she said, 'whoever brought me into being, Edgar Denham will always be my father.' She looked back at him steadily, into clear blue eyes just like her own. 'Please, Sir Michael, drop this court case. Let my father deal with my brothers?'

'I'm so sorry, Daisy.' Sir Michael spread his hands. 'I have my property as well as my reputation as a sadist to defend, and so the answer's no.'

But now he seemed prepared to let her leave, and so she walked out with her head held high.

'What did he say?' asked Stephen, when Daisy got back to the stables, hotter, dustier and so tired that she was almost walking in her sleep.

'You're right, he is a sadist, and he's going to see you cop it.' Daisy grimaced. 'Well, I'll get another job, then I can pay your fine.'

'You will, Daze?' Robert grinned. 'You're such a brick! We thought we'd go to Borstal.'

'If Sir Michael's friends with the presiding magistrate,' said Daisy, yawning hugely, 'you still might. I'm going back to the cottage now – are you two horrors coming?'

'No, not yet. We have to put the animals to bed.' Stephen smiled ruefully at Daisy, and ran his grubby fingers through his untidy mop of jet-black hair. 'Thank you, Daze,' he said.

'Oh, don't mention it.' Daisy rubbed her eyes. 'I'm going home to have a sleep. I'm tired, and it looks like rain.'

Ewan was getting tired of Sadie and Mungo always going on at him.

This Shakespeare business, it had been all his bright idea, they

201

grumbled, and they'd both gone along with it, merely to humour him. But they wouldn't get anywhere with bloody Scottish managements, idiots to a man, who only wanted melodramatic tripe, or the Sir Harry Lauder kind of light variety.

They should be doing proper, modern drama, Sadie said, their mission was to educate the workers. Yes, they'd done that season down in Leeds, had sold their souls to Satan for a while, and saved a bit of money. So now they should spend it putting together a season of their own, doing important drama for the masses. In hospitals, in factories, in barracks – and in prisons, possibly.

Ewan could just imagine prison governors letting the likes of Sadie stand in front of hardened convicts, spouting left-wing propaganda, as the cons looked up her skirt.

'Why can't you get some money from your mother,' demanded Sadie, who refused to accept that Agnes Fraser had no money, and that if she had, she wouldn't have used it to advance her son's career. Sadie simply didn't understand that everything the Frasers owned was all tied up in land, that these days rents no more than covered costs, that there were numerous covenants and entails which meant they couldn't sell this land and raise a bit of money, even if they wished.

'You're just a feudal remnant, Fraser,' muttered Mungo, balefully.

'You call yourself a socialist, but really you're a traitor to the workers,' added Sadie.

Then she dragged him off to bed.

Sadie's favourite hobby-horse was all the senseless slaughter of the workers in the war, in which her father had been badly wounded, and most of his friends had died.

'*My* father was in the war as well,' objected Ewan, stung. '*He* was wounded too. But after they had patched him up, he went back to the trenches.'

202

'Aye, but he was an officer,' grinned Mungo, rubbing his worker's hands upon his worker's greasy corduroys. 'Everybody knows they had it soft.'

'No, they jolly well didn't,' insisted Ewan. 'Officers got killed as well as men.'

'It was filthy capitalist war, and if all the workers had had their proper say, and understood what they were really being asked to do, they wouldnae have fought in it at all,' retorted Mungo, smugly.

Ewan yawned. Mungo's constant flaunting of his working-class credentials was sometimes very tiresome. Not everyone could be a stoker's son. Or was it a boiler-maker's nephew? Ewan couldn't remember, actually. Maybe it was both.

Sadie broke off lecturing him one evening to announce that she had some news.

'What's that, then?' he asked her, wondering what she was planning now, and mentally ticking off the gruesome possibilities.

Rabble-rousing posing as street-theatre in Trafalgar Square? They'd get themselves arrested. A short run of some dull and boring ideological rant in some dusty drill hall? The workers wouldn't come, they all preferred the music-hall or pub. A series of public lectures, with some dogmatic drama on the side?

'I'm pregnant,' Sadie said.

He looked at her and thought how much he didn't want to spend his life with this outspoken, bossy harridan. But now he'd have to do so.

'Right, when would you like us to get married?' he asked, determined to bite the bullet and do the proper thing.

'Marriage is an outdated bourgeois concept,' she replied. 'Anyway, why do you think it's yours? It could just easily be Mungo's.'

'You mean you've slept with Mungo?' Ewan stared like a pole-axed ox, unable to believe it. 'But, Sadie, I thought that you and I were – well, you know.'

'You thought I was your private property?' Sadie shook her head. 'You really need re-educating, don't you?'

'I need my head examined, certainly.'

Daisy thought, I need my head examined, walking across the water-meadows in these stupid shoes. When she eventually limped into the kitchen of the bailiff's cottage, she was wet through, too.

The clouds had gathered as she hobbled up from the stables, the rain had started falling, and now the sky was purple, like a bruise. There were ominous rumbles in the air. It seemed more than likely that they were in for one of those terrific spring or summer storms that sometimes hit the Dorset coast, toppling trees and causing landslides, blowing tiles off roofs and bringing chimneys crashing down.

Rose had come back from the village, where she'd been visiting Mrs Hobson, who'd apparently been anxious that her dear Mrs Denham should meet her eighteenth grandchild.

But now Rose was delighted to see Daisy, and the prodigal daughter was petted and made much of, was made to take off her wet things and put on clean pyjamas, to sit with her blistered feet in a bowl of cool, soapy water, and drink a cup of cocoa. 'You got back in the nick of time.' Rose smiled. 'But were you on the four o'clock? You must have come the long way from the station?'

Daisy realized that Rose could not have noticed that her case was in the porch. 'Well, you're always telling me I mustn't trespass on the Eastons' land,' she told her mother. The twins had just come in, and so she shook her head at them and frowned, willing them to keep quiet about her recent expedition.

The storm raged on all night, the lightning crackled and the thunder rolled, keeping them all awake. The rain came down in torrents, and the gale-force wind howled round the cottage, threatening to bring the chimneys down and take the roof off, too.

In the end they gave up trying to sleep, and all assembled in the kitchen, sitting round a paraffin-lamp, sipping milky drinks and waiting blearily for the dawn.

'I never thought I'd hear noise like this again,' said Edgar, shuddering as a peal of thunder deafened them, and the cottage quaked.

'You mean it's like the guns, Dad?' Stephen asked, bright-eyed with interest.

'It's like the time we blew the Messines Ridge, in 1917.'

'Gosh, Dad, were you there?' demanded Robert.

'Yes, and so were half a million other blighters. Most of them got killed,' said Edgar, scowling at his son.

The storm abated towards morning, growling off to the east and leaving clear, blue-washed skies. Robert and Stephen went out after breakfast, saying they needed to check the pets before they went to school.

But as Daisy filled the usual buckets for the chickens, she saw them set off down the path towards the shingle-beach. They probably hoped to find all sorts of treasures washed up there, fossils newly exposed by falling rocks, and possibly a whale.

They were back ten minutes later in a state of great excitement. 'Dad!' cried Robert, running into the kitchen, his dirty, muddy wellingtons leaving great gouts of orange mud across the clean, flagged floor.

'Whatever's the matter?' Rose demanded, frowning.

'At least take off your boots, you little grubs,' admonished Daisy.

'Where's my dad?' gasped Stephen.

'He's in the milking-parlour, where you should be, helping him.' Rose looked at her sons suspiciously. 'Why, what have you done now?'

'Nothing, Mum!' cried Robert, looking hurt. 'But there's been a cliff fall.'

'Tons and tons of rock and half the road,' continued Stephen, breathlessly. 'It's all come down on to the beach.'

'Oh, my God,' said Rose, and all the colour left her face. 'Daisy, will you go and find your father? But don't tell him it's bad news. I want him sitting down when he hears this.'

CHAPTER 21

But as Daisy got up to go out, Edgar walked back into the cottage kitchen.

He looked relieved. 'The cows are fine,' he said, as he poured himself a cup of tea, sugared it and sat down. 'I was worried they might have panicked, but they're as right as rain.' But then he noticed their long faces. What's the matter with you lot – lost a pound and found a shilling?'

'It's the road from Melbury into Charton,' whispered Rose.

'The cliff has come away, and some of the road has fallen on the beach,' continued Stephen.

'So we're marooned,' said Robert. 'We can't get into Charton now, or to the railway station, not unless we go through Easton Woods.'

'Or along the gated road that's on Sir Michael's land.'

'But you've told us not to go that way.'

'So we can't go to school,' concluded Stephen.

'How will you take the cows to market now, Dad?' Daisy asked him, anxiously. 'How will you drive to Charton, and how will we get all the stuff we need?'

'I don't know,' said Edgar, looking as if he'd just been rabbit-punched. 'As the twins have pointed out, the only other road's on Easton's land. So I suppose—'

'We can't afford to build a brand new road,' Rose interrupted. 'Oh, Edgar, we'll be ruined!'

'No, we won't, said Edgar. 'I'll just have to go and grovel to Easton, ask him to let me use his road until I can afford to have a new one built myself.'

'But that won't be for years!' cried Rose. 'It'll cost hundreds, Edgar – thousands even – to build a proper road!'

'So, I'll be doing very heavy-duty grovelling.' Edgar looked severely at the twins. 'It's a pity you two have upset him. Daisy, you haven't done anything to annoy him, so maybe you could come with me to see him?'

Daisy felt the blood rush to her face. 'Actually, Dad,' she muttered, 'I saw him yesterday.'

'Daisy, you said *what*?' demanded Rose, when Daisy had explained where she had been, what she had done and what she'd said.

'You actually accused the brute of burning down our house?' asked Edgar, who had gone chalk-white.

'I'm really sorry, Dad.' Daisy felt two inches tall, and it didn't help that the twins were sitting staring at her, open-mouthed and goggling, half-impressed and half-dismayed.

'What shall we do?' asked Rose.

'Let me think,' said Edgar.

'I'm glad you didn't marry him, Mum,' said Daisy.

'So am I,' said Rose. 'But that won't get us out this mess, will it?'

'Mum, I was only trying to help,' cried Daisy.

'Well, don't try any more,' said Edgar, curtly.

'You children – what's got into you?' sighed Rose. 'Well, I suppose it's no use sitting here. I ought to go and feed the hens, though how we're going to get the wretched eggs to market now—'

'I'll go and feed the hens,' said Daisy, wishing she'd never gone to Easton Hall, hating the very name of Michael Easton, but cursing herself as well, and wondering what she could do to make amends.

Rose told the twins they needn't go to school, the day would be half over by the time they'd walked the long way round, across a common and through miles of woods. So they went and did their daily chores around the farm, helped Edgar with the cows, then went to seek some comfort from their pets.

At ten o'clock a courier came, bringing an official-looking letter for which Edgar had to sign.

'I suppose I was expecting this,' he said, then handed it to Rose.

Daisy looked over Rose's shoulder, frowning as she read. Sir Michael's lawyer wrote that Mr and Mrs Denham and their children should be aware the Easton estate was private property. Any trespassing on land or thoroughfares would be answered with the full force of the law.

'Do you think we ought to go and see him?' Rose asked Edgar.

'If we so much as set foot on his land, he'll have us up in court.' Edgar shook his head and rubbed his eyes. 'Even if I phone him, he'll probably refuse to speak to me. The bugger means to ruin us, and he knows there's nothing we can do.'

'But there must be something, Dad,' said Daisy. What if we—'

'Daisy, don't do *anything*,' interrupted Edgar, testily. 'Listen, I'm not saying it's all your fault. I realize you were only trying to help. But you don't know the half of what that man is capable. Or how much he hates me.'

Daisy did some things for Rose, collected all the eggs, then put them in the big, square wicker-baskets lined with straw, even though she knew the egg-man wouldn't be able to come round in his van to pick them up.

But, she decided, they could get at least *some* eggs to market. After lunch, she and the twins could carry one basket several miles across the fields to Charton, then they could meet the egg-man in the village. Also, they could bring back a sack of feed.

But that wasn't going to be an effective permanent solution.

She went to see the twins. She found them happily occupied in

209

their infirmary, making pets of all the wild animals which they'd sprung from Michael Easton's traps, and which had indirectly caused this mess. She sat with a lop-eared rabbit on her lap, trying in vain to think of something she could do to help. But she couldn't think of anything that wouldn't make matters worse.

Rose was being so decent about it all, and Edgar had gone so quiet and pale that Daisy felt really wicked. It would be so much easier if they'd raged and shouted, if they'd told her what a fool she'd been. The fact that the wind and tempest were to blame as much as she was didn't make it any better.

At the end of a sleepless night, during which she'd heard her father pacing up and down out in the yard, and her mother begging him to come back in and rest, she suddenly had a brainwave.

'Mum, may I use the telephone?' she asked, after they'd done their morning chores and after the twins had gone, moaning and groaning at the rank injustice of it all, to make their way across the fields to school. 'I need to ring New York.'

'Do you?' Rose looked doubtful. 'You know, it's very expensive to make transatlantic calls. I suppose you want to talk to Phoebe?'

'Yes, I do – and Mum, don't worry, I'll pay for the call.'

'Oh, that's all right, my love. A few more debts won't matter.' Rose raked her greying hair back from her brow and then smiled bravely. 'Go on, go ahead.'

It took an hour to get the call through. The operator rang just as Edgar walked into the kitchen for his morning coffee.

'Who's that?' demanded Phoebe, sounding groggy.

'It's Daisy. Phoebe, don't hang up on me!' Daisy saw Rose and Edgar exchanging curious glances, but she ploughed on gamely. 'I wanted to apologize. I was very nasty to you that last time we met. I'm sorry I ran away that afternoon.'

'Oh – that's all right, my darlin'.' Phoebe coughed, and cleared her throat. 'I reckon I shocked you, yeah? I should've been more tactful. But do you know it's five o'clock in the morning over 'ere?'

'Oh, God, I was forgetting.'

'I'll forgive you, sweet'eart,' Phoebe said. 'So, is that it – we're friends again, an' now can I go back to bed?'

'No, not just yet, there's something else.' Daisy crossed her fingers. 'Phoebe, would you sign an affidavit—'

'Sign an affy what?'

'An affidavit, it's a declaration under oath, to say you had relations with Sir Michael Easton round about the time I was conceived and, that to the best of your knowledge, he's my natural father?'

There was total silence on the line.

Daisy crossed her fingers, praying hard.

But then, 'Well, I suppose so,' Phoebe replied, at last. She sounded quite surprised, but not reluctant. 'After all this time, though – Daisy, you're settled with Rose and Edgar, ain't you? They been very good to you, you told me so yourself. Surely you ain't thinkin' of tryin' to get yourself another dad?'

'No, but – Phoebe, this call is costing us a fortune, can I assume you'll sign an affidavit if need be?'

'Yeah, sure, I'll sign it. I'll get my Nathan on the job, an' he'll sort something out.' Then Phoebe chuckled. 'You left all them bags behind, you know.'

'Yes, I know. I'm sorry.'

'I brought them back with me. We got some lovely stuff in Selfridges, an' in them posh shops in Piccadilly. Look, I'll post 'em on to you, OK?'

'OK,' said Daisy. 'Phoebe, thanks for everything.'

'You're welcome.' Phoebe cleared her throat again. 'Daisy, darlin', write to me some time?'

'I'll do that,' promised Daisy. 'I'll send you lots of photographs, as well. Phoebe, you must come over here again. Come and stay in Dorset, and bring your husband, too.'

'Well, what was all *that* about?' asked Rose, as Daisy hung the receiver in its cradle.

'You'll see, Mum, soon enough.' Daisy buttoned up her cardigan, brushed a few wisps of straw off her tweed skirt. 'I'm going to see Sir Michael again – and Mum, you're coming with me.'

'Oh, I don't know if that's wise,' said Rose.

'Phoebe's going to help us, Mum,' said Daisy. 'So come on, we need to get things moving. Dad, persuade her, will you?'

'Well, I suppose it can't do any harm – or any more harm, anyway.' Edgar suddenly looked more hopeful. 'Daisy's right,' he said. 'We can't appeal to Easton's better nature, the bugger doesn't have one. This is the only way.'

'But – but I don't understand!' cried Rose.

'Daisy, explain it to your mother as you go along.' Edgar plonked Rose's hat upon her head, then kissed her on the cheek. 'Good luck, girls,' he said.

'I'm sorry, Mrs Denham, but Sir Michael's orders are to say he's not at home to you,' began the elderly servant who'd opened the front door at Easton Hall.

'Oh, don't be so silly, Hannah Ward!' Rose looked the woman up and down. 'You've been here – how long, is it? Fifty years? You were in the kitchens once. You used to help the cook. You gave me macaroons and shortbread biscuits, when I was a child.'

'Mrs Denham, please – don't make things hard for me!' The servant flushed a deep shade of brick-red. 'Sir Michael was quite adamant that you and any members of your family were not be admitted. Anyway, he's gone to see his steward.'

'When did he leave?'

'Two or three minutes ago, that's all, but—'

'Did he go on foot?'

'Yes, I believe he did.'

'Then we shall catch him up. Come along, Daisy, we'll go through the shrubbery, that's the quickest way.' Rose clutched her hat and hurried off, closely followed by Daisy.

They caught up with their quarry as he crossed the orchard. They ran up to him, gasping, out of breath.

'Michael, wait!' cried Rose.

'Rose?' As he turned to face them, Michael's blue eyes narrowed, and his face went white with shock. 'Rose Courtenay?'

'Rose Denham, as I believe you know.' Rose met his gaze and smiled. 'Well, Mike – it must be fifteen years or more since we—'

'At least.' But then, recovering from his shock, Sir Michael grinned sarcastically. 'I know it's polite, on these occasions, to tell a woman she hasn't changed a bit. But time has not been very kind to you.' Then he turned to Daisy. 'I wasn't expecting to see *you* again. I can't think why you've—'

'We've had a letter from your lawyer,' interrupted Rose. 'I'm sure you know we've had a cliff fall on our land. We've lost part of the road that goes to Charton. So I've come to ask you to let us use your road, until we can get something sorted out.'

'Why should I?' Michael asked.

'You're our neighbour, and neighbours help each other, or they should,' said Rose. 'Michael, Edgar and I have never tried to injure you, and so—'

'*You* have a short memory, Rose,' said Michael. 'I have nothing more to say to you.'

He turned to go back to the house. But Daisy stepped in front of him, so if Michael wanted to escape, he'd have dodge past her then run away. 'Why are you being like this?' she cried. 'Just because Mum wouldn't marry you?'

'I don't have to talk to *you*,' snapped Michael.

'But I'm your daughter!'

'You are *not* my daughter!'

'Oh, of course I am!' Daisy met Michael's cold, blue gaze. 'Just look at me! Look at my hair, my eyes, my nose – it's obvious I'm yours.'

'Rose, take your brat away.'

'I know what happened now.' Daisy glared back at Michael. 'Mum didn't tell me, Phoebe did, and she's willing to sign an affidavit to say you are my father.'

'Who would believe a chorus-girl?' sneered Michael.

'Everyone would love to believe a chorus-girl,' snapped Daisy, 'especially if the man who seduced her is a baronet.'

'So who exactly are you going to tell?'

Daisy thought, if I mess this up, my family will be ruined. 'If you don't allow us to use your road,' she said to Michael Easton, 'I'll go to all the papers. I'll tell the *News of the World*, the *Daily Mirror*, and *The Times*. I'll give them such a story, and they can have photographs, as well.

'Sir Michael, just imagine it. *One of the largest landowners in Dorset's sordid secret. Love-child and her mother left to starve.* You'll look cruel, vindictive – *and* ridiculous.' Then something Ewan had mentioned long ago flashed back into her mind. 'You want to be Lord Lieutenant of the county—'

'Who told you that?' demanded Michael.

'Never mind who told me,' Daisy said. 'But if you don't let my parents use your road, by the time I've finished with you, you'll be a laughing-stock. As for your chances of being a magistrate, or Lord Lieutenant – they won't even let you shake a collecting-tin on flag days.'

'What about you?' growled Michael. 'After all that, you'd lose whatever threadbare reputation *you* might have.'

'Oh, don't be ridiculous, I have no reputation,' Daisy said. 'I'm a bastard, aren't I? I'm an actress, too. Actresses will go with anyone for half a crown. What did you pay my mother?'

'Get off my property.'

'I'll tell Daniel Hanson that you fucked his girlfriend, and I was the result!' Daisy blushed, astonished at herself for using such a filthy word, but gratified by the look of utter horror on Michael Easton's face. 'He's a London gangster, did you know? He runs all

214

sorts of vice-rings, the police are in his pocket, he breaks people's legs, and he'd break yours.'

Michael Easton turned to glare at Rose. 'You put her up to this,' he spat.

'All Rose has done is love me, look after me and treat me as her own.' Daisy glared at Michael. 'I'll take you to court. I'll claim a share of your estate. Phoebe and I will drag your name through so much muck and mud—'

'You'd get that whore back from whatever gutter you found her in?'

'Yes, I would. Phoebe isn't scared of you. She and I'd put on a damned good show for all your neighbours, and the press. It would be goodbye Buckingham Palace garden-parties, Royal Ascot—'

'Oh, Daisy, careful,' cautioned Rose.

But Daisy took no notice. 'If you don't let us use your road,' she said, in desperation, 'I'll marry Ewan Fraser!'

CHAPTER 22

MICHAEL stared, then suddenly looked so close to losing all his self-control that Daisy was glad he didn't have a gun. 'I'm the head of this family!' he shouted. 'I'll forbid it!'

'We can wait until we're twenty-one!' Daisy shouted back defiantly, determined to outface him. 'I mean it. I'm not making idle threats. I shall do everything I said.'

'All your bloody children should be in asylums.' Michael scowled at Rose, but suddenly all the fight went out of him. 'I'll speak to my solicitor,' he muttered. 'Now, the pair of you, get off my land. Or I shall call the police and have you both arrested.'

'What about the boys?' persisted Daisy. 'I assume you'll drop the charges against them?'

'I've already said I'll speak to my solicitor,' hissed Michael, and he turned and stalked back to the house.

'We did it, Mum!' gasped Daisy, as she and Rose ran down the gated road, not even stopping to catch their breath until they were safely back on their own land. 'He'll see the sense of it, I'm sure. He won't risk all that scandal just to stop the egg-man coming.'

'You did very well, my love, I'm very proud of you.' Rose clutched at her side, trying to rub the stitch away 'But that Mr Hanson – do you really know him?'

'I was in his London show. I told you, Mum. But I walked out on him.' Daisy grimaced. 'So I hope he'll never track me down, especially if he's as mean as everybody says.'

'Oh, don't worry, love, I'm sure your dad could deal with him. Edgar would never let anyone hurt you. But *are* you going to marry Ewan?'

'No, don't worry, Mum.' Daisy looked down at her fingernails. 'Actually, I'd love to marry Ewan,' she confessed. 'But he doesn't want me. He's in love with someone else.'

'Oh, darling, I'm so sorry!'

'It doesn't matter.' Daisy shrugged. 'There'll be other men.'

'What will you do now, dear?' Rose enquired. 'The new season's coming, companies will be casting. . . .'

'I think I should stay here, in Dorset,' Daisy said. 'I can see Dad still isn't very well. But he goes out in all the wind and rain, and he's still trying to do everything himself.'

'I do help him, sweetheart,' Rose said gently.

'Yes, Mum, I know you do, and *you* look like death warmed up, as well. You need some decent help. A couple of farm labourers full time, a proper cowman. A woman to come in every day, collect the eggs, and see to all the hens.'

'We can't afford it, Daisy, you know that.' Rose shrugged. 'Since the war, this country has collapsed. No farmers have it easy these days, and hundreds have sold up. So, compared with some, we're doing well.'

'Why didn't you marry Sir Michael, Mum?'

'I fell in love with Edgar.'

'But, Mum, you could have been so rich! You could have been the lady of the manor, you could have had expensive clothes, and holidays abroad, and everything. Maybe you could have made him kinder, too. Lady Easton must be bad for him.'

'You're thinking how nice it might have been to grow up in great luxury, with your natural father and me – is that it?'

217

'No, Mum, no!' Daisy was horrified. 'My dad's my father, and nobody could have had a better one.'

'I know.' Rose smiled and shook her head, remembering. 'When Michael was denying that you were his, and Phoebe was so anxious to put it all behind her and run off to America, it was Edgar who suggested we adopt you.'

'Otherwise, I'd have ended up in some orphanage, I suppose?'

'I dare say.' Rose met Daisy's gaze. 'I've never regretted anything, you know. I couldn't love you better if you'd been my natural child. I couldn't have been happier than I've always been with Edgar.'

'I'm so glad you married Dad,' said Daisy.

'Daisy, love?' Rose sat down on a stile. 'Nothing is ever black-and-white, you know.'

'Why, what do you mean?'

'You say perhaps I could have made Michael kinder, but I hurt him, too.' Rose looked down at her hands. 'If Lady Easton is a bitch, it's partly down to me.'

'How do you make that out?'

'Daisy, dear, sit down, listen to me.' Rose gazed across the head-land. 'Chloe – Lady Easton, as she's been for fifteen years – was married to Edgar once.'

'To *Dad*?' frowned Daisy. 'Mum, I don't believe you!'

'Oh, it's true,' said Rose. 'But it was a case of having to marry. She was pregnant.'

'What happened to the baby?'

'It was stillborn.' Rose turned to look at Daisy. 'I'm not proud of this, you know. But after the baby died, Chloe and Edgar grew apart. He was in the army, and she was here in Dorset. He was trying hard to stay alive, and that took all his energy. But she believed he didn't love her, and eventually I don't suppose he did.

'Edgar and I had known each other as children. We'd lost touch, but then I met him again during the war, when I was a nurse and he

218

was wounded, and – things happened.'

'So you broke up their marriage?'

'If you want to put it like that, yes – I suppose I did,' admitted Rose. 'Then, after the war, Chloe met Michael, and I guess the two of them. . . .'

'They both hate you and Dad for being so happy, for having children, for having all the things they don't or can't. So maybe they don't love each other – what they have in common is that they hate you.' Daisy shrugged. 'It's getting late. We'd better go and help Dad get the cows in.'

Daisy became the chicken-woman, cowman, general help. As Rose had said, it was bad for farmers everywhere, but somehow they survived.

In her spare time, which didn't amount to much, Daisy sang at weddings, in local concert-parties organized by Miss Sefton, and sometimes she went dancing at the village hall. The word had soon got round about how she'd stood up to the local bully, and she found everybody in Charton wanted to be her friend.

She took out a subscription to *Variety*, and now and then she was tempted to go to an audition. But she was afraid of what might happen if she went away again.

'But I'm fine,' insisted Edgar, whenever she told him he was looking tired, that she'd see to the cows or dig up some potatoes for the kitchen. 'I don't want a lot of flipping women fussing round me, wrapping me in cotton wool.'

But Daisy read the papers, and she'd noticed from the obituaries that servicemen who had survived the war had a habit of dying fairly young. There were a lot of widows in Dorset, and plenty of other women who had helpless invalids for husbands. If anything happened to Edgar, she couldn't leave Rose to cope alone. She'd have to wait until the twins were older to start her life again.

At Miss Sefton's invitation, she started giving dancing classes in the village hall, and sang in the *Messiah* in Dorchester. Rose cut out the notices which praised Miss Denham's pure soprano voice, and stuck them in her scrap-book.

'The *Dorset Herald*'s music critic is in love with you,' she said, as Daisy professed indifference to what the papers said.

'Oh, don't be ridiculous, Mum,' said Daisy.

'You miss the theatre, don't you?' Rose asked Daisy, as they fed the chickens one bright morning, and Mrs Hobson looked for eggs.

'No,' lied Daisy.

'Darling, I think you do.'

'I don't.' Daisy threw the last handful of corn to a little scrum of clucking hens. 'Anyway, you never wanted me to be an actress. So why are you always going on about it now?'

'I didn't want you to be away from home, so young and inexperienced,' said Rose. 'It's very hard to let your children go. But now you're older, if it's what you really want. . . .'

'It's not – not any more,' lied Daisy.

'You'll make some lucky farmer a fine wife,' said Mrs Hobson, bestowing the highest praise.

'I don't want to be anybody's wife,' retorted Daisy.

'Oh, go on with you,' said Mrs Hobson. 'You'd have such lovely babies, it would be criminal if you stayed a spinster. There's a dozen young men in Charton who'd be glad to have you.'

'A lot of them are tenants of Michael Easton, and he hates me.'

'Well, there's nobody round here likes *him*,' said Mrs Hobson. 'If you went looking for a man Sir Michael Easton liked, *and* who liked him back, you'd have your work cut out.'

'I was looking through *Variety* last night,' said Rose, one autumn afternoon.

'I must cancel my subscription, that would save a bit of cash.' Daisy put her feet up on the fender of the kitchen stove. 'It's a waste of money. I hardly ever read it.'

'Have you read this one yet?' asked Rose, shunting it across the kitchen table.

'No, but keep it for a day or two, I might get round to it.' Daisy yawned and stretched. 'Or light the stove with it, if you prefer.'

'Daisy,' Rose said earnestly, 'if you want to do a season anywhere, we could easily manage. The twins are getting older and bigger, they do lots of jobs around the place.'

'You still need me, Mum. I don't want to be anywhere else. This is where I belong.'

'Daisy, you belong here anyway, wherever you go, whatever you want to do.' Rose looked at Daisy, her grey eyes dark and serious. 'Sweetheart, don't bury yourself alive in Dorset if being a farmer's wife is not for you.'

'I need to get the cows in.'

Three or four days later, Daisy was walking home along the cliff path and had nearly reached the rock-fall when she saw someone coming up from the beach. A tourist, she supposed, but he wasn't doing any harm, so she didn't need to tell him this was private land.

As the man drew nearer, though, she realized she knew him.

'Hello, Daisy,' Ewan said.

'Hello, Ewan.' Daisy nodded non-committally.

'Your mother said that if I came this way, I was sure to meet you.'

'You've been to see my parents?'

'Yes, and I was glad to find them well.' Ewan looked at her gravely. 'But enough social chit-chat. I hear you've been upsetting Cousin Mike.'

'*I* hear you're going to be a father.' Daisy looked back at him and hoped she didn't look as flustered as she felt. 'One of the people we were with in Leeds wrote and told me Sadie was about to have a baby. So, congratulations. Ewan, are you married?'

'How would you feel if I said yes?'

'I – I'd be happy for the baby's sake.'

'Sadie's had the baby, and she married Mungo,' Ewan said. 'Oh, at first she wouldn't think about it. She didn't need a husband, she kept saying, her baby would be hers and hers alone, she'd take it with her everywhere, she'd earn the money to keep them both.

'But when it was born, the poor wee thing had Mungo's nose and Mungo's eyes and Mungo's widow's peak. He was so excited that he more or less dragged her to the register office in Dundee, and made her sign her spinsterhood away.'

Ewan smiled a wry, ironic smile. 'They live with Mungo's parents now, in the very best part of Dundee. Contrary to what our comrade Mungo had led us to believe, it seems he comes from solid burgher stock. Mr Campbell is a surgeon with a thriving private practice. He operates on duchesses and earls, apparently. Mungo is going to be an architect. He was only playing at being an actor and a communist, after all.'

'But Sadie – is she happy?'

'Oh, yes, ecstatically.'

'Poor old Ewan,' said Daisy. 'You don't have much luck with women.'

'The way I see it, women haven't had much luck with me.' Ewan shrugged. 'God, I was so childish! But I've now grown up a bit, I hope. I've learned to give and take. I'm not so touchy nowadays.'

'You were always very nice to me.'

'You're very kind.' Ewan pushed his hands into his pockets. 'Damn, I haven't any gaspers.'

'You've given up that pipe?'

'It made me cough,' said Ewan. 'By the way, I also heard we're going to be married.'

'Oh?' Daisy blushed. 'Who told you that?'

'Sir Michael.'

'I was just bluffing, so you needn't worry.' Daisy scuffed the soil with the toecap of her boot. 'Ewan, did he tell you he and I – well, that we're related?'

'*He* didn't have to tell me.' Ewan shook his head. 'I only have to look at you to know what he's apparently been denying all your life. But I'm sure that you can rise above it.'

'Well, of course I try,' said Daisy wryly. 'So we're family.'

'Yes, but the connection's very distant. My father was a second cousin of Sir Michael's mother, if you can work that out. We're hardly kin at all. So, Daisy—'

'Where are you working now?' interrupted Daisy, hurriedly.

'The Palace Theatre, Plymouth. I'm in *Pygmalion* at present, I'm that feckless idiot Freddy. But next we're doing Shakespeare for a month, and I'll be playing Romeo.'

'As if he comes from Surrey?'

'We don't yet have a Juliet.' Ewan took a step towards Daisy, took her hands in his. 'Mrs Denham says you're pining to go back to the theatre.'

'I never told her that!' cried Daisy.

'Mothers know these things.' Ewan pulled Daisy closer. 'She showed me your album. You've been pasting in *my* cuttings too.'

'She had no right to show you that!' Daisy glowered at him. 'Honestly, in our house, *nothing's* private!'

'Maybe she shouldn't have shown me, but I'm very glad she did.' Ewan looked at Daisy earnestly. 'Your brothers are growing up. Plymouth isn't very far from Charton. If there was an emergency at home, you'd only be a couple of hours away. Daisy, will you come and read for Juliet?'

'I – I'll think about it,' Daisy told him.

'Yes or no?' insisted Ewan.

Daisy remembered Sandy Taylor's words. She had the talent, but did she have that inner hunger, did she have that kernel of ambition?

She realized yes, she did.

223

'It's lovely to see you, Ewan,' she said smiling, as she kissed him on the cheek. 'Do you dare defy the foul Sir Michael, and come back with me for supper?'

'Actually,' said Ewan, looking sheepish, 'I might as well confess. Mrs Denham saw my name in a review, in the *West Country Herald*. She wrote to say that when I had a rest day, I'd be very welcome to come over here for supper. So she's already invited me. Come on, Daisy, she said six o'clock.'

'They can wait ten minutes.' Daisy put her arms round Ewan's neck and kissed him properly this time.